CW00798650

PRAISE FOR ERIC DEMAREST

"A rare story that empowers kids from regular walks of life… Heroes are not just comic book legends defined by their powers, but everyday people who simply do what is right. "

"When Matt faces trouble in his hometown, the teen and his friends soon find out they're not losers after all. In this young-adult gem, Demarest creates genuine characters whose loyalty and courage are tested. While doing the right thing isn't always easy, sometimes it's even dangerous."

—Nicole Sorrell, author of *The Art of Living Series*

"A sinister plot that could prove deadly on a grand scale. Matt's not the only one who learns to appreciate a special power. Along the way, they all learn that sometimes a disability is an ability in disguise—it all depends on how you use it."

—*Fran Borin, author of The Ghost Adventures of Orion O'Brien Series*

"The characterization of Tess, a non-speaking autistic girl is not only extremely respectful and accurate, but something to be commended as an example as superb representation of a capable autistic individual."

ABOUT ERIC DEMAREST

Eric Demarest spent most of his childhood living in his imagination. His adult life isn't much different, except now he writes his imaginings down and makes other people read them.

Demarest loves how stories can make us understand ourselves and others more fully. Eric's work has been featured in SPIDER Magazine.

When he's not writing or reading, he spends his time watching science fiction movies and imagining what life is like in the parallel universe where he became a film score composer instead of a fiction writer. Eric Demarest lives in Overland Park, Kansas, with his wife and their cat.

SCAN ME

SUE'S STORY

ERIC DEMAREST
THE HIDDEN ABILITIES SERIES

BUT I'M (NOT) A HERO

ERIC DEMAREST

BUT I'M (NOT) A HERO

ERIC DEMAREST

BUT I'M (NOT) A HERO

ERIC DEMAREST

Published by
5310 Publishing Company
5310publishing.com

Our books may be purchased in bulk for promotional, educational, or business purposes. Please contact your local bookseller or 5310 Publishing at sales@5310publishing.com or refer to our website at 5310PUBLISHING.COM.

BUT I'M NOT A HERO (1st Edition) - ISBNs:
Hardcover: 9781998839049
Paperback: 9781998839025
Ebook/Kindle: 9781998839032

Author: Eric Demarest | Editor: Alex Williams | Interior and Cover Design: Eric Williams

BUT I'M NOT A HERO (1st Edition) was released in June 2023

YOUNG ADULT FICTION / Magical Realism
YOUNG ADULT FICTION / Superheroes
YOUNG ADULT FICTION / Action & Adventure / General

SCAN ME

Narrative themes explored may include: Teenage Fiction; Coming of age; Science fiction; Speculative, dystopian & utopian fiction; Action & adventure stories; Thrillers; Magical realism; Self-awareness and self-esteem; Friends and friendships; Diversity and inclusion

Qualifiers: Interest age: from 14 years; Set in the US Midwest; 21st Century

ACKNOWLEDGEMENTS

Thanks to 5310 Publishing for taking a chance on me. Thanks to my parents for encouraging my big, crazy dreams, and for putting up with my constant daydreaming growing up. Thanks to my wife for staying with me through the ups and downs, commiserating with me through every rejection and celebrating when I finally got my "Yes!" And thanks to the collaborators and friends I've made in my writing group—especially Fran Borin, Nick MacDonnell, and Nicole Sorrell—you have truly made this story what it is. It's been fun sharing our journeys together.

Soli Deo Gloria

To my mom for the imagination, and my dad for the science; and to both of them for teaching me to believe in myself.

1

I USED TO BELIEVE IN HEROES. Used to.

Thought I could be one, what with that thing I can do. My Ability... what a joke that turned out to be. The point is, I learned about reality. And right now, with the same old faded street signs dragging by and Rob's two-shades-of-red, piece-of-shit hatchback sputtering underneath me, I have a strong sense of that reality setting in.

"Kyle Draughton flushed another guy's social status down the toilet today," I say, watching a dog pee on a fire hydrant. "You see his video of Pete's epic fail on the pull-up bar?"

Rob chuckles beside me, one hand casually on the steering wheel. "Yeah, that was awesome."

"That's all you have to say about it? That could've been one of us."

"You mean it could've been you," Rob says with a wink. "I'm too smooth for a flop like that."

I slump down into the duct tape holding my seat together. "I'm just tired of always being one step away from total disaster." Today I got even closer, falling off the bar right after Pete. The only thing that saved me was they were too busy laughing at Pete to notice. "I really thought once we got past freshman year, things would be different."

"Forget it, Matt. In a small-ass, backward town like Chaplain, the cool kids are carved in stone from birth. Everyone else is a loser." He glances over at me with a smile that pops the dimples of his mahogany cheeks. "Of course, when I say loser, I mean you. I'm gonna make homecoming king, but I'll still talk to you after that. Maybe."

A semi-truck rumbles down the hill to the left of us, plastered with a dirty logo for Crossman Industries. Probably hauling another load of brake pads from the factory. I get a vision of myself as a worn-out forty-year-old with a beer gut working on the factory line. "You ever get the feeling you'll be a loser your whole life?" I mumble.

"What're you talking about?" Rob says. "I told you, I'm gonna be homecoming king."

I glance at the sign for the Chinese restaurant, the "G" of Golden Dragon hanging crooked. The laundromat with the cracked window next to that. We're just passing our lame excuse for a hardware store when I hear the truck horn blaring—deep, shuddering, like a freight train.

The semi barrels toward the intersection, running the red light. Rob yells "*Shit!*" and slams hard on the brakes. I lurch forward until the seat belt cuts into my neck and jerks me the other way. We jolt to a stop and I slam back into the seat, blinking through the stars in my vision, just waiting for the truck to plow through us. It growls ahead, metal creaking as it veers to the side. I hold my breath. The truck's grill skids past our bumper—just past. It missed us.

But it's hurtling straight for that blue sedan in the next lane.

The semi crushes into it like a wrecking ball, the bang echoing in my skull. Rubber shrieks as the car skids sideways, sending a guy in the crosswalk diving out of the way. The car misses him and twists into a spin, taking out a trash can on the curb, sending soda cans and fast-food wrappers flying. The shrieking of the tires finally stops when the car slams into a light pole, crumpling the back half to nothing.

I throw my door open and stagger out. I barely register the semi-truck grating to a stop.

"Is he okay?" someone in the crowd asks. People stream out of their cars and the stores, circling around the mangled sedan from a safe distance. I stand there across the street, not daring to move closer. My stomach curdles when I see the blood through the cracked window. A gash rips across the driver's face, down to his peppered beard. He fumbles around, only half-conscious.

Then I shout, my voice breaking, "The car is on fire!"

Flames lick their way out the back, red and orange tongues tangling together. I see the black smoke trailing up, and my throat catches. I can't watch this happen, not again. My eyes dart back to the driver. He's still fumbling, looking for the door handle but can't find it.

"Get him out of there!" someone yells. Another guy echoes him... but no one moves. The crowd hovers back, recording with their freaking phones, everyone waiting for someone else to go. Rob dials 911 with shaking hands, but we can't wait for that. The flames grow thicker, crawling their way toward the cab.

"Damn it, someone's got to do something," I hear myself say. I force myself forward—one step, two steps. Then I stop, paralyzed. I wish I could say it's the heat stopping me, or that it's Rob pulling me back, but that's not it.

I'm just plain scared.

That's when the energy builds in my hands. The tingling, the dull ache I can't even describe, that I haven't let myself feel for so long. A shudder shoots through me; it's happening all over again. The same chance to prove myself a failure. But maybe, just maybe it can be different this time. I've spent so long telling myself not to use this, but damn it, I can do something no one else can do.

I open my hand and reach out—not extending my arm, but my Ability. Even from here, thirty feet away, I can feel the door handle in my mind as solid as if I'd grabbed onto it. My fingers tingle as I see the handle twitch. The door creaks and starts to pull toward me, but it sticks shut. My jaw tenses, I pull harder. The tingle in my hand starts to burn. Come on, damn it. The door creaks again. I take a step forward, then curse myself and stagger back. My stare fixes on the driver's face, on his dazed and hollow eyes. I grit my teeth, straining with my invisible grip like I'm tugging on a brick wall. I pull with everything I have until my hand sears with pain and I can't hold on anymore. I gasp for breath and release just as I see the flash.

The heat of the explosion hits me in the face and knocks me backward, and the windows shatter in a spray of glass. Everyone screams and ducks for cover. I shield my face with my arm before looking back to the driver—but I can't even see him anymore. Just flame, everywhere.

I double over and puke, vomit burning my throat.

2

I WAS FIVE YEARS OLD WHEN I watched the building shake, fire ripping through it, tearing the roof apart and sending flames licking up into the sky. The attic exploded with a raging shudder, belching embers like some horrific firework.

My mom's voice trailed in from the next room. "Turn the TV down, Matt! And from the sound of it, that show is way too violent for you anyway."

"What?" I yelled back, as another explosion rocked the screen. I'd heard her just fine, but like most five-year-olds, I had figured out how to stall.

"I said turn that down!" Mom yelled.

"What?"

"I know you can hear me! Don't make me count to three."

The show was just getting good, but it wasn't worth making Mom count to three. Nothing good would come of that. I reached for the remote from where I sprawled out on the couch, but it was all the way on the other side of the coffee table.

"Matthew Pine, I'm not kidding."

"I'm working on it, Mom!" I stretched out my hand toward it, even though it was still a good three feet away. I was too lazy to get off the couch so I just kept stretching for it, as if it would suddenly move closer. And then... it did.

The remote twitched. Or wait, did I imagine that? My hand felt funny, I knew I wasn't imagining that, a weird tingle like my fingers were waking up after falling asleep.

"I can still hear the TV," Mom said.

I barely even heard her. The fire kept raging on the screen, but I wasn't paying attention to anything except that remote and the weird feeling in my hand. I had to see if I could make it move again.

"All right," Mom said. "You asked for it. One..."

I reached out my hand. My fingers tingled like a hundred pinpricks, and the remote jerked an inch toward me. There was no denying it this time. It kept twitching, rattling against the table. I was doing that. I didn't know how, but I was doing it.

"Two..."

I could feel the remote. It was still three feet away, but I could *feel* it, in my mind. My hand got warm as the remote rattled back and forth, faster and faster. And then I felt this urge to pull at it. Like flexing a muscle I'd never known I had. I clenched my teeth and tried to focus, tried to get a grip on it, like trying to grab a gust of wind—almost... almost...

"*Three!*"

It shot up off the table, through the air, and straight to me. It slapped into my hand, and I squeezed my fist tight around it. The TV switched off, dropping the room into stark silence. I stared at the remote like I'd just caught a cobra.

"Mom!" I bolted up off the couch just as she stepped into

the room.

"You cut that one pretty close, mister," she scolded, folding her arms.

"Mom, look! I grabbed it!" I held the remote up like a trophy.

"What are you talking about?"

"I grabbed it! It moved! I didn't have to get up!" My words came out all jumbled and tripping over each other.

She shook her head, sending her dark hair swishing. "I really need to start watching how much sugar you're eating." She did her best to look frustrated, but there was the tiniest hint of a smile on her mouth. Like we were sharing a funny secret. That's one of the things I miss most.

"No, you don't understand!" I threw the remote down. It thunked against the floor and the batteries popped out.

"Matt, don't break that!" She bent down to pick it up.

She needed to see it, that's the only way she'd understand. Could I even do it again? I looked for something else to use. One of my action figures flopped on the floor in the corner— Mom was always telling me to pick those up, and here was my chance. I reached out and felt the energy tingle again.

"It's working!" I said. "I can feel it!"

"Honestly, Matt, I have no idea what you're..."

She didn't finish, because her eyes followed where my hand was reaching and she saw it. The figure jerked back and forth on the carpet. I was still trying to figure out how to grab onto it. After all, I'd only done this once before. My fingers started to heat up.

"Oh... oh my..." Mom's smile faded and she dropped the remote to the floor again.

The heat in my hand intensified and burned, until I got my grip on the figure. It launched toward me and slapped into my hand. My smile beamed and I held it up proudly. "Isn't that awesome, Mom? Wait till I show everybody!"

    I remember how the sunlight glowed through her hair as she stared at me. Her mouth hung open until her eyes glazed over, then she tipped backward and dropped to the floor.

3

THE BUZZ OF CONVERSATION IN THE Chaplain High lunchroom feels more agitated today. Because there's finally something to talk about. I catch snippets from a dozen kids telling a dozen different versions of that car blowing up, as if I haven't been reliving that moment enough already. What's worse, I see Mr. Baldwin, the school counselor, as I walk in. He puts his hand on Katie Parkson's shoulder, patting her with a measured, practiced sympathy while she sniffs into a tissue. That's the fourth kid I've seen Baldwin with today, making his rounds, making sure we know "we'll get through this together." Katie blows her nose noisily and heads toward the lunch line. Baldwin glances around, looking for his next patient. Hell if I want him patting my shoulder. I quicken my steps before he can make eye contact with me.

Rob's already at the table when I drop into my chair beside him. He smiles at me—seems like he's always smiling—but even he looks down today.

"You sure your stomach's up to the chicken surprise?" he

asks me. His way of asking if I'm okay.

"I guess." I stare at a puddle of grease dripping off the chicken slop. "You find out who it was in that car?"

Rob gives a subtle nod, his eyes still on the table. "Steph Sutton's dad. Worked with mine at the factory."

Everybody here works at the factory. Which means when something bad happens, it hits everyone.

"Sucks," Phillip says. He sits across from Rob, though I wouldn't notice him at all if I wasn't used to seeing him there every day. He slumps down, all but his head behind the table, and his hoodie shades his pale face until he all but fades away.

"*It does suck,*" echoes a voice from the end of the table. It's Tess; well, technically, Tess's phone talking. That's how Tess talks. She holds the phone sort of cockeyed in front of her face, and her fingers flurry over it crazy fast. She's either hitting buttons at random or launching a spy satellite. Her gray-blue eyes stare off, looking preoccupied. "*Steph must be sad,*" she says with a few more taps on her phone.

"Yeah, Tess, I'll bet she is," I say.

Rob shakes his head. "Dude, how do you even know who she's talking to? She's not paying attention to us. All she does is look at her phone." He says it quietly, but not quietly enough.

I lean over to him. "Tess *is* paying attention, and cool it, will you? She's autistic, not deaf, genius." I glance back at her. She keeps tapping, and her expression never changes.

"Sorry," Rob says. "Anyway, Sutton's funeral is in a couple days. I'm going with my dad. You going?"

"I, uh, haven't thought about it." Actually, I'm trying *not* to think about it. I don't know Steph that well, and I never met her dad, but now... I watched him die. How do I get past that? But what I really can't get past is what I tried to do with my Ability.

For a second there, I thought I could actually get him out of that car. Should've known better. I'm not a superhero; they don't exist. I stifle a shudder as my mind suddenly flashes with the image of a truck grill barreling straight toward my face.

"I almost got run over by a truck once," I say, staring off at the far wall. "Did I ever tell you guys that?"

Rob shakes his head. "Nope. I think I'd remember that one."

"I was only about four. I don't remember much of it, but it used to give me nightmares. Last night, after watching the truck smash that car... I had one again."

My mind goes back to the blurred, scattered images. The only color I saw was the blue of the sky; something blocked my view of everything else, I don't remember. But I remember my mom's shriek just fine, as I whizzed toward the street.

"I was on my tricycle," I say. "In my driveway, pedaling as fast as I could. My mom screamed behind me. The next image I get, I was out in the street. All I saw was that truck grill coming at me like giant monster teeth. Pretty sure I peed my pants."

Rob laughs, then catches himself. "Sorry."

"Dude, I was four, and about to get mowed over by a truck! What'd you expect?"

"So, what happened?" Phillip asks.

I shake my head. "Don't know. The next thing I remember, I was back in the driveway. I guess I backpedaled fast enough to get out of there."

The broken pieces of the memory fade away again, but I'm far from relaxed.

"I guess seeing the accident yesterday could really bring that back, huh?" Phillip says. His pale green eyes feel warm when he smiles.

"Yeah. More than I was expecting." I don't tell them about the other flash in my memory, the flash of fire. That's more than I can deal with right now. I look off into the crowd across the lunchroom, needing to forget.

"Who're you looking for?" Rob asks.

"No one," I say, though that isn't true. My eyes graze over everyone until I see red hair emerge from the forest of other colors.

Emily.

She walks with small, timid steps, like she's not sure where she's going, even though she sits in the same spot every day like the rest of us do. Her hair hangs down, partially covering her face. She shuffles over to us and carefully lowers herself into her seat.

Rob gives me a nudge and I glance over at him. A big grin stretches across his face. He looks over at Emily, then back at me, and makes a kissy face.

My cheeks get hot.

"*I wasn't staring at her,*" I mouth to him. Or maybe to myself.

"Hey, Emily," Rob says, still smirking.

"*Hey,*" says Tess. She doesn't look at Emily, but she waves for just a second before her hand goes back to her phone.

"Hey, guys," Emily says. She brushes her hair back, letting her face show now, and straightens up in her chair. She's a different person than she was a second ago. It makes me feel a little better, knowing she can relax around me.

I mean, around *us*.

"What're you guys talking about?" she asks.

"The thing everyone's talking about," Rob says. "The funeral."

Emily exhales. "Look, guys, I spent like two hours crying about that with Steph on the phone last night. I tried to make her feel better, but let's face it, it's not like I could do anything. It just left me torn up inside. Can we talk about something else? Something happy?"

"Sure," I say. I wouldn't mind talking about something else, either.

"Hey, here's something," Emily says. "So after crying my eyes out, I was going through my closet to get my mind off things. Guess what I found?"

She looks at us expectantly. I catch myself staring at her smile; she looks so different now that she got her braces off. I pull my eyes away before Rob can give me any more crap.

"That ribbon you and I won for the three-legged race!" she exclaims.

My cheeks get a little hotter. "That one in fourth grade?"

Rob laughs. "I forgot about that. How did either of you ever win an athletic event?"

"Hey, we had a very advanced technique," Emily says. "Remember? It was sort of a step-hop-hop thing."

"And it helped that Kyle's partner fell over ten feet from the finish line," I add.

"Oh, that's right! I remember he tried to drag her behind him."

I laugh, remembering Kyle pulling Tammy Dirkson along like a sack of potatoes, him yelling for her to get up and her yelling for him to stop. And we step-hopped right past them, somehow staying upright even if it wasn't too graceful. The rope tugged so tight on my ankle I could barely feel my foot by the end, but we laughed the whole way and I didn't care. Then we fell over just past the finish line, and I remember her smile with her hair draped on the grass. She had the buck teeth back then, and her arms and legs were all spindly, but I never thought about any of that. She was just Emily.

"Things sure were simpler then," she says. "That's back when you kept talking about how you were going to be a superhero, wasn't it?"

And suddenly I'm jerked into the present, and I feel my smile fade. "Yeah." I push down the image of the burning house that suddenly jumps into my mind. But it doesn't last long. I startle when I see the blue of a letter jacket cut into my peripheral vision.

We all turn to look at him. Scott Pruitt—one of the football players, but on the scrawny side as far as football players go. There's a long awkward moment as we stare at him and the dumb swoop of hair on his head, wondering what the hell he's doing over here. The cool kids don't come over here.

"Hey, Emily," he says.

He wants *her*? He'd better not be here to mess with her. I squeeze my fists together as I size this prick up.

"Oh… hey, Scott," Emily says, her voice thin.

He doesn't pull some prank, he smiles at her. It comes out awkward, like he'd been practicing it. "I, uh, could use your help," he says.

My jaw drops. I'd be less surprised if Scott had leaned over and kissed me on the cheek.

"M-my help?" Emily stammers.

"Oh, I mean, nothing big," Scott says. He sounds nervous… football players aren't nervous when they talk to us. Actually, they just *don't* talk to us. "I was hoping to get your science notes from last week."

Emily perks up. "Really? From me?"

"Sure, from you. I've watched you in class, and you seem like you really get it." His eyes suddenly jerk wide open. "I mean, I haven't been *watching* you… I, uh, just noticed how smart you are."

Emily blushes as bright as her hair. I'm about to boil over when another letter jacket sidles up.

"What're you doing over *here*, Scott?" It's Kyle Draughton, sounding like he stepped in something sticky.

Scott deflates like a wounded balloon. "Oh... hey, Kyle, I was... getting some science notes."

Emily cringes and hunches down.

Kyle looks us all over, while we try to avoid eye contact. Then he flashes those perfect teeth his daddy bought him. "Let's get out of here, Scott," he says. "It's not like we've got anything in common with these losers. Like Matt, here... shouldn't you be out playing one of your stupid superhero games?"

I ignore him. I've had lots of practice at that. Rob, on the other hand, doesn't ignore jerks so well.

"That's the best you can come up with?" Rob says. "That insult's like five years old. Why don't you go punt a basketball or something?"

"Oh, you've got a mouth on you, huh?" Kyle shoots back. "Laugh it up. I'm gonna enjoy bossing you around at the factory someday. Like my dad does with your dad."

"Whatever," Rob mutters.

But I can tell Kyle hit a nerve on that one.

Kyle's smile spreads wider. "You might as well let it sink in now. You're not gonna amount to anything. None of you are."

It's getting harder to ignore him.

"Come on, Scott," Kyle says, turning away. "I think we've made our point."

Then he glances at Emily.

"Oh, hey, Emily," he adds. "You finally got your braces off. Looks nice." She blushes again and hides further behind her hair.

Kyle struts off, with Scott following behind him like an obedient dog. I watch them go, then look back at Emily. She's still blushing, but she smiles.

I usually like seeing Emily smile, but not this time.

"LAB DAY TODAY," Mr. Plask says. "I know we're all thinking of Miss Sutton's dad right now, but this should help take our minds off of that. The best days in science class are lab days, right?" He smiles, looking at us for a reaction. He never quite makes eye contact with anyone, though it's hard to tell because his glasses make his eyes all big and bulgy. When no one smiles back, he looks down at the floor. "You'll, uh, need to pick lab partners."

A chorus of squeaks fills the classroom as everyone scoots their chairs back to stand up. Normally, I hate picking partners for anything, like picking teams in gym class. When you're a reject like me, your options are pretty limited. Rob's my usual go-to, but he's in math this period. Then I look across the room, and I suddenly think this could work out okay.

"Emily!" I start working my way over to her, pushing through the crowd. She stands there, staring at the floor, as everyone pairs up around her. I'm almost there, just trying to squeeze past Beefy Brett, when *he* swoops in.

Scott Pruitt.

"Hey, Emily, you want to work with me?" Scott says, in that voice he thinks is so smooth. He flashes that dumb smile and Emily blushes a dozen shades of red. Her eyes sneak a quick glance at his face.

I wait for her to tell him to go to hell. Okay, she'll be more polite than that, but she'll say no. Right?

Her mouth quivers for a second... then she nods. I suddenly get an urge to punch something.

Damn it, she doesn't belong with him. She should be with me. I mean, not *with* me, just... oh, forget it. Anyway, I don't have time to fume about this because I still need a damn lab partner. I glance around, trying to see if there's anyone even left at this point. Then I bump into someone behind me.

I spin around and don't even see anyone at first; then Phillip's face peeks out from under his hoodie. I'd forgotten he was even in here. He pulls his hood back, letting his spiky black hair show, and scratches at the one ear that sticks out farther than the other.

"Oh, hey, Phillip," I say, trying to act like I wasn't caught off guard. "You, uh, wanna work together?"

He shrugs. He never says much.

"Okay, everybody," Mr. Plask calls over the mumble of conversation. He roughs at his hair; he's got clumps of it sticking everywhere. "We need to get started. Grab your partner and go to the lab tables in the back."

I follow the herd to the other side of the room, keeping my eye on Scott and Emily. He offers to carry her books and Emily blushes some more, but at least they don't hold hands or anything. I look away before I get any more pissed off. The lab tables are spread with all kinds of crap—Bunsen burners, test tubes, bottles of chemicals, and a bunch of other stuff I should probably be able to identify if I'd been paying attention this semester. I drop my books on one of the tables next to a purplish stain where some idiot spilled something. I'm hoping I don't end up being one of those idiots today.

"All right," Mr. Plask says. "The materials and instructions are laid out there. Now, we're working with hydrochloric acid today. So please, *please* don't drop it." He carries a handful of brown bottles the size of soda cans and then sets them on the tables. "We only have four bottles of the acid, so you'll need to crowd around to pour it into your test tubes."

"Is this really a good idea? Having us play with acid?" I mutter. "What ever happened to making volcanoes erupt with baking soda?"

Phillip shrugs again.

"You'll need four milliliters of the acid," Plask says. "Pour it *carefully*."

The lines form around the tables quickly, and, of course, given my social status, I'm last. I glance at Emily again, over at the next table—she's almost at the front of the line thanks to Scott, though she keeps glancing at everyone behind her like she feels super awkward up there. Scott goes to pick up the bottle and brushes against her shoulder "by accident." She blushes some more, and I grind my teeth until it hurts.

"Why doesn't he go after one of the cheerleaders, like all the other jocks?" I mutter. What makes me even madder is I can't even think of a good reason why this bothers me. Scott's not really a jerk as far as jocks go, and Emily and I are just friends. Right?

Suddenly a shriek erupts from the other side of the room. I spin around to see who it is, expecting to see a little girl being murdered from the sound of it, but it's Beefy Brett. He cradles his arm like a wounded bird, screaming his head off.

Plask flurries over like a hummingbird on crack. "Oh my God, what happened? You didn't spill it, did you? I told you to be careful!"

"I spilled acid on me!" Beefy screams. "Am I gonna lose my arm? You're not gonna amputate, are you?"

"Okay, okay, you'll be fine," Plask says, though his tone doesn't sound convincing. "You only spilled a drop of it. If you'd spilled the whole bottle, that would be different."

"Are you sure?" Beefy cries. "I gotta keep this hand, man!"

"Calm down, just… get to the sink and run it under cold water!" Plask grabs Beefy's arm and tries to tug him toward the sink, but Beefy flops to the floor and keeps shrieking. Plask might as well be pulling on a beached whale. "Can I get some help here?" he pleads.

"I've got you, man," Scott says. He thumps his acid bottle back on the table and rushes over toward Beefy. He winks at Emily on the way—that pisses me off enough—but he also bumps the table.

The bottle of acid totters, and falls.

Cold shock drapes over me as I watch it drop in slow motion. Emily doesn't see it. She's watching the chaos across the room, the same as everyone else. But I see it fine, tumbling toward the ground right next to her leg. I'm stuck in that half second where I know I'm just out of reach and there's no time to warn her. But this is Emily, and I have to do something. My instinct takes over before I even have a say in it.

I reach out my hand. The energy releases all on its own. The bottle stops falling and arcs back up, like it hits a ramp in the air, and snaps across into my hand. And that fast, it's all over. I clench my fist tight around it.

My breath puffs out like I just got punched in the gut. Jesus Christ, did anyone see that? What I tried with the car door yesterday was one thing, no one could tell that was me, but this time I caught it. I *caught* it... in front of everyone. I feel the sweat forming as I dart glances around the room. Emily still has her back to me—she's okay, and thankfully oblivious. Everyone else crowds around Beefy as he holds his hand under the sink, his screaming down to a whimper now. No one's staring at me like the freak that I am. But I am a freak, and I can't turn that off. I slam the bottle of acid back on the table, muttering a curse at myself.

Beefy gives another whimper as Plask wraps a bandage on his hand. Scott slides back over to Emily, and she smiles at him. God, this is going to be a long class period.

Finally the bell rings to get me the hell out of here. I throw my stuff into my book bag and sling it over my shoulder, ready to forget about everything that just happened. I start toward the door when a lanky figure slides in front of me. Mr. Plask.

"Matthew? Or is it Matt?" He fumbles with his hands, looking at the floor. "I was hoping to ask you—"

"Not now." I push past him without an excuse or an apology. I need to get away, from him and everyone else. If only I could get away from myself.

5

"THANKS FOR THE PIZZA, MAN."

"Don't mention it," Rob tells me. "I owed you from last time."

We rumble along in Rob's hatchback toward my house. The sun dips toward the horizon, and I stare out the window and watch the houses flow by.

"You sure you're okay?" Rob squints at me, scrunching lines in his narrow forehead.

A couple more houses pass while I try to make up my mind. "Don't know."

"Me either, man," Rob says. "That car explosion is a lot to take in. I think it got to my dad, too. He worked pretty close with Sutton, I think. Damn shame."

"Yeah." The word sighs out of me. I can't bring myself to say anything else.

"My dad rambled about a bunch of stuff last night when he heard. I guess Sutton was working on some new project. Everybody at the factory is freaking out about it."

"What's up with Emily and that Scott character?" I blurt out.

"Seriously?" Rob shoots me a look. "We see a guy blow up right in front of us, and *that's* what you're on about?"

"Look, I'm plenty shaken up about that, but... this is important too. I mean, it's Emily!"

He scratches his fingers through his thick, short-cropped hair. "What's the big deal? Scott asked her for science notes."

"And then he picked her as his freaking lab partner! And he's so damn clumsy, he almost spilled the..." I trail off. As much as I wish I could tell Rob the next part, he can't know about that. No one can. "Look, he's a football player, and she's, you know, one of us. Football players don't talk to us."

"So? Good for her."

"Good for her?"

Rob gives me one of his sly grins. "Sorry, I forgot you're in *love*."

"Am not," I say, hoping my face isn't turning red. "Emily's a friend. Just like she's your friend, too."

"Okay. Then why do you care who she talks to?"

I stare out the window, watching some birds huddle in a tree. "I don't know."

"Well, you should probably figure that out, then." He grins again, his dimples emerging from the smooth skin of his cheeks. "Hey, you think *I* should ask her out?"

I want to slap him for that, but I can't help laughing. Rob has that effect on people.

We glide to a stop in front of my house. More of a jolt, actually, but we've stopped.

"You really okay?" Rob asks.

"Yeah," I say, trying to sound convincing. "Thanks."

I throw the car door open and start toward the house, in no hurry to get there. The hatchback coughs and sputters off behind me. When I finally reach the front door, I take a long breath before stepping inside.

The living room is dark and quiet. I don't hear Dad, and I don't go looking for him. My steps sound hollow as I plod my way upstairs and into my room, and my book bag thuds to the floor. When I switch on the light, my eyes go to the poster on the wall.

The red cape billows out from behind the guy with the ridiculous muscles, and the red *S* swoops across the yellow background of the flashy, diamond-shaped emblem on his puffed-out chest. I should take that stupid poster down. It used to mean something, back before. Now… it's just a reminder of what I'll never be. I fight a surge of anger and reach for the corner to pull it off the wall, when suddenly my mind flashes to the day I put it up. I had to stretch on my toes then, jittering with excitement. I'd pestered my mom for a week to take me to the comic book store. Right after that day I'd made her faint, I knew I had to go.

"I need to see the superheroes, Mom! I'm just like them now!"

"I told you, Matt, it doesn't work that way."

She didn't understand. The good thing is, five-year-olds can be pretty persistent. So finally I wore her down and she said okay, that she'd take me just to look. Of course we both knew she was going to buy me something.

I'd busted right through the door as soon as we pulled up, tripping over my own feet and the wrinkles in the cheap red and blue carpet. There were so many colors, so many heroes.

"He can fly, Mom! And look at her, how big her sword is! And that guy's shooting lasers out of his eyes, and—"

"Slow down, Matt!" She ran up behind me, her dark hair swishing behind her, and grabbed me by the shirt.

"Don't you get it, Mom? I have a superpower like they do! I'm gonna *be* one of them!"

She turned me around and knelt down in front of me. When she smiled, it felt sad. "Matt, honey, all these superheroes, with their costumes… that's not how heroes really are. These are just for pretend."

"Well maybe they're just pretend, Mom, but *I'm* not! If they're not real, I'll be the *first* superhero!"

"Please, Matt, you have to stop talking like that."

"But I can do the thing, the thing nobody else can do!" I reached for one of the action figures on the shelf and felt the tingle in my hand start to build. I was going to show her, show everyone. Mom creased her mouth tight, and slowly began to shake her head.

"I told you, Matt. You can't show anyone what you can do, and you can't tell anyone either. It has to be a secret."

I dropped my hand. "A secret from everyone? What about Dad?"

Her eyes glossed over, reflecting the colors from the posters all around. "Even him. I'm sorry."

"But why, Mom?" I begged. "You said yourself it's special."

"It is special. *You're* special. But people don't always understand things that are different."

I looked in her face, my little five-year-old head so confused. It would take a few years for me to get it. "If I can't show anyone, then how am I gonna save the world?"

She put her soft hand on my shoulder. "I don't know, Matt. But you *can* save the world, if you want to."

"Like that guy in the poster?" I said, perking up again.

She hesitated. "Not quite like him. You'll find your own way."

The red blurs in my vision now as I stare at the faded poster, gritting my teeth. Mom may have meant well, but she was wrong about that. I'm never going to save the world, and I don't know why I ever believed superheroes were anything more than a pathetic piece of make-believe. I grab the edge of the poster and tear the paper hero right down the middle in a long, slow rip, leaving half of him hanging tattered on the wall. I crumple the other half in an angry ball and toss it to the floor, then I turn and walk out.

A whirring sound and a dim glow come from the kitchen as I head back down the stairs. I cross through the living room, and when I reach the kitchen doorway, I see him. My dad slumps over the counter, staring at the microwave with glazed eyes; the glow casts a shadow across his thin nose, over his cheeks that are starting to sag. His tie hangs loose around his neck. He doesn't say hi as I come in, just keeps staring. I don't say hi either. I pull the fridge door open with a clank of bottles. The microwave keeps whirring.

"We're out of milk, I think," Dad says.

"I picked some up yesterday."

"Oh."

That's all we say. Not, *"How was your day?"* Not, *"You need to talk about how you saw my coworker get blown up?"* I pull a soda from the fridge and pop the tab, feeling the cold fizz burn down my throat as I take a chug.

The microwave beeps and Dad pulls the frozen dinner out. Turkey and gravy tonight, it smells like. He doesn't ask if I've eaten, or even offer to heat one of those up for me. He turns away and carries his dinner to the living room, dropping like a lump into the couch. The TV flickers on. Baseball.

I'm about to start rummaging through the fridge to make a sandwich or something when I hear the crack of a bat, and I glance over at the TV. It's a foul ball, into the stands. The camera pans over and a freckle-faced boy holds up his glove. He caught it. Big grin on his face. His dad pats him on the back, making him grin some more. Then the screen cuts back to the pitcher, but my mind is still stuck on that boy.

That was me, once. I remember that game. I was probably six, and we were way up in the cheap seats. I wore my glove the whole game just in case somebody hit a foul ball. Dad said we were way too high up for that, but I kept my glove on anyway, every second. Made it pretty hard to eat my hot dog like that, and I got mustard all over it. I didn't catch any foul balls, but it didn't matter. I remember grinning like that kid was. And I remember we talked. Probably just stupid stuff about school or video games or whatever, but we talked.

That was a long time ago.

The crowd roars over the TV, snapping me back from my memory. Dad stares at the screen but I'm not sure if he even sees it. I need some air. I need to be... anywhere but here.

I step out the door, taking one last glance at Dad. I don't think he even notices I'm gone.

6

ORANGE BLAZES ACROSS THE HORIZON, THE blue above it
fading to dark. My footsteps are crisp and sharp against the
leaves on the sidewalk. I hear a mockingbird off somewhere,
faint. I don't hear much else. I'm not really sure where I'm
going, and I don't much care.

The houses sit silent. The light from the windows feels warm
as I peer in from out here. I hear the mockingbird again, or
maybe it's a sparrow. I don't really know my birds that well.
Either way, it sounds sort of sad.

A cloud hovers just above one of the houses. Gray and
white, twisting, spiraling up. My eyes are drawn to it... because
it's not a cloud. It's smoke.

It's barely anything, probably someone grilling out on their
deck. But it pulls me in just the same, back to that night. The
orange blaze flickers and grows, and it fills the sky now.

It was five years ago, but it might as well be yesterday. I
walked beside my dad as we headed toward home. We'd
gone to the park at the corner to play catch. Nothing big, just

one of those father-son things we used to do.

"I wish I could throw like you, Dad," I said.

"Me?" He laughed. "I'm not the best role model when it comes to athletic ability, Matt."

"Sure you are. Give me a couple years, and I'll throw like you."

Dad smiled, and roughed up my hair. I used to love moments like that with him. He was my hero.

That's when I saw the smoke. The thick gray mass, hovering, slowly rising. Orange light glowed beneath it on the horizon. Dad's steps quickened. The glow rose up as we crested the hill until I could see the outline of the house, flames pulsing and flickering all around it. The realization burned like hot lead in my stomach.

"That's *our* house!" I screamed.

I dropped my glove and took off running, shoes slapping against the pavement, my legs flailing out of control.

"No, Matt!" Dad yelled behind me. "Come back!"

"But Mom's in there!"

The smoke scratched my throat as I sucked in jagged breaths, as I kept running as fast as I could, each step thudding painfully through my feet. I had to get to her. I had to save her. I got as far as the driveway before the heat drenched over me. I skidded to a stop, involuntarily, squinting against the blaze. I forced myself forward one more step, but I had to throw my arm up to shield myself as the heat scorched against my face.

Dad caught up behind me and threw his arm around my neck, pulling me back. I thrust myself forward, straining against him.

"Let me go!" I pleaded. "I have to go in there!"

"I can't let you."

"I have to!"

"I can't lose you too, Matt!"

"Then… then you'll go in. You'll save her!"

I looked up at him. His mouth twitched like he was going to say something, some heroic thing, right before he would go charging in. I'd seen enough movies, I knew how it was done. But Dad's face was pale, lifeless. His eyes glossed over, blank pools covered with tears, until the tears trickled down.

He wasn't going in.

"Don't worry, Dad," I told him. "It's okay. I can do something no one else can. I can get her out from here!"

This was it. My moment to prove I was a superhero.

I reached out my arm, cringing at the heat on my hand. I felt for the front door, for the doorknob. Across the distance I felt it take shape in my mind, and I grabbed on and pulled. Pulled with everything inside me, as my hand tingled and burned, as I thought about Mom; her smile, her voice, her hand on my shoulder. She'd told me not to use my Ability, but this was for her. With one last tug, the door came flying open.

"I *did* it!"

"Did what? Matt, I…" Dad sobbed, but he didn't know it was going to be okay.

I reached out again, and… and…

That's when all my delusions came tumbling down. I wasn't a superhero. I wasn't even an ordinary hero; because I suddenly realized I couldn't move anything as big as a person. I couldn't pull my mom out of there. My Ability wasn't strong enough to save her. So I stood there, shuddering as the roof wrenched on its frame with a crack and sparks flurried upward. I almost, almost, went running in there to pull her out with my bare hands. But I didn't… because I was too damn scared.

Heroes aren't scared.

In that moment, covered with flame and soot and smoke, I realized I wasn't special. My Ability wasn't special. It was nothing... in fact, it was worse than nothing, a cruel joke, because it had made me *think* I could do something. But now, there was no more pretending.

A siren wailed as a fire engine sped past us, blaring its horn in deep shudders. The truck screeched to a stop and the firefighters piled out in all their gear.

"Stay back," one of them ordered, a loud muffle through his mask. "We'll handle this."

I almost believed him. Almost believed they would save her, where Dad and I had failed.

But no. They scurried around with their hoses, spritzing water on the flames, setting out flimsy barricades to keep us "safe." But the fire kept rising, churning, billowing, and my mom was still in there. Until the roof caved in entirely, and the house swallowed it up into its burning shell.

There are no heroes.

THE AIR SITS ODDLY QUIET AS I step slowly toward the church. I tug at my tie, trying to ease the lump in my throat, but I know it's not my tie causing it.

My dad walks beside me, not saying anything. We hadn't even discussed coming here, beyond Dad saying, "Sutton's funeral is at ten tomorrow," before he shut himself in his room last night. He fidgets with his jacket like it itches him. I don't have a suit, and my shirt could use a good ironing if I knew how to do that, but at least I'm wearing a tie. I tug at it again as I force down a swallow.

We step through the church doors. The air smells stale, and the light is a mix of yellows and reds from the stained-glass window. Layers of paint on the walls pretend to hide the cracks. A projector and screen were shoehorned into the front a few years ago, looking out of place. Now the screen glows with a slideshow of happy photos of Carl Sutton and his family; barbecues, birthday parties, old shots from his college graduation and his wedding day. Sappy violin music murmurs behind it over the static in the speakers. The only other sounds are a few muffled coughs and whispers.

The place is packed. They sit stiffly in the pews in their starched suits and dresses, looking like they're made of wax. I spot Rob sitting with his dad about halfway up. They give me a solemn head nod. I nod back. I'd like to sit next to Rob to make this whole thing feel a little less weird, but he's packed in on both sides.

Dad shuffles forward through the pews until he comes to an open spot. He slumps into it, his head hung down. His face is washed out and gray, and I don't think I've seen him blink once. I slide into the pew next to him. My shoulders pinch against the hard wood. I lean forward, trying to find a comfortable position.

This is the first funeral I've been to, since… you know. I can't bring myself to look at the casket. The box at the front of the room with Steph's dad in it. When it was my mom in there, I'd kept staring at it, right up until we dropped it in the ground and threw dirt on it.

The casket's closed now, of course. No one wants to see what Mr. Sutton looks like, what's left of him, after what happened.

I hear someone crying and for a second I almost think it's me. As I wipe at my eyes to make sure, I see Steph Sutton in the front pew, her shoulders shaking. Someone hugs her, whispers something to her. I notice red hair. It's Emily. She pats Steph on the shoulder and shuffles to her seat. I suddenly feel like I shouldn't be watching, and look away.

Something thumps in the aisle behind me. Several thumps, muffled and heavy. By the time I figure out they're footsteps, the last one lands right beside me. I glance over, expecting to see Mutton Chops—that's what I call him, anyway, the big dude with scruffy whiskers who cuts meat at the grocery store. It is a big guy standing there, but not Mutton Chops; it's not anyone I've seen before, actually, and given the size of this town, I've seen everyone in here before. As the guy adjusts his suit, I catch a glint of a silver cufflink with an eagle carved in it. The eagle doesn't look happy. The guy doesn't look happy either. His suit jacket cinches tight around the shoulders because, well, he's got big shoulders. His neck is thicker than it should be, too. With the dark glasses he's wearing, he looks like he's either in the Secret Service or he's a mob boss. I suddenly realize I'm staring at him, and what's way worse is he's staring back.

"There's a spot here, Mr. Crossman," the guy says in a rough grumble of a voice.

Another man with unnaturally smooth skin and curly blond hair steps up beside him. His suit has a sheen on it, and so does his gold watch. I don't recognize him either, but I recognize money when I see it. That should be enough of a clue, but I've got so much on my mind it takes a second before it smacks me between the eyes.

Crossman. As in *Crossman Industries*. This is the guy with his name on the factory. We've all heard rumors about him, made-up stories about him living it up in his ivory tower off in the city somewhere, but we've never actually seen him. I try to hide the fact that my eyes pop wide open, and I make a point to stare straight ahead. My dad does too.

"I'm not sure there's room here, Deckert," Crossman says.

The mob boss—Deckert—looks me over through his dark glasses. I get the distinct feeling that he's deciding which of my bones to break first. "Move over," he grunts.

If he was anyone else, I'd tell him to go to hell. But for him, I slide over as fast as I can, knocking shoulders with my dad until he shuffles over too. Deckert drops into the pew with a thud, shaking the whole thing, and shoves his mass into me. My face squashes into his shoulder. Somehow I still feel like I'm the one who should apologize to him. Crossman acts like he didn't see Deckert's sumo wrestling match with me, straightens his jacket, and slides smoothly into the end of the pew.

My phone buzzes and I peel my face off Deckert's shoulder. I pull the phone out to see a text from Rob.

ROB—who's the guy with the $$$ and the massive dude sitting next 2u?

I make eye contact with him across the room. Rob raises his eyebrows and jerks his head toward my bulky companion, then taps on his phone again.

ROB—not from around here

I make sure to shade my phone with my hand so Deckert doesn't see as I text back.

MATT—Crossman

I see Rob's eyes go big even from here. His fingers flurry.

ROB—no way! tell him your dad needs a raise. Mine 2!

I slide my phone away, making sure Deckert doesn't see. I don't have to worry about my dad seeing it or scolding me for texting at a funeral, he's still staring off in a trance.

The music begins to fade out as the projector screen goes dark. The pastor gets up, a shriveled man with a thick gray beard. He climbs the steps to the pulpit, looking like he might fall over any second.

"We are gathered today to remember," the pastor says in a surprisingly deep voice. "Carl Sutton will be remembered as a loving husband and father, as well as a good friend to many. He will be remembered as..."

The voice carries over the haze in my head. I keep getting

images of dreams I've had of this room ever since my mom was the one in the casket. But in my dreams, everything's on fire.

Snapping back from my dream, I hear the pastor say, "Would you like to say a few words, Mrs. Sutton?"

Everyone's eyes go to the woman sitting next to Steph in the front row. Her skin stands out a ghastly pale against her dark hair. She steps slowly toward the pulpit, taking what seems an eternity to get there. When she finally reaches it, she grips the sides as if it's the only thing holding her up.

"Carl would hate all this attention," she begins. Her voice sounds empty. "He was a quiet man. Simple, but caring. Always looking out for everyone else. Even little things, like making the coffee in the morning. He got this fancy new machine because he knew I'd like it, and every morning he'd have a cup waiting for me by the time I got downstairs. This morning, when I went to make some… I suddenly realized I don't even know how to use the thing. I just always figured he'd be there, to…"

She trails off, and slumps down over the podium. I feel like I should avert my eyes or something. Then, suddenly, she snaps back up. And it's not some renewed will to go on, there's anger on her face. No… make that hate.

"*You* did this!" Her voice cuts like a razor now. "You're the reason he's dead!"

She stabs a finger—at me. I jolt back like she just shot me, trying to figure out how this is my fault. But then, maybe it is. I failed, I didn't get him out of that burning car. Then the shock fades and I realize she isn't pointing at me, she's pointing at the guy two seats over in the fancy suit. Crossman.

"This is your fault!" she screams, fire rising in her voice. "You parade in here throwing your money around, buy these worthless flowers as if that makes everything better."

I hadn't even noticed the flowers, but now that she mentions them, I see they're draped all over the casket. Not that they make any difference anyway. The guy in there is still dead.

"You think they'll make us forget?" she screams. "Carl told me things. I know what kind of man you really are!"

Everyone sits in stunned silence as her shoulders heave with angry breaths. It's ghastly quiet in the pews now, no one daring to make a peep. Steph in the front row looks like she has no idea how to react either.

"Mrs. Sutton," comes the pastor's deep voice. "Perhaps we should—"

"*No!*" she screams. She locks eyes with Crossman. "You're going to answer for what you did, you son of a bitch!"

She storms down from the pulpit, straight for Crossman, and given that I'm sitting two seats from him, she might as well be coming at me. Each of her steps drops like a hammer, and she looks about to strangle him with just her eyes. I don't know if she's planning to punch Crossman or spit in his face. I freeze like a deer about to be run over by a dump truck. Crossman doesn't move either. Just before she gets to us, Deckert pries his shoulder off of me and pushes both himself and Crossman out of the pew. At first I wonder if he's offering Crossman as a sacrifice, but then he pulls Crossman behind his massive bulk.

Mrs. Sutton storms up to Deckert, looking like she could barrel right through him even though he's three times her size. "You going to hide behind your guard dog, Crossman? You Coward!" she yells.

Deckert stares her down, his face passive. "You need to stop."

"Get out of my way!"

Deckert grabs her arm—not violent, but I can tell his grip is firm—and he leans toward her. He says something in her ear, low and quiet. Then he straightens up again. His expression never changes.

Mrs. Sutton stands frozen for a moment, her face raging, until the anger drops away and leaves her face empty. Then she sobs. Violently, uncontrollably. Deckert steps toward the back of the church, still gripping her arm, dragging her along with him. She shakes, heaving with sobs.

"Stephanie!" she cries out. "I can't lose you too, Stephanie!"

Steph jumps up and runs after her. She lets a look linger on Crossman as she hurries past him, then she follows her mom out the door. No one else dares to say anything, or blink even.

My phone buzzes.

ROB—WTF?????

I don't even know how to reply, so I don't.

"I, ah…" the pastor tries. He doesn't get any farther than that.

"Perhaps I should say something." It's Crossman, looking out of place where he stands in the aisle. He moves half a step toward the front of the room, hovering there for a moment. He adjusts his suit, looking like it itches him even though I'm guessing it cost more than my dad makes in a year. Then he makes up his mind and strides quickly forward.

The pastor awkwardly shuffles to the side, almost bowing to him. Crossman rests his hands on the pulpit and looks out over the pews.

"We are all part of a legacy." His voice is smooth but quiet. I guess I expected him to sound more commanding. "Some of us, like Carl Sutton, like… my father… are taken before their time. But their legacy can live on. I didn't know Carl except as an employee. I regret that; I'm sure he was a good man." He stares off, seeming to lose himself for a moment. "The point is, his legacy can live on. The work he was doing was incredibly important. We're on the verge of unveiling something at the factory, something that will change things, improve things, for everyone in Chaplain. You all knew my father," he says, though I'd certainly never met the guy. "This work was *his* legacy, and I need to fulfill it." He gets a distant look in his eyes when he says that. There's another awkward cough at the back of the room; it startles Crossman out of whatever stupor he's in. "Carl will be part of that. He'll be remembered as part of that legacy."

He adjusts his suit again, then steps down and strides back to the pew. He slides in next to me. I make sure to avoid eye contact with him. My phone buzzes with another text.

ROB—that legacy shit seems nuts

I sneak a sideways look at Crossman, still staring off like he's watching the ghost of his dead dad.

MATT—or obsessed

I glance at my dad to see a drop of sweat sliding down his forehead.

8

I TRUDGE THROUGH THE LIBRARY DOORS, past a clump of guys from metal shop and most of the volleyball team. They all carry books, but they don't look too intent on reading them. They're too busy talking. I shuffle past and they ignore me. A couple basketball players stroll by outside the window, glancing in. I don't know whose idea it was to build the library like this, in the middle of the school surrounded by windows so we're all on display in here. My books slap down on the study table as I slide in.

"Has your dad been acting weird lately?" I ask.

Rob looks up from his notebook. "Hello to you, too. And what do you mean?"

"I don't know, weird. Sutton's funeral was what, a week ago? And ever since then, my dad's been…"

Rob taps his fingers on the table. "You gonna finish that thought?"

"Scared," I mumble.

He chuckles. "Of what, monsters under his bed?"

"Dude, I'm trying to be real here. I think he's scared of Crossman."

"Well, Crossman is his boss, or his boss' boss anyway. What, you think your dad's afraid of getting fired or something?"

"No, I mean... I don't know, something bigger. Something's not right with him. Like, really not right."

Rob's dark eyes stare at me. "You're serious?"

"Yeah, I'm serious. Have you noticed anything with your dad?"

He shakes his head, but his mouth tightens. I've known Rob long enough to know he's holding something back.

"Nah, man," he says with forced casualness. "You know how adults get." His mouth creases some more as he scratches his hair. "But, okay, I do see how that stuff Crossman said at the funeral was nuts."

"I know, right? That wasn't normal. Why'd he talk about legacy so much?"

"Maybe it's something to do with his dad," Rob says. "Whatever he's working on now, he said his dad started it, right? Maybe that's what it is. He's trying to prove to his dead dad that he's not a screw-up. Rich guys have to deal with that stuff too, you know."

"Maybe... I still think there's more going on."

I turn as Emily walks up beside us. For a second I see her in slow motion; her fiery hair swishing, her freckles popping out from her cheeks. My whole body flushes when I see her. I want to say something to her but I feel like I just swallowed a sock. What the hell's wrong with me? I've known Emily a good ten years and I never had trouble talking to her before. I force the feelings down and open my mouth.

"Hey, Emily," I manage to get out. My voice doesn't sound nearly as cool as I'd hoped.

Her eyes dart toward me for just a second, before she glances back the other way. She shuffles the last step to our table, tottering awkwardly.

"You gonna sit down?" Rob asks.

She shoots another glance to the side. I follow her stare—I should have known.

Scott Pruitt.

He's crowded into a table with Kyle, Beefy, and half a dozen other football players. Emily shifts on her feet, still looking his way. Scott doesn't see her; Kyle slaps him on the back, laughing about whatever dumb crap he thinks is funny today. After one more glance back, Emily gives up and slides into the chair across from me. I feel my face drop as I try to pretend I didn't see and that I don't care.

"What's up?" she asks with an exhale, forcing a smile.

"Matt's going on about that crazy funeral," Rob says. "You know how he gets."

"I don't 'get' like anything," I huff back. "It's messed up. What about Steph's mom? She said Mr. Sutton told her things about Crossman. What kind of things?"

"I dunno," Rob says. "Probably just the usual bitching people do about their boss."

"But when that bodyguard dude dragged her out, she screamed how she couldn't lose Steph too. What was that about?"

Emily perks up at that. "You know, there is something odd…"

"Don't you start too," Rob quips.

"It's just that I haven't heard from Steph," Emily says. "I mean, I figured she'd be out of school for a while, but she hasn't texted me since the funeral."

Rob shrugs. "So she needs some space."

"Steph and I have *never* gone more than two days without

texting. I've texted her a dozen times this week, but I haven't heard anything back. I'm worried about her."

"I'm, uh, sure she's okay," I say. "And I'm sure she appreciates you, you know, checking on her." I smile, hoping it doesn't look awkward. Emily doesn't seem to hear me; she glances back toward Scott. My smile fades.

The door opens and a tall skinny figure ambles in. It's Mr. Plask, his eyes darting in all directions like he's watching out for the boogeyman. I grab one of my books at random and pull it up to hide my face.

"What's your problem?" Rob says.

"*Shhh!* It's Plask. I've been avoiding him all week. He's been giving me all kinds of weird looks lately."

"He gives everyone weird looks because, well, he's weird."

"Yeah, but he's—"

It's too late. He's already spotted me with those bulgy eyes. He rubs his hands together, then starts toward me.

"Matthew?" Plask says. "I mean, Matt? I was hoping to talk to you..." He quickly scans Rob and Emily. "Oh, I, uh, don't want to interrupt..."

Perfect, an excuse to get out of this. "Yeah, we were—"

"We were just leaving," Rob says, giving me a sly wink. I'll have to pound him for that later. He gets up without bothering to take his books with him. Emily follows, looking at the floor. Plask fiddles with his hands some more before sitting down.

"Look," I say, "I know my grade in your class isn't great, but I'm not flunking. Well, yet."

"What? No, this isn't about your grade." He roughs at his hair like he's got fleas. "I need to... damn it." He pushes himself up to leave; then he drops back down, firms his face up, and looks me square in the eye.

"I saw what you did," Plask says.

I laugh, not knowing how else to react. "Saw me what? You think I stole answers for a test or something?"

"The bottle of acid."

Oh my God...

My throat closes up, and I can't hear or see anything in the room except for Plask staring at me. He *knows?* About me, about my Ability? This is why Mom told me to hide it. "I don't... don't know what you're..."

"You controlled it. How did you do that? How long have you known?"

"There's nothing to know. I can't... I didn't do anything."

He leans in, making me flinch. "It's okay, Matt," he says. "I won't tell anyone else. I just... this is incredible. It's such a gift."

"A gift?" My shock hardens to anger. "You don't know anything."

Plask's eyes twitch behind his glasses. "You could make such a difference with it, Matt."

I hesitate for just a moment before I push my chair back and stand up. "I don't know what you're talking about."

I walk out without looking back.

9

THE SUN'S GLOW FEELS COLD, AND I shove my hands in my pockets. The breeze blows a stray brown leaf past my face. I take a wandering step, and another; I don't know where I'm going, and I don't care. I end up by the football field, but like I said, I don't care. I just need to be somewhere I can think. And of course I don't want to go home.

Does Plask really know? Really? I've gotten so used to carrying this secret alone. Because people won't understand, Mom was right about that. I should've done a better job hiding it.

But what's really eating at me… Plask called it a gift. Like it's something good, something to be grateful for. What the hell does he know? If I really had a gift, if I'm so damn special, then I would've been able to save my mom. But I'm not special, and she's dead.

I stare out at the field with its uneven yard line markers and patches of crabgrass. Kyle and Scott and the rest of the team are doing some stupid drill, throwing balls back and forth, scurrying around like it actually matters. One of the balls flies off stray, toward me, up over my head. And suddenly I'm not sixteen anymore, I'm nine again. And the clouds are gone, the sun is high in the sky, and the air is warm and sticky. I run on my spindly legs in the shoes I haven't grown into yet, chasing the ball that Rob threw. I glance over to see Kyle Draughton pedal up on the glossy red ten-speed he's been showing off to everyone, and a sly smile creeps over my mouth. Wait till he sees this. The ball is sailing out of reach, no way I can catch it, but... they don't know what I can do.

My hands tingle as I let the energy build in them. I hesitate, thinking about Mom, thinking about my promise to her. But promises are hard to keep when you're nine.

I pull at the ball and it curves at an impossible angle, arcing back toward me. I reach out. It drops right into my hands, and sticks there like a magnet. My steps stagger to a stop and I almost fall over, but even so I caught it. I smirk over at Kyle and watch his jaw drop. Then the jealousy erupts on his face, and my smirk gets bigger. Rob blabbers, "Did you see how I made it curve? I didn't even know I could *do* that!"

But Rob didn't make that ball curve, and it wasn't some fluke. *I* did that. I had an Ability, and it was going to make me way more than a dumb football star.

A chill breeze hits me and the clouds are back, and I'm my clumsy sixteen-year-old self again. The football thuds to the ground just past me.

It wouldn't have mattered if I'd caught it, anyway. I'm not a superhero. There's no such thing.

***

"YOU SURE IT'S COOL with your mom if I come over?" I ask, Rob's hatchback rumbling beneath us.

" 'Course it is. You know my mom, the more the merrier."

"Thanks. I just…"

"Don't want to go home?"

I can't bring myself to answer, and stare at the gray sky out the window.

We pull up to Rob's house. I creak the car door open and step out into the breeze. "You sure she won't mind?"

"Dude, I told you. Chill."

We step inside, and I'm immediately struck by two things: the squeals of Rob's two younger sisters and the smell of meat loaf.

"Adeline, Cassandra, I've told you to hush up and I won't tell you again," comes his mom's voice from the kitchen.

That means they're borderline in trouble. When their mom veers away from the usual Addie and Cassie, it's never a good thing. By the time she gets to the middle names, even I've learned to make myself scarce. Rob's mom smiles a lot, but you don't want to get on her bad side.

"Hey, Mom." Rob strolls into the kitchen, undaunted, and kisses her on the forehead. "I brought Matt with me. Hope that's okay."

She turns to me and her face lights up. I don't know how she does that; I'm the one imposing and you'd think I did her a favor.

"Well of course it is," she says. "Come here, Matthew. How are you?"

She strides to me and grabs me up in a hug, patting flour all over my back. She hugs me like this every time I see her, but it still disarms me. My dad's not much of a hugger. I haven't been hugged like that since… Mom.

"You, uh, don't need to feed me or anything, Mrs. Jones," I say.

"Don't be silly, Matthew. We've got plenty of food, and you're gonna eat some of it." She reaches out and manages to catch the younger daughter in mid-run without even looking. "Adeline, you set another place for Matthew here, and what did I tell you about keeping your voice down?"

"Yes, Momma," says Addie. She flips her pigtails around and winks at me before scurrying off.

A tall figure shuffles out from the hall. Rob's dad looks down at the floor, mumbling something to himself. His bald spot stands out against his graying hair, the dark skin catching a sheen from the light overhead.

"There you are, dear," Rob's mom says to him. "You washed up for supper?"

He looks up like he'd forgotten where he was. "Hmm? Uh, yeah."

She ignores his reaction and gives him a peck on the cheek. "Rob brought his nice friend Matthew with him. You remember Matthew, don't you?"

He gives me a look, and I'm not sure if he's trying to remember who I am or figure out a place to ditch my body after he murders me.

"Good day at work, Dad?" Rob asks.

He finally breaks his stare with me and shifts his gaze to Rob, looking at his son like he's a stranger. "Fine. Just fine. I'm just… going to wash up."

"I thought you said you'd already washed up, dear?" Rob's mom says.

His dad mumbles something unintelligible and shuffles off.

I grab Rob's arm and lean in to talk into his ear. "What's with him? Don't tell me this is normal."

Rob starts to say something, then looks away and shrugs.

"Dude, I'm serious," I say. "The last time I was here, your dad was cracking dumb jokes about how his barbecue sauce is made out of unicorn tears. Now look at him! You're really not seeing this?"

"All right," he exhales. "He's a little off. But it doesn't mean anything."

"*My* dad's been off—or more off, anyway—since the funeral. I'm guessing that's the same with yours, right?"

Rob doesn't answer, but his silence says plenty.

His mom bustles to the table with a heaping plate of corn on the cob. "How has your father been holding up, Matthew? I know Mr. Sutton's passing has been tough on everyone at the factory. I hope he hasn't taken it too hard."

"Uh, no," I say. "He's been... his usual self."

"Oh, good," she says, either oblivious or ignoring my tone. "It's just such a horrible thing. I can only imagine what it's been like for Barbara... Mrs. Sutton, I mean. I wish I could talk her through everything or just give her a big hug, but she hasn't returned my messages."

The words jolt through me. "You can't reach her?"

"No, and I've had coffee with Barbara three times a week since I can't remember when. I don't know why she won't let me talk to her, especially now that she needs help the most."

My eyes shoot over to Rob as soon as his mom hurries off to get the rolls. "She can't reach Steph's mom?" I say. "And Emily can't reach Steph?"

"Dude, you need to let it go." Rob turns away, but I see his mouth tighten.

10

I WALK SLOWLY PAST THE LOCKERS, past all the other kids crowded around. I'm not really paying attention to them, or to much of anything. Then my stomach clenches.

It's Plask, walking this way. I put my head down and slide in behind a herd of guys getting out of the gym. Plask ambles by, looking around nervously like he always does. He doesn't see me. I let out a breath.

I can't deal with talking to him, knowing that he knows about me. That he knows the secret I wish I could bury. And that he thinks it's a freaking gift. I don't know what I'm going to do during science class; maybe I'll just skip the rest of the year.

I make it to the lunchroom and drop my tray onto the table with a long sigh. Every part of me feels drained. Not only do I have the whole Plask thing, but it's also everything with Mr. Sutton and the factory too. Right now, I just need to talk about something else, anything else.

"Where is everybody?" I ask.

Rob looks up from his tuna casserole with a crease in his forehead. "Well, *I'm* right here. Thanks for noticing. And Tess is over there like usual. I'm sure she appreciates being overlooked."

I glance over at Tess, her eyes glossy with the glare from her phone screen. Her sandy brown hair hangs down around her face, but she never bothers to brush it back.

"Uh, sorry, Tess," I say.

"*It's okay,*" she says, her typed words spoken by her phone.

"And Phillip," Rob goes on, "is over there, also deeply hurt by not being mentioned."

I startle as I notice Phillip sitting across from me. It's like he suddenly materializes underneath his hoodie, his green eyes peeking out from his pale face.

"So, as I was saying," Rob continues, "*everyone* is already here. Unless, of course, you mean your girlfriend."

"Emily's not my—" I bite my lip to stop myself. So what if I desperately want to see her, and I can't even explain why? Rob doesn't need to know that. "Look, that's just how lunch works here, isn't it? We all eat together, all of us, every day. That's normal. I need things to be normal right now."

Rob looks at me for a minute, then shakes his head. "Hate to break it to you, Matt. There's nothing normal about any of us."

I ignore him and scan the room. Finally I see Emily, walking toward us. I slide out the empty chair beside me for her, regardless of what Rob will say about it. But Emily stops in the middle of the room, glancing hesitantly in the other direction.

Toward the cool table.

"What's she doing?" I mutter.

Rob smirks. "I think she's looking at her *other* boyfriend."

I clench my fists to avoid saying something I'd regret. I keep my eyes trained on Emily, watching as she shifts on her feet, hesitantly debating which way to go. She drops her eyes and takes one step toward us, but she turns the other way.

Her steps slow but she keeps going all the way, right up to Scott. Her lunch tray wobbles in her hands, jostling her mound of mashed potatoes. "Uh, Scott? Hi, uh... I was wondering..."

"She wants to sit with them," I mutter, my face starting to burn. "With *him*."

Rob whistles. "Gutsy move. Didn't think she had it in her."

"They won't let her sit there. They have their table, we have ours. That's the way this works."

I look to Phillip, hoping for support. "We'll see," is all he says.

Emily stands there, turning every possible shade of red. Scott looks up at her, blushing a little himself. "Oh, hi, Emily! What's up?"

"Hi! Yeah, hi, I, uh..." She glances around desperately, then grabs her milk carton and shoves it out toward him. "You want my milk?"

Instead of laughing at her or telling her to drink her own damn milk, Scott puts on that crooked smile again. "Sure," he says. "In fact, maybe you could..."

He glances over at Kyle, his smile faltering. *He's asking permission.* For a second I think that'll be the end of it, because Kyle will tell Emily to get lost. But Kyle looks her up and down, his eyes landing on her chest like a total perv, and nods. Scott pulls a chair over, and Emily slides into it.

"Son of a bitch," I mutter.

"Wow," Rob says. "Good for her."

"Good for her? Are you kidding?"

"*Big news,*" says Tess, tapping away.

"Not now, Tess," I say, more forceful than I should. Then I take a breath ripe with guilt. "Sorry. You're right. I guess Emily sitting there is big news."

"She's not wrong about that," Rob says. "And anyway, yes, good for Emily. I knew one of us would graduate to the cool table. I always thought it'd be me, but there's still time."

"But people don't graduate, or upgrade, or whatever! You said so yourself. The cool kids are carved in stone around here, and the rest of us are losers, right?"

"*Channel 4 News,*" Tess says. "*Sending a reporter.*"

"I don't think it's *that* big, Tess," Rob says. "And Matt, you're just jealous because it's not you over there."

"What?" I say. "You think *I* want to sit with those morons?"

"No, I mean you wish Emily was stuttering to ask *you* to share her milk."

I gape at him.

"*Hey, listen,*" Tess says. "*Channel 4 News reporter, coming today.*"

"Seriously, Tess, I can't deal with that right—"

I stop short because Tess turns her phone around. She turns it slow and holds it out toward me. Her eyes keep staring off in the same direction.

"What's the matter, Tess?" Rob says. "Did the wi-fi disconnect on you?"

"I think she's trying to show us something," I say.

"It's something with the Channel 4 News logo," Phillip says. Geez, I'd almost forgotten he was here again.

I reach slowly toward Tess's phone, unsure of how she'll react. "Is this something you want to show me, Tess? Is it okay if I take this?"

Her face stays peaceful and expressionless and she doesn't look at me, but she nods, sending her hair swishing. I gently pull the phone from her hand and scroll down the page.

"No way," I blurt out.

"Okay, what is it?" Rob says.

"Channel 4 *is* sending a reporter here—to the factory. Crossman's meeting with some investors or something." I keep reading, and suddenly tense up. "Wait, it's about a new product launch. That must've been what Crossman was spouting off about at the funeral! How'd you find this, Tess?"

"Anybody can pull up the Channel 4 website," Rob quips.

"This isn't on their website. It looks like their interview schedule, like something confidential. Seriously, Tess, how'd you find this?"

Phillip leans in to take a look, and his face gives away that he's impressed even though he doesn't say anything.

"Is there a reason you're showing me this?" I ask her. Tess doesn't say anything. I realize she *can't* say anything while I'm holding her phone. Suddenly I hear a shrill voice beside me.

"How *dare* you!"

A bony hand yanks the phone away from me. I turn to see Mrs. Turner, the geography teacher. "You stole her phone!" she yells, stretching the wrinkles around her mouth. "You know she can't take care of herself, and now you go and do this?"

"I didn't steal her phone," I blurt out. "She wanted to show me something."

"Don't give me some story," she snaps. She shoves the phone back into Tess's hands and storms off, all without ever looking or actually saying anything to Tess.

"Sorry about that, Tess," I say. "Don't listen to her."

"You can take care of yourself just fine," Phillip says.

Rob raises an eyebrow but doesn't say anything.

Tess's fingers go back to her phone. "*Thanks,*" she says. "*It's okay.*"

"Either way," I say, "we still need to talk about this meeting with Crossman."

"What's there to talk about?" Rob says. "It's just a stupid photo-op."

"If a reporter's coming in from the city, it's big. And whatever this launch is, it's got both our dads spooked, and neither will tell us why. Maybe this meeting can finally explain some things."

Rob starts to snap something back, but he hesitates.

"I know this has been on your mind, too," I say. "Look, my dad is always distant. He's just worse now. But has your dad ever been like this before?"

"My mom's been off too," Phillip says.

Rob grits his teeth through a long exhale. "Okay, yeah, I'm worried about my dad."

"So you're coming?" I ask him.

He hesitates one more second, then shrugs. "Sure, what the hell. But I'm guessing they won't just let anyone show up to this thing, so what's the plan?"

11

THE AIR WHIPS PAST THE WINDOWS as we rumble in the hatchback on the way to the factory. Part of me is agitated about what we'll find. Part of me is nervous about how this meeting is going to go. And part of me, I'm not gonna lie, is a little excited about skipping class and getting outside. At least I won't bump into Plask again.

We pass the edge of town and there aren't any more houses or buildings, just trees. Lots of them. Then a valley opens up off to the side of us, and the factory comes into view down below.

You can tell it's a factory just by looking at it. It's not ugly, exactly, it's just... well, okay, maybe it is ugly. All concrete blocks—no bricks or glass or anything decorative like that—painted a mix of gray and dark brown. They should probably paint it again with the way it's fading and the lines of rust that trail down from the metal roof, but no one seems to care about that.

The road winds its way down the hill into the parking lot. The good news is there's no gate or security guard to stop us; this place isn't important enough for that.

"So where to now?" Rob asks.

"How should I know?" I shoot back.

"If you don't know, how the hell should I? This was your idea!"

"Look, just... pull into the corner over there."

We slide crooked into a spot, and Rob kills the engine with a cough. "You see Crossman anywhere?" he asks.

I crane my neck to look around the cracked pavement; dirt-spattered cars and pickup trucks all around. Nothing Crossman would be caught dead pulling up in. Then I notice something shimmering up front by the building, and I see three black SUVs with tinted windows. They gleam with money, suddenly making the rust and faded paint of the factory seem embarrassing.

Crossman stands next to the SUVs, shaking hands with an olive-skinned guy in a suit that looks as nice as Crossman's. A woman in a grey pantsuit stands next to them.

"Those must be the investors. Tess was right." I grab the door handle to get out.

"Hold on," Rob says. "What's your plan?"

"What do you mean?"

"They're not going to let a couple snot-nosed kids walk right up and bust in on their meeting."

"I, uh..."

"You got nothing, huh? I told you we shouldn't have come here."

I punch the dashboard, sending up a cloud of fresh dust. "Damn it, Rob! Can you not fight me on this one, for once? Plan or no plan, I need to know what's going on. With Crossman, and this factory that seems to control everything around here, and Steph, and my dad..." I turn to look him in the eye. "Don't you want to know what's going on?"

Rob gives me a long look. "All right, we'll figure something out."

He throws his door open, and I do the same. I start walking toward Crossman and the other suits, not admitting to Rob that I have no idea what I'm going to do when I get there, when I hear a rumbling beside me.

I spin around to see a white van barreling into the lot straight toward me. I jump backward, just in time to get a good look at the giant number 4 on the side of it and the equally giant decal of a face plastered next to that—black hair perfectly swept back over tan skin and an unnaturally wide smile. I manage to read the caption *"Antonio Rivera, keeping you in the know!"* right before I land on my ass.

"Hey, slow down!" Rob yells at the van. He hurries over to me and pulls me up. "You okay, man?"

"Yeah," I say, watching the van dart its way to the front of the building. "Looks like Tess was right about the reporter."

The van screeches to a stop and the door slides open immediately, revealing a smaller version of the face that's painted on the side. Antonio steps out, quick and smooth. He sweeps his hand through his hair, which hardly seems necessary since it's already fused in place with a mountain of hair gel.

"Move your ass, Tom!" he barks. "It'll be your head if I miss this shot because of you."

A dumpy guy with a bald spot and a gut crawls out behind him, huffing to wrangle a video camera. Antonio strides quickly ahead of him, turning that fake smile on with a switch as he approaches Crossman.

"Antonio Rivera, Channel 4 News," he says, with an air of *you should already know who I am.* "Could you all shake hands again so I can get it in my shot?"

Crossman frowns slightly. "I'm sorry, this is a private meeting."

"Of course." Antonio smiles back. "Don't let me interrupt. Tom, are you rolling?"

"I mean that I didn't invite the press," Crossman says. "I'll be holding a press conference later, at a more appropriate time."

"Oh, I'm not here for anything as formal as a press conference. I just happened to be in the neighborhood." Antonio's smile never breaks, even though they both know that's a bold-faced lie. "Why don't you give me a few quotes, since I'm already here?"

Crossman turns to the investors. "Let's move our discussion inside." He waves them toward the door. Antonio crowds in to follow behind them, but then a massive bulk of a man emerges from the door and blocks his path.

"Deckert, I'm taking our guests inside," Crossman says. "Can you please keep this gentleman company out here?"

Deckert nods, as best he can with his tree trunk of a neck. He gives Antonio a subtle but firm shove backward, and Crossman and his bankrollers slip through the door.

"You can't keep me out here!" Antonio puffs out his chest like a peacock. "Don't you know who I am?"

Deckert folds his arms, not even bothering to answer. Antonio moves to step around him, but Deckert gives him another shove.

"This is our chance," I tell Rob. "We can slip in while the sumo wrestler's busy with the news guy."

"That's actually a good idea, for once," Rob says.

"Come on!"

We hurry up to the side of the building, ducking behind cars on the way. I wait until Antonio starts on a fresh tirade before I slip past them and bolt through the front door.

The lobby sits empty. Muted brown carpet stretches through the small room. There's a receptionist desk in the corner, but whoever's usually sitting there is gone now, probably fetching coffee for the VIPs.

"Where'd they go?" I ask.

"How should I know?" Rob says.

"Well, where would they have a meeting in here?"

"I guess I wasn't paying attention on take-your-kid-to-work day."

I ignore the sarcasm and look around. Big double doors sit on the left; I hear a bunch of hums and rattles coming from behind those. I'm guessing the machinery is back there. Crossman wouldn't take his fancy clients back there to get grease on their suits. I glance to the right, down a hallway that sounds a lot quieter.

"This way." I start down the long hallway, past some doors that look like they go to offices, and I flatten up against the wall when I see the suits through a window, sitting at a conference table.

Rob slides up next to me. I shove my finger in front of my mouth to shush him and put my ear up against the wall, straining to listen.

"These new brake pads will change the face of automotive technology," Crossman says, his voice muffled through the wall. "They're lighter and thinner, and they've performed spectacularly in safety tests thus far."

"So that's the big deal he was talking about," I mumble. Now it's Rob's turn to shush me.

"I've read the reports," the other rich guy says. "The pads performed well in normal conditions, but when the vehicle's power assist fails, the results are below required specifications."

"That was only in preliminary tests," Crossman says, a hint of defensiveness in his voice. "We're working through that now. As you know, we're a self-regulating industry, so testing can be handled very quickly."

"Self-regulating or not," the woman cuts in, "the pads still have to meet minimum safety standards."

"I understand," Crossman says. "But remember, a vehicle's power assist fails quite rarely, less than five percent of the time, so that needn't be our primary focus. In normal conditions, the pads performed so well that—"

"I can't invest in your product unless they meet *all* the requirements," the woman interrupts.

"Y-yes, of course," Crossman sputters. "No need for concern. I have no doubt that the next series of tests will show..."

I don't hear the rest of the conversation, being interrupted by a deep voice that booms behind me.

"What the hell are you doing in here?"

I spin to see Deckert towering two feet from me. With his arms crossed, his shoulders pull so tight at his suit they look like they're going to bust right out of it. The glaring eagles on his cufflinks look like they want to shove their talons through my neck.

"I, uh..." My mind whirls. I've got nothing. Maybe Rob was right about needing a plan, but it's way too late for that now.

Rob steps up, flashing his best smile, not an ounce of stress on his face. "Hey there. We just came to say hi to our dads. They both work here."

"We don't let kids in whenever they feel like it," Deckert grunts.

"Nice place in here," Rob goes on, like he didn't even hear him. "Really first-class operation."

Deckert doesn't look impressed. "Mr. Crossman's holding a confidential meeting in there."

"Is that what that is?" Rob glances back at the window with a look of surprise that's almost believable. "Gosh, we didn't want to interrupt anything."

"You get anything on video?" The way Deckert says it, it sounds more like an accusation than a question.

"Video?" I say, trying to keep my voice from cracking.

"I said the meeting was confidential," Deckert rumbles. "I'm not gonna have you posting any of this on the internet or selling it to that dumbass reporter out there."

"Oh, I don't even know how to work the camera on my phone," Rob says casually. "Like I said, we just wanted to say hi to our dads. You know, give them some encouragement for all the great work they do here."

Deckert steps closer, looming over him. Even Rob's smile cracks a little.

"I'm gonna need to see your phone," Deckert says.

"We'll, uh, just be on our way," I stutter.

"You won't be going anywhere. You've gotta deal with me now."

My mind flashes with images of how this is going to play out, none of them good. Then... I get an urge. That tingle in my hands that I've been fighting for so long. I try to push it down, but I hear Plask's words in my head. *It's a gift. Make a difference.* Damn it, if I can't use my Ability at a time like this, then what's the point?

My eyes search for anything I can use. They lock onto a bulletin board on the opposite wall, big and heavy. I clench my teeth together, getting myself ready to pull the board off the wall and right into Deckert's head.

Then one of the office doors swings open, startling me. I glance over to see the last person I expected, or hoped for— my dad.

"Matt?" He scurries over, his face flushed with surprise. Not the good kind. "What are you doing here?"

"We, uh, came to say hi to you," I say. "So... hi!"

"Hi, Mr. Pine," Rob says, his smile still smooth as ever.

Deckert takes a step back. "This is your kid?"

"Yes, I'm... I'm sorry," Dad apologizes.

"They shouldn't be here. Crossman's having a private meeting."

"Of course, of course," Dad says, nodding emphatically. "I'm sorry. I'll take them home right now."

Deckert looks us over, his face cold and unmoving. For what feels like a long moment, I don't think he's going to let us leave.

"Don't let me catch you in here again," he finally says.

I let out a breath of relief, already hurrying toward the exit. The sunshine hits me as I burst out through the doors.

"That was close," I exhale. "For a second there, I thought—"

"What the hell are you doing?" Dad snaps at me.

"We told you. We came to say hi."

"Don't give me that! Since when do we ever say hi to each other?"

My mouth tightens. "Yeah, why would we start caring about each other now?"

"What?"

Rob coughs. "I'll, uh, wait in the car," he says, already on his way.

"Do you have any idea what you almost got yourself into?" Dad says. "What you almost got *me* into?"

"No, I don't actually, because you won't tell me anything," I say. "I was just trying to find out what the hell's going on around here."

"There's nothing going on."

I stifle an angry laugh. "I'm not a little kid anymore, Dad. I'm not stupid."

"Well, you don't need to know about it."

"Don't I?"

"Damn it, Matt, it's my job to protect you!"

"Sure. You've done a great job of that so far."

We stand there breathing heavily, staring each other down.

"Go home," he orders. "We'll talk about this later."

He turns and storms back inside. I watch him, fuming.

We both know we're never going to talk about this again.

12

VOICES MURMUR THROUGH THE HALL, LOCKERS slamming, backpacks rustling. I barely pay attention to any of it.

What the hell was I thinking yesterday? When that dump truck of a dude Deckert loomed over me, I had an uncontrollable, ridiculous urge to use my Ability. To attack, of all things. That wouldn't have worked. Would it? I can't go playing superhero like that. That's all I'd be doing, anyway—playing.

My thoughts are interrupted as I bump into someone. Someone skinny.

"Oh… sorry, Phillip." I didn't see him there, as usual.

"Hey. What happened? The factory?" He never says much, but somehow fills in the rest with his facial expressions.

"Oh, yeah, I wanted to tell you about that," I say. "These two investors in fancy suits showed up to meet with Crossman. A Channel 4 News van showed up, too. Tess was right about that."

"She's smart. More than people think."

"She sure surprised me. I still don't know how she found it, but we wouldn't have known about the meeting without her."

"You get in?"

I nod. "We snuck in while the Channel 4 guy was arguing with Deckert, Crossman's bodyguard or whatever. We were able to overhear a little of the meeting." I catch myself glancing around to make sure no one's listening. "We found out what Crossman was talking about at Sutton's funeral, that big new thing he was so obsessed about. They're launching some new brake pad material that's supposed to change the world, at least to hear Crossman tell it."

Phillip's eyebrows go up, almost all the way to the black spikes of his hair. "Could be big."

"Could be. I don't think it's a done deal yet, though. One of the investors got all fussy about safety testing. The pads didn't pass one of the tests, and Crossman was all defensive about it."

"Then what?"

"Then Deckert showed up. We didn't get to hear any more after that." I feel my stomach twist a little. "Actually, for a minute there, I wasn't sure if he was going to let us leave at all."

"Whoa," Phillip exclaims.

"I know. That guy's bad news, man. My dad happened to stumble in, and Rob talked our way out of there somehow."

"What'd your dad say?"

"Told me to leave it alone, that he's trying to protect me." I let out an aggravated sigh. "He's scared to death but won't say why. Just like everyone else in this town."

Phillip doesn't respond, at least not with words. His face says a few things. I'm trying to get my thoughts together when someone catches my eye down the hall.

Emily.

I could really use a talk with her right now, never mind what Rob would say about it. I'm about to call out to say hi when I stop myself. She's... different today. It takes me a second to put my finger on it. She's not walking like Emily. She's striding, confidently. And there's something else.

She's wearing lipstick. A deep crimson. And as she brushes her hair behind her ear—she never brushes her hair back—I catch that her nails are painted too, the same crimson as her lips. I'd think it looks nice on her, if I wasn't so shocked. She strides straight down the hall, right past me, without missing a step or even looking at me. Like I'm not even here. Like I'm beneath her.

"Wow," Phillip says. "That's new."

I stare after her in shocked silence.

"You okay?" Phillip asks me.

No, I'm not okay. I watch her walk on ahead with the cheerleaders. They smile at her and talk to her like she's one of them, like she's always been one of them.

"...wonder what they're talking about," I mumble.

"The lake party," Phillip says, matter-of-fact.

"What?"

"They're talking about the lake party. Tonight."

"Oh..."

It's not like I don't know about the lake parties, or even what goes on there. Mostly alcohol, and the stuff alcohol tends to lead to. Or so I've heard, anyway, since I've never been to one.

"Okay," I say, "but people like us don't hear about those until afterward, 'cause it's not like we're invited. So how'd you hear about it?"

He shrugs. "People talk when they don't know I'm around."

I look back at Emily. She's laughing with her new friends,

acting like they've known each other as long as I've known her.

"She's going, isn't she?" I ask Phillip.

He won't look at me straight on.

"Isn't she?" I repeat.

He hesitates, then nods.

"Damn it," I huff. "People like us don't go to those parties." It's not like there's an official guest list or anything, it's just understood. Rejects aren't invited. "Emily's one of us. She shouldn't be there."

"Maybe you're not upset that Emily's going," Phillip says. "Maybe you're upset because you want to go. With her."

"What?" I say, trying to hide my shock. "Of course not. I don't want to go to that stupid party." Even I don't believe myself.

I'm picturing Scott getting drunk and trying to go to second base with Emily, or worse. She'd never let him do that, would she? But what really scares me is... what if she *wants* to? I'm about to boil over when I feel a hand on my shoulder.

"Seriously, Phillip, I'm—"

I turn, and it's not Phillip. It's Plask.

"What are *you* doing here?" I bark at him. It comes out a lot meaner than it should, but I can't deal with him right now.

"I... need to talk to you," he says.

"Well, I don't need to talk to you."

"Please, Matt—"

"I don't have time for this. My friend and I have a thing to get to. Right, Phillip?"

I take a step away, expecting Phillip to take the hint and follow me. He doesn't. He gives me a look that somehow says I should talk to Plask, that maybe it's a talk I need to have. I try to debate him with my eyes, but Phillip wins that one.

"Okay, fine," I sigh. It's probably just as well. I can't avoid

Plask forever.

"Let's, uh, go to the science room," Plask says, glancing around at everyone. "Wouldn't want anyone listening in on… your assignment."

"Wouldn't want that," I mutter. I give Phillip a glance as we move on down the hall. "Might as well get this over with."

Plask takes a couple steps into the classroom and turns around toward me. "Matt, what I need to tell you is—"

"You don't know what you saw."

He startles back a step. "What?"

"You think you saw me do something, but you didn't. I didn't."

"Matt, I—"

"I can't do anything special." I suddenly realize I'm coming across way too heavy. I force a laugh, trying to sound natural, but it doesn't work too well. "I mean, how crazy would that be?"

Plask looks at me long and hard, debating. Maybe I'm actually convincing him that he was just seeing things that day. Finally he nods at me, slowly.

"Sure, Matt, sure," he says. "Of course it would be silly to think someone could do… something like that. I guess I'd just always believed, that maybe… and then, when I saw—or I thought I saw—" His eyes search me, making me cringe. "I thought maybe I'd finally found something, someone, that could make a difference."

I force myself to keep staring at him. Plask breaks his gaze, and wrings his hands together. When he speaks again, his voice is quiet.

"I wasn't always going to teach at this school, you know," he says. "This tiny, backward little town." He glances up sheepishly. "Sorry, I don't mean that. Well, maybe I do. It's just… I had a life before this. I had plans. I wasn't going to be a teacher at all. Did you know that? I was going to do things, big things. Space program." Plask's eyes flicker with something, then turn dark. "Didn't work out."

His words fade, and the silence settles over us like an itchy blanket. I'm just starting to wonder if maybe he's right after all, if I do have something special, when a big guy barges through the door.

"Hey, Plask," the guy says, "Stokes is looking for you."

It's Mr. Childress, the assistant principal. He has his auburn hair slicked back more than usual today, like he's trying to impress someone. Probably someone female.

"Oh... hello, Robert," Plask says. I notice something in his face change.

Childress frowns. "For God's sake, Plask, my name's Bob. Can't you get that?"

Plask shrinks a little. He's not making eye contact with him. "Right... Bob, sorry. You said Principal Stokes wants something?"

"You didn't enter your grades from last week. Stokes is ticked." Childress looks sort of smug as he says it, like he tattled on the class nerd. He sweeps his hair back with his hand, though it looks pretty greased back already. I don't think he even notices I'm here.

Plask shakes his head, not just once but repeatedly. "What? No, no, I got those keyed in. I know I did, it was—"

"Look, Plask, I don't have time for this," Childress says dismissively. He glances at his watch. It looks flashy but cheap. "I have to go. I'm meeting everyone at the bar for a drink."

He turns to leave, and strides out the door.

I look back at Plask. For another second he's still hunched over, eyes down, bent into himself. Then he coughs and straightens up, trying to pretend that didn't just happen. But it did happen, and it goes without saying that he isn't invited to the bar with everyone else.

He's a reject, like me.

I feel an angry heat building inside me. Adults should be past this kind of shit. By God, that's not going to be me someday, still stuck at the losers' table when I'm fat and middle-aged.

"Forget that prick," I tell Plask.

He looks up at me like he'd forgotten I was here, and shrugs. "Doesn't matter."

"It does, and it stops here." I start toward the door. "I've got to go."

Something stirs in me. Something I'm probably going to regret later. Something I know I'm going to do anyway.

13

"FINALLY, THIS IS ONE IDEA OF yours I can get behind. I'm all about crashing a party." Rob mans the helm of his hatchback as the twilight slips its way down the sky. "Doesn't seem like you, though. Why are you doing this?"

"Just something I have to do," I say. "Time for a change."

"A change from what?"

"From being a reject and getting shoved out of everything. It's time to stand up for myself."

"You make it sound so noble. Didn't seem to bother you last week."

"Yeah, well, I've given it some thought."

"You mean you've given Emily some thought."

I'd punch him for that, except he's the one driving. "Okay," I admit, "maybe she's the reason I'm thinking about it, but so what? Either way, I'm getting in."

"If you say so."

"Hey, if Emily's getting in, why can't we? It can't be that hard. We've just never tried before."

Rob chuckles. "You don't think Emily's ticket in has something to do with the fact she's cute? I mean, you've got your boyish good looks and all, but she's a lot cuter." He winks at me. "But I'm sure I don't need to tell *you* how cute she is."

Okay, I really am going to punch him in a minute.

We crest the hill and start down into the valley where the lake sits. It's not much of a lake, really; most people would call it a pond, but it's all we have in the way of water around here so we call it a lake. As we get closer, I see a bonfire throwing sparks up into the dying light. The firelight silhouettes a crowd of figures; that's all I can make out from here, except for the cluster of cars and trucks parked haphazardly in the grass.

"So, how you want to do this?" Rob says. "Pull right on up, or wander in the back way?"

"The back way," I tell him.

"I figured." He smirks, but he doesn't jab me with anything else.

We pull up to the ridge and the engine dies off. As soon as we get out, I hear the distorted thudding of bass from a car stereo. We're maybe a hundred feet from the party, and we start through the woods toward it. Well, "woods" is a bit strong. Just like it's not much of a lake, it's not much of a woods either. But there are some trees and bushes and stuff, enough that in the thickening night, the other kids probably won't see us right away.

We get to the edge of the clearing and I stop behind one of the trees that's actually big enough for some cover. I take a good look out at everyone; it's like looking into another world, one where I don't belong or know the rules.

The car bass throbs, the dry leaves under my feet shivering

with each beat. A few cheerleaders dance to it, everyone else is just sort of milling around. A keg sits in the back of one of the pickups, and a couple of coolers lie around. Everyone's drinking out of red plastic cups.

"I need to get a closer look," I tell Rob. I make sure no one's looking this way and hurry out of the woods, darting behind one of the pickup trucks. I peer out from around the dent in the fender.

Rob saunters up and leans casually on the truck beside me. "Dude, you're being ridiculous."

"Quiet!" I shush him. "There she is."

Emily's a few feet away, wearing a pair of skin-tight jeans she wouldn't have been caught dead in two weeks ago. She holds a drink like it's something foreign to her, sipping at it timidly. The fire casts warm shadows across her face.

But I don't have a chance to get lost looking at her, because Scott slides in and lays his arm across her shoulder. And she smiles, damn it.

"Are we gonna hide out here all night, or what?" Rob prods me. "They got free beer!"

"*Shhh!* No. Well, maybe. I don't know yet."

I hear the roar of an engine, the way it sounds when someone's revving it up for show. Then a truck peels up, spinning dirt from its oversized tires.

"Nice truck," Rob says.

Aside from the dirt that just got thrown on it, it's polished to a sheen and just as gaudy. But as nice as it looks, I already know I don't like it. I also know whose truck it is.

Kyle Draughton's.

He steps out of the cab, grinning like the smug little prick he is. Everyone immediately swarms around him like obedient little lemmings. Kyle puffs out his chest, fist-bumping the guys and making eyes at the girls. Everyone swoons a little as he walks past. Even Emily.

Scott shuffles awkwardly. "I'll, uh, get us some more drinks," he tells her.

"Sure," Emily says, though it looks like she's barely made a dent in the one she has. She takes a big gulp to catch up.

"Look at her," I whisper. "She doesn't fit in there."

"Looks like she fits in fine to me," Rob says.

He's wrong about that. Rob doesn't know Emily like I do. Sure she's come out of her shell and dresses fancy now, but she's still the same girl I've known since we were in kindergarten. See, there she goes glancing around at everyone, insecurity on her face. Those aren't her friends. Not like me.

I glower inside as Kyle struts his way toward Emily. "Hey, sexy," he says. "I was hoping you'd make it tonight."

She blushes at him. Kyle looks her up and down, slobbering her whole body with his eyes like he's tasting a piece of meat. It only makes her blush and smile some more. "I was... kind of hoping to see you, too," she says.

My jaw hits the ground.

Kyle smirks like he knew she was going to say that. He turns and struts away. Emily hesitates a moment, chewing her lip... then she follows him. She freaking *follows* him, hurrying to catch up. Never mind that she came with someone else. Never mind that she has *real* friends that she ditched and dumped to the curb.

Without another thought, or probably because I'm *not* thinking, I step out from behind the truck into the firelight. My heart thuds anger in my ears and washes out my vision with red, and I don't see or hear anyone else as I march a straight line toward Emily. I've kept quiet long enough. I grab her arm and yank her back toward me.

"Matt?" she exclaims, her eyes wide. "What're you doing here?"

"What're *you* doing?" I demand, surprised at the forcefulness of my own voice.

She startles, and in the flicker of the bonfire—just for a second—her face flashes back to the old Emily. The Emily I know, or that I used to know.

"What are you talking about?" she says.

"All of *this!*" I shout. "With your clothes, your makeup, and whatever the hell you've turned into!"

Her eyes drop down and she pulls her hair in front of her. The way she used to.

"Am I not good enough for you anymore?" I yell. "Ever since you squirmed your way into this crowd, you've made it a point to avoid me. Damn it, we've known each other since we were five, and now you act like you don't even know me?" I see a pang of hurt cross her face, but I'm not done yet. "But even that wasn't good enough for you, was it? Even after Scott noticed you and turned you into this, you ditched him too as soon as you got a better offer." I see her flinch and glance off to look for Kyle. "That's right," I keep going, "you think I didn't see what happened just now? You're working yourself right up the ladder. Never mind that Kyle's an asshole."

Then the hurt leaves her face, and it sparks with anger instead.

"What makes you so perfect?" Emily snaps back, her voice sharp. "You think I'm such a bad person for making new friends? What makes the old friends so great? Sitting at the loser table every day, everyone pretending we didn't exist. Is that really good enough for *you?*" Her voice comes out like barbs between her gritted teeth. "If you had a chance to be special, you'd do it in a second, too, and you know it."

I feel the words stab me in the chest, cold and sharp. We stand there, the firelight playing across her face as she breathes heavily with rage. My own rage is spent now, leaving me drained and empty. The edges of my vision are coming back into focus, and I realize that everyone hushes quiet, staring at us. The cheerleaders stop dancing and the football players stop drinking. A pop of sparks from the bonfire sends a flurry of embers up into the sky.

I stand there stammering. Emily keeps glaring at me with an anger I've never seen in her before. Everyone else stares at me too, and I see Kyle stomping over with clenched fists.

I have to get out of here. I tear myself away from Emily and run, not daring to look back. I grab Rob and pull him with me through the trees, and we escape in the hatchback until the bonfire is little more than a spark in the darkness of the rear window.

14

BY THE TIME I GET HOME, it's late. Really late. I hold my breath as I put my hand on the doorknob, wondering for a second if I can just stand out here all night. I don't have the energy to get into it with my dad. I'm just working up the will to push the door open when I hear the muffle of voices coming from inside.

Voices—as in more than one.

I hear my dad talking, something about reports or numbers, I think. I press up against the door to make out the rest. The cold of the wood shocks my ear.

"I know you've seen a lot of things come through lately," comes another voice. A man's; he sounds familiar, but I can't quite place it. "You may have seen something… confusing, before we straightened it all out. I need to make sure we're clear on everything."

"We're clear," my dad says with hesitation. "But I don't understand why we couldn't have talked about this tomorrow at the factory, Mr. Crossman."

I get another jolt, not from the cold this time. That's

Crossman in there? In my house? At—I check my watch—12:37a.m.?

"I needed to make sure you understand what's at stake here," Crossman says.

More hesitation. "I understand."

"Do you? Because there's a lot of good that will come from this deal, and a lot of bad... a *lot* of bad... that could come if it doesn't go through."

"Y-yes," Dad stammers. "I understand."

"Just so we're clear."

A chill shivers through me, and it's not from the gust of cold breeze. I'm wondering if I should walk away when the doorknob yanks out of my hand and the door opens. I prepare myself for Crossman, but the figure standing nose to nose with me is way worse and twice his size. Twice mine, too, for that matter.

Deckert.

"What are you doing here?" he rumbles.

I stumble back a step. "I, uh, live here."

Deckert stands there staring me down, his shoulders bulging at his jacket. "Have I met you before?"

I gulp down a swallow that feels like a softball going down my throat and pray he doesn't connect the dots between me and that meeting I snuck into at the factory. I'm also really glad I didn't hit him in the head with that bulletin board, because I'm guessing he'd remember that. "Nope, I don't think so."

"Goodness, Deckert," Crossman says. "Let the boy in. We're guests here, after all."

Deckert finally steps to the side, motioning me in with his arm. He sure as hell isn't acting like a guest. I give serious thought to turning around and running away as fast as I can, but I don't think that's really an option at this point. I reluctantly step through the door.

Dad hurries up to me. "Why the hell did you come home *now?*" he hisses at me under his breath, glancing toward Deckert.

Crossman strides toward me. "This must be your son, then? It's so nice to meet your family." He smiles at me in a way that makes me squirm.

Dad turns toward him. He stands partially in front of me and stiffens there. Crossman sticks out his arm toward me, reaching around Dad. I give his hand a limp shake and let go as quick as I can.

"Your father does important work for me," Crossman says. "This is an exciting time, you know. Important for everyone to recognize their place through it all, so we can accomplish what we set out to do."

I stare at him, no idea what I'm supposed to say. My dad still doesn't move from his spot in between us.

"I'm sure you look up to your father," Crossman says.

I glance toward my dad, who won't look at me. "Sure," I mutter.

"Of course you do. I looked up to mine. He's the one who started us on this journey. And I'm going to make sure we finish it." He steps close to my dad, staring right through him. "It's important to everyone here, including our families. Including *your* family. We don't want to let our families down, do we?"

The silence hangs there. I can hear Deckert breathing across the room. Then Crossman smiles again and turns to leave. "Come, Deckert," he says, his voice smooth as ever. Deckert lumbers out the door with him, giving me a cold stare as he leaves. The door snaps shut behind them.

I turn toward my dad, who's still frozen. "What the hell was that?"

He starts breathing again but won't look at me. "Nothing."

"Don't give me that. That *wasn't* nothing."

"Just go to bed."

"What was Crossman doing in our living room? Was he trying to scare you or something? Because it sure worked on me."

"You shouldn't have been here," Dad says. "Why did you come in when you did?"

"I live here."

"It's past midnight!"

"Okay, fine, I know it's late. I was out, but now I'm back. Which brings me back to *why was Crossman here?*"

"Don't," he snaps. "Don't ask questions."

"Why shouldn't I? I've got plenty of questions about all the shit that's going on around here. Like what Crossman thinks you saw, and why he wants you to forget it?"

"I said don't!" Dad yells. "I'm handling this."

"You're handling it? How exactly are you doing that? By sticking your head up your ass and pretending everything's normal?"

He glares at me, but it's not anger in his eyes. It's something else. "We'll talk about this later."

"Whatever."

I start up the stairs with my rage still fuming. I hear the bottle of scotch clank on the table as I reach the top.

EMILY'S SMILE HAUNTS ME, BLOCKING OUT everything else. The way the firelight plays across it, the way her skin stands out against the dark sky behind her. I can't look away. I'm trying to decide if her smile is real. I trace her lips with my eyes, looking for any hint of something fake. It *has* to be fake. Because next to her, next to that beautiful face cast in firelight and shadow, is Kyle Draughton. That stupid, sleazy grin. The way he's looking at her like he's two seconds away from shoving his hand up her shirt.

She can't be happy with him. Can she?

The image in front of me shakes as something knocks into my elbow and the phone fumbles in my hand. I look up to see Jake Crawford sliding past my desk. He doesn't say anything to me, but he doesn't have to; his smirk says plenty, the same as the dozen others I got on the way in here. He chuckles and drops into a seat. I force the effort to ignore him and look back at my phone, scrolling to the next photo on Emily's feed.

"Let's get started, everyone," says Mrs. Thompson at the

front of the room. "What did everyone think about the reading last night?"

"It sucked," Jake says, and hi-fives his buddy Tom.

Mrs. Thompson sighs and brushes a clump of frizzy hair out of her face. "Don't get me started, Jake."

I hold my phone under the desk and look back at Emily's photos. Selfies in the firelight with Amy and Tracy and the other cheerleaders.

"Can anyone tell me," Mrs. Thompson goes on, "how the Battle of Antietam marked an important change in the Civil War?"

I stare at the images, looking for a break in Emily's smile... but there isn't any. She's happy. Happy with her new friends. And those friends have sent her smiley faces and funny cat GIFs and comments she'd never have gotten from them a couple weeks ago.

—*you look great, girl!*

—*so glad u made it!*

—*u and kyle look HOT 2gether! so jealous!!*

I fight back a barf and scroll past.

Tom raises his hand. "Is Antietam the one where they tried playing rock-paper-scissors instead of shooting at each other?"

"All right, that's it," Mrs. Thompson snaps.

I scroll through more of Emily's feed, through all the comments and emojis, when I stop dead at a pic Jessica Kittner posted. Of me, yelling my tirade at Emily. The moment I want to forget ever happened, stuck up there forever for everyone to comment on.

—*I don't remember inviting this A-hole to the party!*

—*what did this loser want with you, Em?*

I look for Emily's reply. For just a second, I think she'll back me up, tell those pricks off. But the only response she gives is a laughing face emoji. I stare at it until the black lines and yellow face all blur together.

"The Battle of Antietam," Mrs. Thompson lectures, "was important because it halted the Confederate invasion into Maryland. Up to that point, the Union was…"

I flip back to Emily's selfie with Kyle, sticking my thumb over his face so I don't have to look at him. I keep staring at her smile, wondering if I've blown any chance of her ever smiling at me like that.

***

"HEARD YOU CRASHED THE lake party last night."

I look up to see Phillip slide into a seat across from me at the library study table.

"Did Rob tell you?" I ask him.

"I hear things from a lot of people."

That figures. I glance over at Tess at the end of the table. "You hear anything about me, Tess?"

"*You don't want to know*," she says.

Sounds about right.

Rob drops some books on the table and slides into a seat. "What we talking about?"

"Mostly, how I made an ass of myself last night," I say.

"You said it, not me. Oh, and thanks for including me as an accessory to that, by the way."

I stare at a stain on the table. "Sorry."

"I'd ask what got into you," Rob says, "but I think we already know what that is. Or *who* that is."

I glance at Emily across the room. She won't even look at me, as if I don't exist to her anymore. I probably deserve that.

But that smile, the one in her photo, is gone now. Her mouth tightens as she talks with her new friends, and her eyes feel empty.

"She's upset about something," I say.

"Yeah, probably because you unloaded on her last night," Rob says.

"That's not it," Phillip says.

We both turn to look at him.

"She got a postcard from Steph Sutton," he says. "Says she moved to Michigan with her mom, but Emily doesn't believe it. Says Steph would never leave without saying goodbye. She still can't get her to text back."

"Oh, is that all?" Rob quips. "Who'd you hear that from?"

He shrugs. "People say a lot of stuff when they don't know I'm around."

"I think you found your superpower."

"Never mind that," I say. "You realize what this means? There's *definitely* something going on."

"Here you go with your conspiracy theories again," Rob says. "So what if Steph and her mom moved. Her dad just died! Maybe they wanted to make a fresh start somewhere. Move closer to family or something."

"That's not what I mean. Who sends postcards anymore? If you were going to move, is that how you'd tell me?"

Rob pauses with his mouth open. I can tell I made a point there. "Okay, it's a little off. So what?"

"They still have cell reception in Michigan," Phillip says.

"Exactly!" I exclaim. "Why can't Steph send a text, or her mom call yours? Something's up. Something with Crossman and the factory."

"Hold on there," Rob says. "What's Crossman got to do with Steph flaking out and moving?"

"I don't know how it all fits yet, but..." I let out a breath as I debate telling them. "Crossman was at my house last night."

Rob perks up at that. "Wait, he was at your house? When?"

"After we got back from the party."

"That was like midnight! He was in your *house?*"

"What was he doing there?" Phillip asks.

"Talking to my dad. Trying to scare him, I think. I didn't catch it all, but Crossman said something about some report Dad may have seen that could have been 'confusing.' "

"Confusing how?" Rob asks.

"I don't know. Crossman kept going on about how important this project is and how he's going to make sure it goes through. That big guy Deckert was with him, too. It was all kinds of creepy."

"Did your dad tell you what he was talking about?" Phillip asks. "The report or whatever?"

I laugh, even though it's not funny. "Of course not. My dad never talks to me, not even about normal stuff. He clammed up as soon as Crossman left. Damn it, that's the whole problem! No one will talk about whatever it is that's going on, but there *is* something going on, and Steph disappearing is part of it."

"Steph didn't disappear. She moved," Rob says.

"You sure about that?"

I'm interrupted by Tess turning her phone around toward me.

"Tess?" I ask. "Are you trying to show us something again?"

Her face is calm and still. She holds the phone out farther toward me.

I squint at the screen. "It's somebody's cell phone account, like call history and stuff."

"Probably just Tess's," Rob says.

"I don't know whose it is. There's no name, just the phone number."

"Like I said, she just pulled up her own account. What's the matter, Tess, you running out of data?"

"It's not hers. Whose number is this, Tess?"

"She's not going to answer you," Rob mumbles.

I pull out my phone. "I'm going to call the number and find out whose it is."

"Are you kidding?" Rob says.

"Tess wouldn't show this to us if it wasn't important. I'll just ask who it is and pretend I dialed the wrong number." I punch in the digits and hit Call. Perfect—it goes straight to voicemail.

"Hey, this is Steph. You know what to do."

I drop my phone in shock. "Holy shit, it's Steph Sutton's phone!"

"It's *Steph's* number?" Rob jolts upright. "Did she answer?"

"No, it went straight to voicemail."

Rob yanks Tess's phone out of her hands. "How'd you get into Steph's account?"

"Don't take it from her like that," I say, but Tess doesn't give any reaction.

"She was trying to show it to us anyway, wasn't she?" Rob says.

Phillip crowds in beside us. "Look—Steph hasn't sent any texts or made any calls for like a week and a half."

"Who goes that long without using their phone?" I say. "And look at when she stopped. Isn't that right after the funeral?"

Rob presses his lips tight together. He slowly hands the phone back to Tess.

"Don't you owe her an apology?" I tell him.

He looks up at me like a little kid caught stealing cookies. "Oh… uh, yeah. Sorry, Tess. And, uh, finding that was impressive, actually."

Tess's fingers flurry over the phone. *"No problem."*

"That phone data fills in a lot of blanks," I say. *"Now* do you believe me?"

Rob shakes his head. "It still doesn't prove anything, and it certainly doesn't prove this has anything to do with Crossman."

I pound the table with a thud. "Damn it, I don't care if it proves it! I *know* there's something going on, and I'm gonna *do* something about it!"

The last words spill out of me like hot tar, and then a tense silence hangs.

"What do you want to do?" Phillip asks.

"I'm going to Steph's house," I say without a second thought. "To see what really happened to her."

"Are you *serious?"* Rob exclaims.

"You bet I am."

"Look," he says, "even if something did happen, you think it's your place to do something about it?"

"Someone should." I look over at Emily. She's crying now, and one of the other girls pats her shoulder. I drop my eyes.

"You're doing it for her, aren't you?" Rob says.

"So what if I am?"

Phillip gives a subtle nod, calm as always. "I'll go with you."

Rob hesitates, then sighs. "All right, fine. You guys want to break open a conspiracy? You won't get anywhere without me."

16

THE HOUSE LOOMS DARK IN FRONT of us. Long metal tubes of the oversized wind chime on the porch swing slowly, gonging together with a sound that's hollow and cold. I pull my jacket a little tighter and rub my arms.

"We gonna do this, or are we gonna hide here all night?" Rob asks.

"I'm just checking things out first," I shoot back, peering out from the bushes across from the Sutton house. "There's no For Sale sign. If they really moved, wouldn't there be a For Sale sign?"

"Doesn't mean anything," Rob says.

I glance at Phillip, his black hoodie almost completely blending him into the night. He nods toward the house, just as I hear an owl hoot somewhere.

"All right," I say, firming up my resolve. "Let's go." I step out from the bushes and start toward the house, keeping to the shadows, and hurry to the side door. I glance around for any prying eyes, then creep up and press my face against the cold glass in the door.

"See anything?" Phillip asks.

I squish my face in closer. "Not really. It's dark in there."

"God, you're pathetic." Rob shoves me out of the way, and before I even have a chance to react, he smashes his elbow through the glass.

"What're you doing?" I half whisper, half yell. "I wasn't planning on breaking and entering!"

"You're not going to see anything staring in a dark window," Rob says. "Do you want to find out what's going on or not?" He casually reaches through the broken glass and unlocks the door, swinging it open. Phillip shrugs and goes in.

"I hate how you're always right," I mutter, stepping in myself. I switch on my phone's flashlight to cut through the blackness. The beam looks stark and unnatural as it probes the shadows down the narrow hallway to the kitchen.

"What're we even looking for?" Rob says. "Everything looks normal to me."

It does look normal. *Too* normal. "That table shouldn't be there," I say. "If Steph moved, why is the furniture still here?"

Rob hesitates a moment, which means I made a point. "Maybe they're having it shipped later."

Something buzzes past my ear. I swat at it instinctively, bringing a whole swarm of things to graze my hand. I turn my light toward it to see a cloud of bugs, little dots floating in the light. As I step to the counter, the cloud gets thicker and my nose tickles with the smell of rotted fruit.

"Ugh," Rob grunts. "Fruit flies. I'm guessing those used to be bananas."

"Those have been here a while," I say.

"Maybe they forgot about them when they left."

"No. The Suttons didn't move."

"Well, if they didn't move, then where are they?"

"Guys, you'd better see this," comes Phillip's voice from down the hall. I hadn't even realized he'd left the kitchen.

We hurry through to the living room, and my breath catches. A long black shadow drapes across the carpet from a chair that lays toppled over. Broken shards of something scatter through the carpet, what's left of a vase or a mirror.

"I told you something happened here," I say.

"Maybe... they just dropped that on accident," Rob says, but his voice shakes.

My flashlight plays over the shards, and I see a glint stand out in the pile. Something small and silver. I reach in and pick it up. It's round, and as I run my thumb over it, I feel the rough edges of something carved in it.

"What's that?" Rob asks.

I squint through the glare of the reflection, trying to make it out. Finally I see talons and a beak.

"Holy shit!" I drop it like hot coal. "That's Deckert's cufflink!"

"What? How do you know what his cufflinks look like?"

"Because he mashed himself into me at the funeral, that's why. He had silver cufflinks with pissed-off eagles on them, just like this one."

Rob picks it up out of the mess on the floor. "Are you sure it's the same one?"

"Of course I'm sure!" I grab it back from him and shove it in my pocket. "I got a look at them when we were at the factory, too. Deckert was here, Rob."

"Uh, guys..."

I turn toward Phillip's voice. His shadow stands motionless over a blotch on the floor. It looks like someone spilled something, a dark spot the size of a spare tire. I step over to him. My flashlight beam falls on it, and the stain fades from black to red… it's hard to tell in the dim light, but it sure looks red to me. And I smell something, a sick, sweet smell like wet rust. As it hits me, I taste bile in the back of my throat.

"Oh my God, that's blood!" I exclaim.

"Blood?" Rob steps over to take a look. "Are you sure?"

I wave my hand in front of my nose to get that smell away. "Trust me, it's blood."

"I can't tell what it is in this light. Let's not jump to the worst-case scenario."

"Worst-case scenario? Rob, look around! Steph sure as hell didn't move to Michigan. Crossman sent Deckert here, and something very, very bad happened."

"Okay," Rob exhales, rubbing his face with his hands. "Okay, clearly *something* happened here. But we don't know it was Crossman, and we don't know it's as bad as whatever you're imagining."

"You're right, we don't know that. *Yet.* I'm searching the rest of the house."

"Like hell you are," Rob says. "I don't like the look of this. We're getting out of here, now."

But I'm already running up the stairs. "You take the first room. I'm gonna search the one at the end of the landing."

"Got it," Phillip answers as he climbs up behind me. He gives me a nod as he disappears into the first doorway.

"Damn it…" Rob angrily bounds up the steps. "Five minutes, and we're gone."

"Five minutes." I reach the landing and turn to start across the balcony. The darkness of the entryway looms over the railing beside me, except for what's painted gray by the moonlight through the front windows. I'm almost to the room on the far side when I hear something click. I stop dead.

The front door cracks open. My eyes dart down to the door,

then to Rob at the top of the stairs. His eyes bulge in the glare of my flashlight. He ducks backward into the dark doorway where Phillip is. I glance back to the front door as it swings open—there's too much ground for me to get across the hall to Rob, and no time. I spin and duck the other way, sliding into a closet and pulling the door shut. I can still see through the slats in the door, which means whoever's coming in can see my flashlight. I frantically jab at the button, snuffing it out just as I hear footsteps cross the threshold.

"Did you hear something?" comes a man's voice. I crack the closet door ajar to get a better peek and I can see him outlined against the moonlight, tall and skinny.

"What are you talking about, Stiles?" The second voice is deeper, and the man it belongs to is thick and heavy as he steps inside. "This place is dead. Let's do what we came for."

It's not Deckert; I'm quick to notice that. It's also sure as hell not Steph or her mom.

The two shadows move off and out of my field of view. "Shit!" the smaller one, Stiles, blurts out. "What happened in here, Tanner?"

"Boss doesn't like questions. That's what started this whole mess."

I can't even breathe as I strain to listen. Did Crossman send them? He must have. But why, especially when Steph and her mom are already gone?

"What're you doing over there?" comes Tanner's deep voice.

"I told you, I heard something," Stiles answers. "I'm gonna check everything out."

"Well, hurry up. I'll be all set here pretty quick."

I hold my breath as Stiles starts up the stairs toward us.

THE STAIRS SQUEAK AS STILES CREEPS his way up. Moonlight outlines his silhouette, cropped by the slats of the door that hides me.

"Come out, come out, wherever you are..." He shines a light into the bathroom, peering around until he's satisfied there's no one in there. Then he aims the light in my direction. I squint and pull back from the door. The light blinds me through the slats.

"This seems like a good hiding place, don't it?" he says, reaching for the door.

Shit...

Then I hear something, a sneeze or a cough, coming from the other end of the hall. Stiles spins and starts back the other way. Toward Rob and Phillip.

I freeze, unable to move as Stiles steps slowly toward them. My thoughts scream inside me. I can't do anything but hide in here and watch. Except my hands tingle, and there's that voice in my head.

You can do something no one else can do.

No. I can't let that out again, and it wouldn't work anyway.

I hear a click and see something glint in Stiles's hand. The long dark barrel of a gun. He takes another step toward the open doorway.

Don't you want to make a difference? I hear Plask's voice ask me.

It's not that simple. I'm not some action hero.

You have an Ability.

I grit my teeth and push the thought down. It doesn't matter. It couldn't save my mom.

Another step. Stiles is almost to the doorway now.

You can save the world, if you want to. But this time, the voice is my mom's.

"I do want to, Mom," I whisper to myself. "But I don't know how."

You can't if you don't try.

"What if I fail?"

You have to try anyway.

Suddenly something hardens inside me. It doesn't pull my fear away, I'm still scared out of my mind, but it doesn't matter. I throw the door open, quick and silent. Stiles doesn't hear me. I hesitate for one more second, having to will my foot over the threshold. Stiles still has his back to me. He's right at the doorway now, right where my friends are. I take a step toward Stiles, and another, until I'm running toward him.

My hand tingles with energy as I reach out, and his gun drops to the floor.

"What the..." Stiles looks down at his hand.

I'm almost on top of him, and it just comes to me. I reach for the door in my mind, and the tingling in my hand rages to a full burn as I pull as hard as I can. The door slams shut, hitting Stiles right in the face. His head snaps back with a grunt. I take the last stride to him, and for good measure I put my hand on the back of his head and smack his face into the door again. He goes limp and drops to the floor.

When the adrenaline surge fades, I stand there wondering if that really just happened. But I look down at the unconscious thug in front of me, and there's no denying it. I did that.

The door swings open, revealing Rob's silhouette. "What the hell just happened out here?" he whispers.

"No time to explain." I say that because it's true, plus there's no way I can explain it anyway. "Get him into the bedroom."

I can't really see Rob's face, but I can feel the way he's looking at me. He hesitates for a second, but Rob grabs Stiles and helps drags him into the room. Stiles will have a pretty good headache when he wakes up but it doesn't look like I did any permanent damage. Phillip materializes from the shadows. "You okay?" he whispers.

"Yeah, but this isn't over yet," I answer. "There's still one more of them downstairs."

"Then let's get out of here before he finds us," Rob says.

We hurry down the stairs. I cringe as the stairs creak under us, my legs shaking and heart pounding to remind me I'm still terrified. Rob goes straight for the front door. I glance back toward the living room, scanning for movement, trying to find Tanner.

"Come on already!" Rob hisses.

"I hear something," I tell him. It's a whirring from the kitchen. A glow emanates from there, too. I take a hesitant step toward the kitchen doorway. The light shines from above the stove—the microwave.

"What the hell are they cooking at a time like this?" I mutter.

"Matt, we've got to go," Rob says. Then he hesitates. "Wait, do you smell something?"

I stand there squinting at the microwave. Something shimmers inside, and there's a sort of crinkling sound. Rob sniffs again beside me. "Do you smell... gas?"

The tickle hits my nose just as he says it. By the time I realize those shimmers in the microwave are sparks, it's too late.

The explosion blows the microwave door clean off, erupting flames like dragon's breath, and I'm hit by the force of the blast full on. I fall backward, landing just as the door smashes into the opposite wall. My head hits the floor, and I'm not sure if I see stars or if those are more flames.

I painfully roll myself over. The fire churns its way onto the cabinets, belching smoke up to the ceiling. I pull my shirt up over my mouth and stifle a cough against the smoke and the gas fumes. The flames light up the room like daylight, and I see a glimmer of something red and shiny on the other side of the room, underneath the sink where the cabinet door hangs open. The thought takes a second to get through the haze in my head—*fire extinguisher.* I reach out, and the extinguisher skids across the floor toward me. I catch it and fumble before I get the pin pulled and figure out where to squeeze the trigger.

Foam blasts out in a torrent. I wrangle it in my hands like a hissing cobra, straining to aim the spray. It hits the burning shell of the microwave and smothers the flames, but a fresh surge of fire belches out and leaps around the foam, spreading in all directions. I turn the spray back and forth, but the fire spreads faster than I can keep up.

I feel a hand on my shoulder and roll over to see a dark face with a shirt pulled up over the nose. It's Rob, dragging me away from the burning kitchen. Phillip's behind him, shielding his face too.

"Fire's too big, man," Rob coughs, his voice muffled through his shirt. "We've gotta get out of here."

The extinguisher sputters its last, allowing the fire to keep spreading. Rob's right, we need to get out of here. I haul myself up and move toward the front door just as I see a form stumbling down the stairs. It's Stiles, blood dripping out his nose and over his sneer of a mouth.

"You little bastards!" Stiles yells with a cough. He lunges toward me.

I reach toward the window. My hand tingles, and the curtain rod pulls away, dragging the curtains with it. The fabric drapes over Stiles, who stumbles backward. Rob sees it and grabs him in a bear hug, pinning him inside the curtains. Stiles shouts a stream of muffled profanity through the fabric.

"Come on, let's get out of here already!" Rob yells. I pull the door open and we pile outside onto the porch. I'm about to breathe a sigh of relief—and just plain breathe, now that we're clear of the smoke—when I see another figure stepping up.

"Stiles, I told you to get out here already!" Tanner bellows. Then he sees us. "Who the hell are you?"

Rob glances at him with wide eyes, but he's still stuck wrangling Stiles inside the curtains. I look for Phillip, but he's disappeared.

"Damn it, kid, I didn't plan on this," Tanner says, "but the boss said no witnesses." He reaches for his back pocket, but his hand comes back empty. "Where the hell is my gun?"

I catch a glimpse of Phillip emerging from a shadow, holding something that glints of metal. I don't know how Phillip got it away from him. He tosses the gun into the bushes.

Tanner sneers at me and grabs my arm, his grip tight as a bear trap. I see the long tubes of the wind chime hanging from the corner of the roof. I reach for one of them, but Tanner yanks me back. My hand begins to tingle again, moving the tube even though I can't reach it, swinging the tube toward us like a baseball bat. It cracks Tanner square in the head. With a grunt, he loosens his grip and stumbles to his knees.

"Run!" I yell, already sprinting on my way. Rob throws Stiles down, flopping him on the porch in his cocoon of curtains, and takes off in the opposite direction. Phillip's already disappeared again.

I glance back as I reach the street, just as flames breach the roof and lick their way up into the sky. With sirens piercing the night, I keep running, on and on, as if I can ever leave this night behind me.

18

MY LEGS FALTER WHEN I FINALLY burst through my bedroom door, and I stumble to a heap on the floor. I gasp for air, but my heart's beating too fast to get in more than shallow breaths. My shirt sticks to me with a film of sweat and smoke. I peel it off as fast as I can, trying to rid myself of the smell, of everything.

My phone buzzes in my pocket, making me jump like I got stung. I pull it out with trembling hands, almost dropping it as I wipe the sweat out of my eyes to read the text message on my screen.

ROB—u get home ok?

I can barely hold my fingers steady to type back.

MATT—home. definitely not ok. u?

ROB—same. u hear from Phillip?

MATT—not yet. lemme get him on.

I shoot him a message, my eyes locked on the screen for his response.

PHILLIP—...

Those three dots flicker, and my heart jumps into my throat wondering what Phillip is typing. It feels like an eternity until his response pops up.

PHILLIP—home and ok

I feel a weight drop off my back, and ease myself up to sit against the bed. *I'm* the one who talked them into going in there. If either of them hadn't come out...

MATT—glad ur ok

MATT—sorry

ROB—nothing 2b sorry about

PHILLIP—yeah. in this 2gether

MATT—thx, guys. means a lot

ROB—dont get mushy, we need to figure this out

PHILLIP—did u recognize those guys?

I see their faces in my mind, what I could make out through the shadows and smoke.

MATT—not really. sorta familiar but dont know who they r

ROB—same here. guessing they work at the factory

I hesitate before I can get my fingers to type the next line.

MATT—think they know who we are?

ROB—nah, we had shirts over r faces. what I want 2 know is how the hell u knocked that guy out

I look down at my hands, wondering the same thing.

MATT—hard 2 explain

ROB—love 2 see u try. some freaky stuff bck there. stuff i'm trying 2 convince myself I really saw

I stare at the screen, trying to think of a response, but there isn't one.

ROB—u there??

MATT—...

ROB—u saw that stuff 2, Phillip?

PHILLIP—saw some things

MATT—...

MATT—you srprised me 2, Phillip. how did u get that guy's gun?

PHILLIP—I'm good at blending in

ROB—dont change the subject, Matt. What did u do bck there???

MATT—look guys

MATT—...

I'm about to tell them. Tell them everything. I owe them that much, especially after what we went through tonight. But this is too much for a text message or phone call.

MATT—this is somethng need 2 tell u in person

ROB—ok, but you ARE going 2 tell us

MATT—I will

There'll be questions about why I never told them before, over all the years I've known them; I don't know how I'll answer those.

PHILLIP—u think Crossman sent those guys?

MATT—course he did

ROB—we dont know that, they never said his name

MATT—who else would it be?

ROB—better ?? is why they burned the place down

PHILLIP—2 hide what hpnd there

PHILLIP—the blood

That thick smell still hangs like vomit in my throat.

MATT—you think he killed Steph & her mom?

ROB—idk. He sure wanted 2 shut them up, tho

PHILLIP—shut them up about what?

MATT—whatever dirt Mr. Sutton told her about Crossman

ROB—she was just spouting off at the funeral. she can't really have known about a scandal

PHILLIP—what if she did?

My mind is spinning with possibilities when my phone buzzes with another message, this time from someone else.

TESS—are you ok?

Below that is a pic of a burning house. Steph's house.

I stare at the flaming image, knowing this *just* happened and wondering how in the hell Tess got this.

MATT—where did u get this pic?

She doesn't reply. I look closer at the screen. Red and blue lights frame the edges of the photo. Holy crap, this is from a police dashcam! Now I *really* need to know how she got this.

MATT—where, Tess?

TESS—I know you were there. are you ok?

MATT—I'm ok, we all r. thanks. did u get this from police car? how?

No response, not even the three little dots. I think about sending the photo to Rob and Phillip, but I decide against it. My screen flashes back to the group text.

PHILLIP—should we tell Emily?

MATT—…

MATT—dont know

ROB—not just her. do we tell ANYONE?

I wish I knew. What the hell do you do after something like this?

ROB—look, Matt, I want 2 say thx. dont know if we wld've made it out without whatever u did bck there

I can barely make out that last line because I'm crying. There's too much. I'm not sure if I'm scared or proud or confused or maybe all of those together. I made a choice tonight.

I look over at the torn remnant of the superhero poster on the wall. Feeling my mom's smile on me, I pick up the crumpled half off the floor and spread it out to put it back together.

19

IT WAS A SUNDAY. Don't know why I remember that. I sprawled across my bedroom floor with action figures strewn everywhere, like any good five-year-old. Was I five, or was I six here? I guess it doesn't matter. The superhero poster Mom had bought me at the comic book store hung proudly on my wall, and he watched me from behind the paper as I practiced my Ability, getting myself ready to be just like him.

I tried moving my bed and my dresser, but they wouldn't budge and kinda made my hands hurt. That was okay, I was sure big stuff would come later. I'd just have to build up to it. But for now, I stuck with little toy cars and rubber balls. I could move those just fine, but even then, it was a lot harder to control than it looked. One of my action figures jerked around as my hand tingled, the figure sliding and bouncing across the carpet. I could get him to jump up to my hand or move him side to side a little, but what I really wanted to do was get him to hover, do summersaults in midair, that sort of thing. I bit my lip as I tried to concentrate, but he just ended up shooting past me and smacking into the wall like I'd done a dozen times already. Oh well, I'm sure the guy in my poster didn't fly so well the first time he tried. I reached for the comic book lying across the room. My hand tingled, but... nothing happened. Not even a flutter of the pages. I couldn't even feel it, not the way I could feel the other stuff in my mind. It felt sort of fuzzy. I frowned and reached for my action figure again, and he flew back over into my hand just fine. I dropped him to the floor and reached back for the comic book, determined this time. The tingle in my hand grew and started to burn, my face got hot as I strained and pulled—

The door opened. Dad stepped in and I blew out the breath I was holding in.

"Hey, buddy," he said. "Whatcha playing with there?"

"My action figures." I glanced back at the comic book, feeling like it was sticking out its tongue at me. I'd get back to that later.

My dad knelt on the carpet beside me. "They're all superheroes, huh?"

"Yeah! They're so cool, with all their powers! I'm gonna be..." I trailed off, remembering my promise to Mom. It had to be a secret. "I mean, I like to pretend that I could be a superhero, too."

"Very cool. Lots of pretending." Dad picked up one of my action figures, a lady with giant wings, but it seemed like he didn't know what to do with her. He set her back down. "Hey, I got you something."

He pulled out a bag, and took out an action figure—but the little plastic man wasn't wearing a cape or a mask or anything, just a yellow hard hat.

"What's that, Dad?"

"This is a little guy for you to play with. He's a construction worker."

I looked down at my collection of heroes, trying to figure out how this guy in a hard hat was going to save the world with them. He didn't even have a bulldozer.

Dad sensed my skepticism and reached back into the bag. "Oh, he's got some friends, too. See? This one's a police officer. And here's a firefighter. Wouldn't these be fun to play with?"

I took the police officer, looking at the little handcuffs painted on her belt. Those were kinda cool, but the heroes I had could break those cuffs real easy. "I guess so. Thanks, Dad."

"I know you like all your superheroes, but these are *real* heroes."

I hesitated longer than I should have, then nodded.

Dad brushed back the string of hair that was always getting in his face. "Matt, pretending can be fun, but that's all superheroes are. They're not real. You can't grow up to be a superhero, but you can grow up to be a firefighter, a doctor, fly a plane, or lots of other heroic things! Real-life heroic things. Isn't that exciting?"

Dad didn't get it. He didn't know what I was going to become. I wished he could understand.

He slapped my shoulder. "You're gonna grow up to do something really cool, Matt, just like these guys. Have fun with them." He hesitated a moment. "Tell you what... why don't I play with your superhero people for a while, and you can play with these new guys?" Dad smiled at me, and cautiously picked up my action figures. I fought the urge to grab them back. He carried them with him as he walked to the door.

I watched him walk out, frustration and resentment churning in my gut. I *was* going to be a superhero. Not a pilot or a police officer, a superhero. I needed him to know that. Suddenly, I didn't care about my promise to Mom.

I stretched out my hand and felt the tingle, reaching for one of the figures in Dad's hand. In one quick motion, it whipped out and flew across the room to me. I gripped it tight.

Dad spun around. His jaw dropped, and he stared at me. He looked at the figure, then at me, and back again. I smiled, proud. But that's when Mom stepped into view in the doorway. She'd seen. How do moms always do that? She looked at me with tight eyes. Whatever disappointment she felt was masked with tension, preparing for an impact. She turned to Dad, watching him intensely.

He stared at her. It was only for an instant, but there was something questioning, confused, in the way he looked at her. Something stirred in my memory, somewhere I'd seen my dad give that look before... but the memory dissolved, and his eyes seared into me and made me squirm. The whole thing must've taken all of a couple seconds. Finally he laughed, forced and awkward.

"Silly thing must've slipped out of my hand," Dad said. "Didn't mean to throw it back at you like that. Lucky you caught it."

"But Dad," I said, "it was—"

"I should be more careful," he said, cutting me off. He smiled, but it felt like a mask he was putting on.

Mom probed his face with her eyes. "You okay, honey?"

"Of course." Dad reached out to pat her arm, with the slightest hesitation... then he walked away.

I stood there, waiting for what Mom would say. She closed her eyes and let out a long, slow breath, and slowly stepped toward me.

"I'm sorry, Mom," I said. "I know you told me to keep it a secret. But Dad said there aren't real superheroes, only regular ones, and I knew if he could just see what I can do—"

"It's okay," she said. "I knew, sooner or later, it would come out."

I felt my forehead crease as I looked back at the empty doorway. "But he acted like he didn't even see it. He did see it, right?"

"Yes, he did. But I told you, some people... a lot of people... won't understand."

"What if I show him again? I could—"

"No, Matt. I'm sorry." Mom's eyes were firm but sad. "Your dad doesn't believe in superpowers. He doesn't *want* to believe, so he pretended not to see. I don't think he's ever going to understand. That's why you need to keep it a secret, Matt. If you show other people, it could be much worse."

"Worse, how?" I was so damn naive back then.

She shook her head. "I hope you never have to find out."

"So... I really can't show anyone?" I looked down at the superhero in my hand. "I just wanted to save the world."

"I know, Matt. But I told you, these toys aren't the way heroes are. I think... maybe it's time for you to stop playing with them."

It was all I could do to keep my mouth from quivering as I stared at her. I slowly released my fingers, letting the figure, my little plastic hero, drop to the floor. I knew if I looked down at him, I'd cry.

Mom knelt in front of me, putting her soft hand on my face. "Matt, honey, you *can* save the world, if you want to. When it's time to use it... you'll know. But you have to be careful. Some people won't understand, and some will try to stop you."

I looked up at her, confused. "Why would people try to stop me if I'm doing something good?"

"Because you're different, and that can scare people." Her lips tightened, almost too faint to notice. "And not everyone is good."

20

THE LUNCHROOM FEELS NUMB AROUND ME. Or I guess it's me that feels numb. I hear the trays clatter and the footsteps on the cheap tile floor and the gossiping voices, but they're all blurred, snuffed out by the haze in my head.

Emily sits there, across the room, at the cool table. All made up like she does now, the new her. Kyle's beside her. Not Scott—Kyle. I can tell she's upset; the little movements of her face I've gotten to know so well. Kyle doesn't care. He can barely get his eyes off her chest to even look at her face.

The slap of Rob's lunch tray pulls me out of my fog. "Everybody's talking about the fire at Steph's house last night," he says.

"Do they... know?" I ask him.

Rob shakes his head. "They don't know we were there or any of the crazy shit that went down. Just the usual gossip about a house burning down."

I glance back at Emily. That house wasn't just any house to her. It was her friend's house, the friend she hasn't heard from since her dad's funeral. I can see the hurt on her face; but since she isn't speaking to me, all I can do is watch from across the room.

Phillip slides silently into his seat beside me. "You all okay?"

I nod, even though I'm pretty sure I'm not. "I really am sorry I dragged you guys into that," I say.

"You didn't know it was gonna blow up like that." Rob grimaces. "Sorry, bad choice of words. The point is, you may have gotten us into it, but you also got us out. Which reminds me—*how* did you get us out?"

"Look, guys…"

"I need to know how you laid out a dude twice your size," Rob says.

"He was actually kinda scrawny, as far as thugs go."

"You know what I mean. No way you did that without some kinda voodoo. And the other stuff I saw in there makes me wonder if you *did* have some kinda voodoo."

I glance from Phillip to Rob, and end by looking to Tess at the end of the table. My chest feels tight as I try to pull in a breath, knowing what's coming next.

"There's something about me you don't know," I say. "No one does. I can… do things. Things other people can't. That's why when we were kids, I wouldn't shut up about how I was going to be a superhero. But then I realized it wasn't as big as I thought, and… I didn't use it for a long time."

They all stare at me. Well, Tess won't look at me straight on, but I can still tell she's waiting for my next word.

"Use what, man?" Rob asks.

How do I explain something like this? "You remember when we would play football, how the ball would curve?"

"Oh yeah, I forgot about that!" The dimples pop faintly back into his cheeks. "That was so cool. I still don't know how I did that."

"That's the thing, you didn't. *I* did. And the weird stuff at the house last night... I did that too."

Rob's dimples disappear again, and he stares at me without blinking. "Dude, just tell us already."

The point of no return. I reach out, my hand tingling as I pull at Phillip's soda can. It slides toward me, grating slowly against the table until it reaches my hand. Then the grating stops, and the silence deafens me.

I don't hear the voices murmuring or the trays clattering across the room. Everyone beyond the edges of our table might as well not exist. I glance between Rob, Phillip, and Tess, but I can't even look them in the eye. I just count my own heartbeats until I can't stand it anymore.

"Guys?"

I let go of the can and rub my hands together, trying to wipe off the sweat.

"Please say something," I plead. "Anything."

"*Telekinesis*," says Tess.

"Tele-ka-what?" Rob says. "More like holy f—"

"Have you always been able to do that?" Phillip cuts in.

"Pretty much," I say with an exhale. "The first time was when I was about five."

"Hold up," Rob says, his voice rising. "Five? Since you were *five?* You mean to tell me—"

"*Can you do that again?*" Tess asks.

"Yeah," Phillip says. "I'm gonna need to see that one more time."

I reach for Rob's fork, and it flies over to my hand. I set it down on the table.

"*Shouldn't be possible,*" Tess says.

"No shit," Rob says. "But forget that for now. You've known

since you were five? I've been sitting next to you at lunch every day since kindergarten, and you never once bothered to tell me you could've picked me up with your freaking brain?"

"No," I say, fighting the redness in my face. "I mean, it doesn't work like that. I can't move anything big, and I can't even control it that well."

"That's not the point! You're still talking about moving stuff with your..." Rob scratches at his hair, his hands jerky and agitated. "How could you lie to me like this?"

My mouth goes dry, and I can't look at him.

"*He didn't lie if you never asked,*" Tess says.

We all turn to gape at her.

"Uh, thanks, Tess," I say, "but I don't think that helped."

Rob's face flushes to crimson. "I shouldn't have to *ask* about something like this! There is no freaking excuse for you to—"

"Bet it was hard carrying something like that," Phillip interrupts.

"You're taking his side?" Rob snaps at him.

Phillip shrugs. "Just saying."

"Look, guys," I say, "I wanted to tell you—"

"But you didn't," Rob cuts in.

"You're right. I didn't." I blink the tears out of my eyes. "I showed my mom, the first time it happened. I wanted to use it, I... thought it would make me a superhero. Mom said it didn't work like that, that people wouldn't understand. She made me promise to hide it."

Rob's face calms, the red fading. "You promised your mom?"

"Not easy when you're five," Phillip says.

"No, it wasn't," I say. "It was even harder to not use it. I cheated on that a little, like when people couldn't tell it was me. The football."

"But then you stopped altogether, didn't you?" Phillip says. "Why?"

I open my mouth, then hesitate. My mind flashes with the fire; the smoke scratching my lungs, the heat on my face. "It was... that night, when my house burned. When my mom..." A tear escapes my eye and slides down my cheek. "I wanted to use it, that night. I thought that's why I had it, to save her. I pulled the front door open from where I stood in the driveway, but that was it. That was all I could do. I stood there with the heat burning my hand, and I realized my Ability wasn't what I thought it was. Who was I kidding, that I was going to be a superhero? That I thought I could..."

My voice chokes to a stop. I feel a hand on my arm; it's Phillip. He doesn't say anything, but he doesn't have to.

"I didn't want to use it after that," I say. "It was a reminder of how I'd failed. I just wanted to hide from it."

"But you didn't hide from it last night," Phillip says.

"No. I couldn't. I was the one who convinced you guys to go in there, and then all hell broke loose and... I had to do something. But I knew I couldn't take that guy on my own."

"Damn straight," Rob says.

"I knew I couldn't pick him up or throw him or anything," I go on, ignoring him, "but somehow I suddenly knew what to do. How to use my Ability as an advantage anyway. And for the first time in a long time, it felt right."

"So you're going to use it now?" Phillip asks.

"I guess... yeah. After last night, I've decided to use it. When I have to."

"Use it for what?" Rob says. "You're not gonna do something stupid like hunting down those guys from the house, are you?"

"Wasn't planning on it," I say, stifling a shudder. "But we're waist-deep in this now. We can't pretend everything's fine anymore."

My phone buzzes, interrupting my thoughts. I glance at the screen, then at Tess.

"What is this, Tess? Why'd you send this to me?"

"Tess sent you something?" Rob says. "She's never sent me anything."

"She likes me better than you," I quip back to him. I scan through the text on the screen. "It's something from the fire department. Holy crap, it's their report on the fire last night!"

Rob crowds in beside me to get a look. "How the hell did she get her hands on that?"

"This is impressive, Tess," I say. She doesn't look at me, but I think I see a faint smile.

"What's the report say?" Phillip asks. "They have to know it was arson, right?"

Rob shakes his head. "Nope. See there? Says faulty electrical wiring."

"Are you *kidding* me?" I glare at the screen. "Those guys turned the microwave into a bomb! Are they really too stupid to notice that?"

"Maybe it's not that they're stupid," Phillip says.

When he says that, something in me feels cold. "You mean... you think they're covering it up?"

He shrugs, but there's a hesitation in it.

"We have to do something about this," I say.

"*You're* gonna do something?" Rob shakes his head. "Man, you really are on a superhero kick."

"I'm just saying," I huff, "that *we* know what really happened. We can come out with the truth."

"That's a bad idea, man," Rob says. "If the fire department is covering it up, all the more reason to stay out of it."

"I don't care if it's a bad idea. We need to do something."

Rob laughs an irritated chuckle. "So now it's 'we,' huh?"

"Well, I just thought—"

"No. You had a chance for us to be a 'we' ten years ago, the first time you found out about your magic trick. But you kept it to yourself, so you can keep this to yourself too." He pushes up out of his chair.

"Rob, please—"

"Save it," he says, waving me off. "I need some time to think." He walks away without looking back.

"Don't worry about him," Phillip says. "He'll be okay in a day or two. Just a lot to digest."

I blow out a long breath. "No joke. Thanks for sticking around."

"I'm staying too," Tess says.

I smile at her. "Thanks, Tess."

"So now what?" Phillip asks. "You really want to do something about this? The fire?"

I look back at Emily, watching the anxious lines on her face. "Hell yeah I do. For the sake of Steph, her mom, and everyone else Crossman has hurt."

21

THE FADED CONCRETE BUILDING STANDS COLD in front of me. I take a deep breath watching the red sun slip behind it, draping it in shadow.

"Are you sure coming to the police station is a good idea?" Phillip says beside me. "Maybe Rob was right. Should leave well enough alone."

I shake my head. "Somebody's gotta do something about this."

"Maybe so, but why us?"

"We're the ones who know what happened."

Phillip absently tugs on the strings of his hoodie. "Yeah, but only because we were trespassing. Police ask questions about stuff like that."

I turn to look at him. "Look, man... maybe this is stupid, but it's something I have to do."

"Okay," Phillip says without any hesitation. "Then let's go."

I give him a nod of thanks and start forward across the street, not looking back so he can't see the doubt that's still on my face. I reach the front door and grasp the cold metal of the handle. One more breath to convince myself, and I pull.

The starkness of the fluorescent lights makes me blink. Everything feels washed out in here, sort of faded, even though everything's so bright. The clacking of computer keys fills the room, the sound every bit as stark as the lighting. I step across the hard floor until I reach the front desk.

"Can I help you?"

The woman doesn't look up from her computer monitor, and her fingers keep clacking. Her dark hair scrunches behind her in a ponytail, her forehead creased with lines from squinting at her screen.

"We've, uh, got some information about a crime," I say. "Do we fill out a report or something?"

"What is it?" she says with a sigh.

"It's about the fire last night. At the Sutton house."

She shakes her head, her eyes still on her monitor. "That wasn't a crime."

"But it was. We saw someone set that fire."

The clacking stops, and she swivels in her chair to look at me. The lines on her forehead crease tighter. "You know filing a false police report is a chargeable offense?"

"I, uh, didn't know that, actually. But it doesn't matter because this is the truth."

"Really?"

"Really." I force myself not to blink as I meet her stare.

"We did see someone set the fire," Phillip says.

She spins to look at him. "When did you get here?"

"Ma'am?" I say. "Or, uh, officer? This is really important..."

"Susan," comes a new voice, "what are these young men talking about?"

I look over to see a tall man walking with a slow steadiness that borders on creepy. He's thin, muscular, and dark, a good three shades darker than Rob. What creeps me out more than his walk is his face; I'm trying to figure out if he's giving me a massive scowl or if that's just the way he looks with all the wrinkles he's got.

"Chief Ross," the woman says, sounding like she's a little spooked by him too. "These boys say somebody set the fire at the Sutton place last night. Do you want me to take a report?"

"No," he says, his voice low and smooth. "I'll talk to them myself. Would do me good to meet with some of our fine citizens." He smiles in a way that looks like it's going to crack his face. He extends a long arm out toward an office in the back.

I make a quick glance at Phillip, who gives me an *I-hope-you-know-what-you're-doing* look. I take a breath and shuffle behind Ross to the office. The stark light pulls behind us as we step in, replaced by the glow of a desk lamp.

"Sit," he says, which comes out more like a command than an attempt to be polite. I do sit; the chair is a hard plastic that bites into my backside. Phillip squirms into his chair beside me.

Chief Ross folds his hands on the desk in front of him. "I've seen the fire chief's preliminary report about the fire last night," he says. "Says it was an unfortunate accident. Faulty wiring."

"I know what the report says, sir, but—" I stop when Phillip jabs me with his elbow, reminding me we're not supposed to know about that report. Shit. "I mean, I know what people are saying about it," I try to recover. "But that's not what happened. Someone set that fire."

Ross sits there staring at me, his hands never moving from where they're folded. "This type of thing can be difficult to deal with. I'm sure it's easier to accept if we invent someone to blame."

"We're not inventing anything," I say. "We saw two guys break into the house just before the fire started."

The wrinkles around Ross's eyes tighten. "And where were you when you saw this?"

I catch Phillip giving me a sideways glance, but I can remember our cover story just fine without his help. "We were across the street. We'd been studying and decided we needed to take a walk, you know, to clear our heads, and we noticed these two guys standing by the Suttons' door, messing with it."

"Mm-hmm," Ross says. "Well, there are a lot of innocent explanations for something like that. They could have been delivering a package."

"No way were they delivering anything. They busted the door open and went inside."

"They 'busted' it open." His tone is dry, unclear whether he means that as a question.

"Yeah," I say. "Smashed right through the glass." After all, I can say with certainty that the glass on the door got smashed. I just don't mention that it was Rob who did that. "We hung around to see what happened. You know, uh, from across the street. Those guys were only in there a few minutes; when they came out, there was a big bang from inside the house, and then the fire started."

"So these men—whoever they are—you didn't actually see them start the fire." Ross leans forward, almost imperceptibly. "As I said, this kind of tragedy can be difficult to accept. Sometimes we invent things in our mind; embellish the details to change the story. To help us understand it."

"I'm not inventing anything!" It comes out louder than it

should, and I immediately dial it back. "Look, I can tell you everything about those guys. We even heard their names, Stiles and Tanner."

Ross's eyes twitch at that. Maybe I'm finally getting somewhere. Then his look grows static again. "I'd say we can look into it, but I don't see that there's anything to look into."

I feel myself burn inside. Can't he see what's going on? "Sir, this is serious," I plead. "They burned down the Suttons' house. And do we even know where the Suttons are? All we got was a postcard saying they moved, but nobody can reach them. Doesn't that sound strange?"

Ross laughs. "Is that what you're worried about? Let me set your mind at ease, son. I spoke with Mrs. Sutton just the other day."

"You did?" says Phillip. He sounds like he believes him. I don't.

"You talked to her?" I ask. "Why won't she talk to anyone else? And Steph won't, either."

"They suffered a terrible tragedy," Ross says. "They've decided they need to start over, put the past behind them."

"I don't buy that for a second," I say. "There's more going on here."

"Oh?"

"Yeah. A lot more. Can't you see that? The guys that broke into the Suttons' house didn't do it on their own." I bite my lip, then throw everything to the wind. "Crossman sent them."

Phillip inhales a quick breath, then the room falls deathly quiet.

"That's not funny," Ross says.

"I think," Phillip says, "what he was trying to say was—"

"You're right. It's not funny," I say. "It's the truth."

Ross rubs his hands together, slowly. I hear the rough skin

grate together like sandpaper. "You have to be careful about suggesting something like that. You might... offend the wrong person."

Phillip laughs nervously. "My friend comes up with these theories sometimes. He likes to, uh, pretend."

"You shouldn't even pretend about something like that," Ross says firmly.

I clench my teeth. "I'm not—"

"We won't." Phillip jumps out of his chair and pulls me up with him. "Thanks for your time, sir. You're right. I'm sure we were imagining things last night. We'll just, uh, get out of your hair."

I think about pulling back as Phillip tugs me out of the room, think about telling Ross how I really feel, but I don't. Something about Ross's face makes my tongue go numb.

"Remember what I told you," Ross calls out from behind us. "Don't even pretend."

22

"WHAT'D YOU EXPECT? I told you to stay out of it."

Rob's less-than-tactful statement lands like a lump in my stomach as we plod past the lockers, where a couple guys suck face with their girlfriends before class. At least Rob is talking to me again, even if his attitude still has an extra edge to it.

"It's not just that the police chief wouldn't help," I mutter. "I think he's involved."

"Don't go starting on your conspiracy theories again."

"I'm serious. You should've heard the way he was talking. Crossman's paying him off, I know it."

Rob grabs my shirt and presses me up against the lockers. "*Shhh!* How stupid are you? If the police chief is covering for Crossman, you think it's a good idea to go spouting off about it?"

"So now you're on his side too?"

"I'm not saying that." He lets go of me and steps back. "I'm just smart enough to know when I'm in over my head. It's time to drop this."

He turns and walks away, expecting me to follow him. I don't. He can drop this if he wants, but I can't, not after the other night. I squeeze my fists together, feeling the energy in them. Which reminds me... there's someone else I need to talk to about that.

The door creaks softly as I step into the science room. "Mr. Plask? You in here?"

He hunches over his desk with a scattering of papers sprawled all over it. His eyes dart up at me. "Matt? What are you doing here?"

"I need to talk to you. I should've done that already, actually."

I step toward him when I hear a clinking of glass on the other side of the room. I glance over to see a couple of metal shop guys messing with some beakers and bottles. They look at me for a second, indifferent, then go back to the beakers.

"Pete and Tom are making up a lab assignment from the other day," Plask says with a tone of apology.

"It's about the bottle of acid," I continue.

He makes an anxious glance at the shop guys. "Maybe we shouldn't..."

"No. I have to do this now." I take a deep breath to steady myself. "You were right about me. About the... thing I have."

He sucks in a breath. "The thing I saw? It's real?"

I make a quick glance to make sure the shop guys aren't looking, then I reach for Plask's pen. It flies silently to my hand. Plask's eyes bulge like they're going to pop out of his face.

"I didn't want people to know about it," I say, setting the pen back down. "It's not something most people would understand."

"I understand," Plask says quietly.

One of the beakers slips and makes a dull thud against the table.

"Do you know where you got it from?" Plask asks me.

I shake my head. "It just showed up one day, a long time ago."

"Do you know how it works?"

I hear a gush of spilled liquid. One of the guys mutters an f-bomb. Plask doesn't even notice.

"I haven't been using it," I say. "I wanted to get rid of it, but it's… not something I could throw away."

"You didn't want it?" Plask's eyes dig into me as he tries to understand. I choke back a ball of emotion.

"No," I cough. "I didn't. But a couple nights ago, I… pulled it out again."

Plask smiles. I'm vaguely aware of the shop guys mopping up their mess. "What made you change your mind?" he asks.

"Something happened. Something big." The beakers clink behind me. I glance at the guys, making sure they're not looking this way. "I feel like maybe I—"

"No way! She *didn't!*" comes a shrill voice from the doorway. I spin to see Rachel and Cindy strolling in.

"She *so* did, right to my face! And then she…"

I turn back to Plask. "So, yeah, maybe this is why I—"

"Out of my way, skanks," says Lisa Carlson, shoving her way in through the other girls.

"We, uh, don't call each other that," Plask says to the girls, though he's not very commanding about it.

"The thing that's happening," I press on, "I think it might be why I got this… present. But there's a lot going on, and I might need some help—"

Beefy smashes himself in through the door, barreling through everyone else. "What are all my bitches up to?" he booms.

"We really don't talk to each other that way," Plask says, popping up from his chair and scurrying toward the cluster of bodies. "Can you take your seats? Uh, please? And Tom and Pete, you need to wrap up…"

I huff a frustrated breath and plod my way out.

* * *

MY MATH TEXTBOOK THUNKS on my desk and I flip through the frayed pages to last night's assignment. Like I actually care about that right now. Mr. Harkin carefully looks out at the classroom over his glasses, taking attendance.

Kyle barges in, laughing and slapping his buddy Clint on the back. Harkin gives them a glare as they plop into their seats.

"Hey, man," Clint says, nudging Kyle. "Emily sure looked hot at the lake the other night, huh?"

I grit my teeth.

Kyle shrugs. "Yeah, she's hot, I guess. Of course, I got to see a whole lot more of her off in the woods."

I mutter something I'm not proud of under my breath. Good news is, Mr. Harkin doesn't notice because his hearing went a long time ago.

"Time to get started, class," Harkin announces in that raspy voice of his. He tries to pretend he doesn't use the desk for support as he stands up. "Let's talk about last night's homework."

Clint leans a little closer to Kyle. "I thought you were with Heather?"

"Yeah, but she whined too much," Kyle says. "She was kinda hot, but she's not worth all the work."

"I hear ya, man."

"The assignment," Harkin says, oblivious, "was to calculate how much fuel it would take for a jet to circle the earth." He stops, his bushy white eyebrows scrunching down. "Is that right? Or was that from Monday?"

"We didn't have an assignment last night," Beefy rumbles. We did, of course, but can't blame him for trying. With Harkin's memory, it's always worth a shot.

"You're right, Mr. Harkin," Jessica says. "The problem with the jet fuel was last night's assignment."

"Suck up," Beefy coughs under his breath.

"Okay, right," Harkin says. "I liked that problem. Of course, your book oversimplified it. With this problem, you have to remember atmospheric drag, and…"

He starts into a bunch of advanced calculus stuff, way beyond what we're supposed to learn. He tends to do that. How he can be so forgetful and brilliant at the same time, I'll never know.

"So, was the lake a one-time thing?" Clint asks Kyle. "Or are you and Emily, like, together?"

"Dunno yet, man. Just having some fun for now."

I'm about to climb over and punch him, when Harkin slaps his forehead. "I almost forgot! We have a quiz today. Why didn't you remind me?"

Everyone groans collectively, me included. Harkin's quizzes are legendary.

He strides down the rows and dramatically slaps a paper on each desk as he goes by. "I think you're going to like this one," he says. "Make you scratch your head a bit."

Harkin drops me my paper and I stare at the first problem on the page. I think I'll be scratching my head for a while.

I notice Kyle pulling something out of his book bag, and

glance over at him. He spreads a crumpled paper out on his desk next to the quiz. Then I notice his paper looks a lot like the quiz—except it has an extra line at the bottom of each problem.

"The prick got a cheat sheet from somewhere," I mutter. I glance over at Harkin, hoping he sees it, but he never notices anything.

Kyle casually jots down his stolen answers with a dumb smirk on his face. Somebody should wipe that smirk off. I could always raise my hand and blurt out that he's cheating, but that would be pathetic. I'm enough of a reject as it is.

Then I get an idea. There's something else I can do. Maybe it's not as heroic as laying out that guy at the Suttons' house, but I'd still be doing the world a public service to bring Kyle down a peg. No one even has to know it's me. I reach out my hand and feel the tingle, pulling on his cheat sheet… except I can't feel it. I can feel the desk and the books just fine, but that sheet of paper is like a fuzzy haze in my head. I tug harder, my hand beginning to burn, when Kyle grabs the sheet up, scratches in his last stolen answer, and shoves the cheat sheet back into his book bag. Damn… I smolder that I missed my chance to ruin his day. Kyle taps Clint on the shoulder.

"The other thing about Emily," Kyle says into his ear, "is she's *way* better than Heather. If you know what I mean."

My fist squeezes tight around my pencil until it hurts, and the pencil about snaps in two. I tell myself Kyle's blowing smoke, that Emily would never do that. Not with him. But then, I didn't think I'd ever see her with lipstick and nail polish either. I slam my pencil down on the desk; it's not like I care about finishing the damn quiz, and not like I was going to do very well on it anyway. I pull out my phone and flip to Emily's social media. At least Harkin's too oblivious to notice.

I whip through the photos, looking for any hint that Kyle actually did anything with her. Not that Emily's going to have a naked pic of her and Kyle on her feed—God, I hope not, anyway—but I'll be able to tell somehow. Right? I realize how stupid I'm being but keep scrolling anyway, trying to calm myself. Then I get to an old selfie Emily took with Steph. Just giggling together, sitting on what I'm assuming is Steph's bed. Back before that bed, and the house around it, all burned. Back before all of this.

Steph's eyes haunt me as I stare at the photo. Feels like I'm looking at a ghost.

* * *

MY KNOCK SOUNDS HOLLOW on the door. I shuffle awkwardly, waiting until it opens.

"Hi, Matt." Mr. Baldwin brings out his standard-issue school counselor smile. "Glad you could make it."

That's a subtle dig at me, since I tried to ditch our last what-are-you-going-to-do-with-your-life meeting. I say I 'tried to' ditch it because Baldwin tracked me down anyway. He's massively annoying like that.

"Wouldn't miss it," I snip back at him.

He ignores my tone and motions to a chair, then adjusts his sweater vest. He always, always wears sweater vests.

I step into the office and immediately cringe a little because Baldwin stares at me from every angle in here—not just the real him, he's got a couple dozen photos of himself staring too. At an amusement park, at the beach, at a campground in the mountains. His wife and kids smile just as creepy.

"Make yourself comfortable," he says.

I sit down, but I'm not comfortable. My hands fidget on the desk, then I fold them together to keep them still. Baldwin slides into his chair on the other side of the desk, sitting perfectly straight like his shirt still has the hanger in it.

"So last time," he says, "we talked about your interest in—"

"I don't want to talk about that."

His face freezes in mid-syllable, like he's deciding whether to snap at me. Instead, he forces another smile. "Do you want to look at some colleges or vo-tech schools instead?"

"No. There's something else." I scratch at my neck, wondering if I want to go there. Oh, what the hell. "I've got a problem. Counselors are supposed to help solve problems, right?"

His smile strains but doesn't break. "Sometimes."

"Well, this is a big problem. There's something going on at the factory."

Mr. Baldwin cocks an eyebrow, like he might actually be interested. "That's an odd thing to say."

"Maybe so, but there *is* something going on."

"Well, of course there is," he says. "I've heard they're introducing a new product. Everyone's talking about it. Seems very exciting."

"I'm not talking about that. I mean, I think it has something to do with that, but there's something else. Something... bad."

He looks at me sideways. "Bad how?"

"I don't know yet, exactly. But everyone's been acting weird. My dad, Rob's dad, Phillip's mom. Everybody's scared."

"Scared of what?"

I hesitate. "Crossman."

"Mr. Crossman? What's there to be scared of about him?"

"Plenty. Were you at Mr. Sutton's funeral?"

"Yes."

"Then you heard the way he was talking. That's not how you talk at a funeral. And you saw the way Steph's mom ran out?"

"Mrs. Sutton suffered a terrible loss, Matt. We all deal with grief differently; I think we should excuse her outburst considering the circumstances. And Mr. Crossman was just trying to restore a reverent mood after she left. That's not so scary, is it?" Baldwin folds his hands as if he's challenging me.

"Okay, but there's more," I argue. "No one's talked to Steph or her mom since the funeral. Emily heard they moved, but why would they go silent like that? It doesn't make sense."

"Maybe they felt the need to start over. Leave the past behind."

"That's exactly what Chief Ross said, but I don't buy it."

Baldwin's eyebrows shoot up. "You talked with the police chief?"

Maybe I shouldn't have mentioned that. "Uh, long story."

He stares at me a moment, his eyebrows slowly sliding back down. "All right. But why are you so worried about the Suttons? I didn't realize you knew Steph that well."

"I don't, but that doesn't matter. I know people who *do* know her, like Em—" I stop myself and take a breath. "Look, the point is, there's something going on with them. For crying out loud, they burned their house down!"

"Yes, the fire was a tragedy, especially considering the timing. But tragedies happen, and at least it was fortunate that the Suttons had already left and no one got hurt." He pauses, and a question flashes over his face. "And what do you mean 'they' burned the house down?"

I debate whether I should have said that or how much more I should say. Oh, screw it. "I think Crossman's behind it."

Baldwin laughs.

"It's not funny!"

"Wait, you mean you're serious?"

"Yes, I'm serious! Haven't you been listening?"

Baldwin leans forward. "You're saying that Seth Crossman—the owner of Crossman Industries—burned down the Suttons' house?"

"Yeah."

"Matt, you can't say things like that."

"Why can't I?"

"Mr. Crossman is a very important man in this town."

"You mean he's rich. That doesn't mean he can do whatever he wants."

"No, I mean *important*. The factory employs a large portion of Chaplain—I'm guessing your father, too. You can't go spouting accusations against someone like that without reason."

"I've got plenty of reason!"

"Do you? Why would Mr. Crossman possibly want to burn down the Suttons' house?"

"I don't know yet, but I think it has something to do with Mr. Sutton dying in the first place."

Baldwin instantly gets a compassionate look on his face; a rehearsed one, like a stock image he pulled out from somewhere. "Oh, of course," he says. "Now I understand."

"You do?"

"Absolutely. His death has been hard on all of us. And my goodness, you saw it happen, didn't you? I'm sure that must've been very hard on you."

"Well... yeah, but that's not—"

"It can be hard to process when someone we know dies," Baldwin says, ignoring me completely.

"I've had to deal with that before," I say, a hard edge coming over my voice.

"Oh, yes... of course you have, with your mother. And I'm sure Mr. Sutton's death has brought all those memories back, hasn't it?"

"No!" I fight back an image of a burning coffin from my dreams. "It's not that. It's... look, there's something behind all this. Something behind how Mr. Sutton died."

Baldwin leans forward, folding his hands carefully. "Maybe it would help for you to talk to someone about this. Talk about how this has made you feel. I think that would help. Don't you think that would help?"

He smiles again. I wonder what kind of messed-up therapy shit I just doomed myself to.

23

MUFFLED LECTURES DRIFT THROUGH THE CLOSED classroom doors while I plod through the empty hallway. Normally I'd feel guilty about skipping class, but right now I couldn't care less. I walk by the glass of the library and glance in, half the kids with their noses shoved neck-deep in books and the other half joking around not even pretending to study. Then I notice one figure sitting alone, her face washed with the glow of her phone. Tess. I find myself stepping through the door and making my way toward her.

"Hey, Tess. You mind if I sit with you?"

"*Sure,*" she says.

I drop into the chair. "I don't know what to do, Tess. I feel like there's a storm brewing, or maybe it's already here, and I'm the only one paying attention to it. You ever feel like that?"

I glance at her. She shrugs, trails of sandy hair falling around her shoulders. Her eyes stay glued to her phone.

"You probably don't," I say. "I never know what you're looking at over there. But there's something going on, and I need to get to the bottom of it. The problem is, I'm scared about what's down there."

"*It's okay to be scared*," Tess says.

"Maybe so, but what do I do about it? First Mr. Sutton gets killed. God, I don't think I'll ever get that image out of my head. Then my dad gets all weird; I mean, he's always weird, but this is different. And Rob's dad is acting strange too. They know something that's scaring the shit out of them, but they won't say anything." I squeeze my fists as the frustration builds. "If that was all it was, I could deal with it. I might even be able to pretend everything's okay. But then Steph and her mom disappear, and their house burns down, and, oh God, the blood on the carpet..."

I rough up my hair, wishing I could scratch that memory out. Tess keeps tapping. "Somebody should do something about this. Like, an adult should do something. I mean, what am *I* supposed to do? I can't talk to my dad about it, and Rob won't talk to his dad. I just got done with Mr. Baldwin—all he did was tell me how I'm not dealing with my grief, like I need a support group to get me in touch with my feelings or something. Screw him."

Tess pauses for a second, but doesn't say anything.

"I even tried going to the police," I go on. "They're supposed to investigate stuff like this, aren't they? But the chief just told me everything's fine. That I can't go saying bad things about Crossman. Damn it, everything's *not* fine. The police won't help, the fire department is either stupid or lied on their report, and no one else will listen to me... what am I supposed to do?"

"*No easy answer*," Tess says.

"You're right about that one." I watch her, tapping away silently. "You never do say much, do you?"

"*Guess I got used to it*," she says. "*Most people don't talk to me. They don't even think I'm listening."*

That comment lands hard. I watch her gray-blue eyes staring off, and I realize that even I caught myself wondering that when we first met. "I'm sorry about all that, Tess. They just... haven't gotten to know you. You're a great listener, actually. Thanks for letting me vent." I blow out a long breath. "I just wish I could talk to someone who could actually *do* something about all this."

My phone buzzes. I pull it out, and there's a photo of a middle-aged woman on it. She seems familiar, but I can't quite place her.

"Who's this lady, Tess?"

"Someone who can do something."

I stare at the photo, trying to figure out where I've seen her before. Her brownish hair is halfway turning gray, and she's trying to hide her wrinkles under some makeup. She looks done-up, business-like, as if she just stepped out of a board meeting. That's when it hits me.

"This is one of those investors!" I blurt out. "She was there with Crossman when Rob and I snuck into the meeting at the factory!"

Tess nods.

"Wow. I mean, if she's helping pay for those new brake pads, then I guess she could maybe do something," I say. "But how am I supposed to talk to her?"

My phone buzzes again, and a text message flashes across the photo. Ten digits, nothing else.

"Holy... Tess, is this her phone number?"

"Talk to her," Tess says.

"Are you kidding? What would I even say?"

"You said you wanted to."

I tug at my shirt collar to get more air. "Look, I know what I said, but this isn't what I meant! It's not that simple."

I look at Tess, waiting for another reaction. Her blank stare tells me plenty, and I know she's right. I take a deep breath to prepare myself before hitting Call. The ring sounds thin and tinny in my ear.

"Katherine Franc." The woman's voice is quick and even, all business.

"Hi… I, uh, wanted to talk to you about Mr. Crossman."

"Who is this?"

Her voice is so direct that I almost tell her, but I figure that won't go anywhere helpful. "I know some things about what's going on," I say. "Crossman did some bad stuff, and the police won't do anything, so I need your help to make it right."

She takes a long, cold pause. "How did you get this number?"

I fight the urge to laugh. "You wouldn't believe me if I told you. Look…" I spill everything, the whole story—except for the parts that could land me in jail—ending with the thugs at the Suttons' house and the blood on the carpet. Then I hold my breath and wait for her to say something. The line crackles with a pop of static.

"How do you know about the bloodstain?" she says.

Shit. There isn't an easy answer to that question. Oh, what the hell. "I was there the night those guys broke in."

"So you broke into the house too." It's not phrased as a question.

"Well, okay, yeah. The point is, Crossman's up to no good. I think it has something to do with the new brake pads he's trying to launch. He asked you for money for those, right? So can you do something about this?"

"I'm not even going to ask how you know about my investment," Katherine says. "The more important question is how you're inferring that the men who *allegedly* burned down that house have anything to do with Crossman."

"Who else would've sent them?"

Her eye roll is almost audible. "That's hardly a logical connection."

"Why would anyone else want to burn the house down?"

"Why would Crossman want to?" Katherine pushes back.

"Because there's something about this brake pad deal he doesn't want people asking questions about."

More static.

"Don't you care about what Crossman's doing?" I ask.

"I care about protecting my investment."

"Does that mean you'll do something?"

The line clicks dead.

***

MY FOOTSTEPS CRUNCH ON the dry leaves that scatter the sidewalk. A big, bearded guy in coveralls steps out of the hardware store up ahead, juggling an armful of wrenches. A stray dog skitters across the street, headed for the dumpster behind the sandwich shop. I shove my hands farther into my pockets.

Is everyone in Chaplain a coward, a crook, or just plain stupid? They have to see what's going on. But no one's got the balls to do anything about it.

A car engine purrs beside me. I don't really pay attention to it as I keep walking, staring straight ahead. The purr continues, slow and even, staying right with me.

"What are we going to do about this?" comes a low voice.

I startle out of my thoughts and look over to see it's a police car creeping along beside me, matching my pace. Chief Ross stares at me through the open window, his wrinkles creased down to a point over his eyes.

"Um... excuse me?"

"I told you not to go slandering Mr. Crossman," Ross says. "Told you it could be dangerous. Remember?"

Something about the way he's looking at me makes me feel dizzy. "I, uh..."

"People get these crazy ideas in their heads," he says. "Start spouting off conspiracy theories. It can get them into trouble."

"I'm not causing trouble." My voice comes out thinner than I'd like it to.

"Someone is. See, I got a call from Mr. Crossman. Seems one of his investors is asking questions about the fire at the Sutton place. Says someone saw a couple guys go in there."

"She said that?" I can't believe it. Did that call actually work?

Ross's forehead creases a little tighter. "There you go again. I never told you it was a 'she,' did I?"

I glance down at the sidewalk, hoping he doesn't see the panic on my face.

"Most people here have been smart enough to leave well enough alone," Ross says. "But then there's you." He points a long finger at me. "You've been asking questions you shouldn't be. Talking to people you shouldn't be."

I open my mouth but can't decide on a response. The car keeps creeping along beside me.

"If someone digs around because of something they *think* they saw," he says, "it gets everybody riled up. Other folks start digging, too. And if people are foolish enough to keep digging, well..." He cocks his neck until it cracks. "I'd hate to find out what would happen. But you're a smart kid, aren't you? I'm sure you can be smart about this."

Sure, I can be smart. But then I think about Carl Sutton's

bloody face in the burning car, and the bloodstain on Suttons' carpet, and the hurt on Emily's face wondering what happened to her friend. I straighten myself up. "I know what I saw."

Ross clucks his tongue. "I was afraid you'd say that. I don't know how you could be so mistaken. What to do, what to do..." He lets out a long breath that makes an eerie whistle. "Chaplain has suffered so much tragedy already. Carl Sutton passing, and then the fire. I don't know how much more this town can take."

I force myself to stare back at Ross, even as the back of my throat fills with acid and fear. "Do what you have to, and so will I."

His face is cold as frostbite. His eyes never leave me as the car creeps forward painfully slow. I manage to hold myself upright until it finally turns the corner out of sight, then I buckle over and spit vomit on the ground.

24

LOCKERS CLANK SHUT ON EITHER SIDE of me. Ben Carson flies through the crowd on his skateboard, until he bumps right into Principal Stokes. Stokes mutters something to Ben that doesn't sound like a compliment, before he bends over—which takes some effort, given Stokes's waistline—and snatches the skateboard up. A couple of the other skateboarders snicker at Ben's expense, but everyone else just ignores the whole thing and keeps on marching toward the door to get the hell out of here.

I barely feel anything as I plod along with them. After that run-in with Chief Ross, I was sure I'd end up arrested... or at the bottom of the lake. It's been two days since then, and I'm still here; I guess that's a good thing, but I haven't heard any other developments about the fire either. The whole thing is eating at me from the inside.

Rob comes up and shoulder-bumps me, knocking me off balance.

"What the hell, man?" I blurt out.

"So you *are* still pissed," Rob says. "I was wondering."

"I'm not pissed. I'm just..." I search for a more flattering adjective.

"Nah, pissed fits. Look, I'm sorry your trip to the police station didn't go the way you wanted, but I told you it was a bad idea in the first place. Besides, it's not up to you to fix everything."

I'm debating whether Rob might be right like he usually is, when Phillip comes barreling straight toward us, shouting, "Guys! You gotta see this!"

I've never heard Phillip yell that loud. Or yell, period. The green of his eyes seems hyper intense.

"What's wrong?" I ask him. "You okay?"

"Fine," he says. "But this is big. Look what the police just posted!"

He shoves his phone in front of me and hits play. I see an all-too-familiar face, dark and creased with wrinkles. Chief Ross looks like he's trying to smile but not doing a good job of it.

"I have an important announcement about the recent fire on Sycamore Street," he says. "The cause of the fire was, in fact, a crime."

I hold my breath. Did he cave?

"Thankfully, we were able to apprehend those responsible," Ross says. "Two local men, John Stiles and Tanner Drake, are now in custody."

"They actually arrested those guys?" Rob asks.

Chief Ross continues talking; his expression never changes. "These men apparently saw the opportunity of a vacant house and attempted to turn it into a methamphetamine lab. They failed to take proper safety precautions with their equipment and started the fire, destroying the house."

"A meth lab?" I blurt out. "Are you kidding me?"

"I don't have to tell any of you how dangerous a meth operation would be for Chaplain," Ross continues. "Fortunately, we were able to shut it down. The men we have in custody acted alone. There is no indication that anyone else was involved. I'd like to thank my officers for their fine investigative work, as well as the good citizens of Chaplain for their support." The video cuts to black.

"See?" Rob says. "I told you it'd work out."

"Work out?" I look at him, trying to figure out if he's actually serious. "You call this worked out?"

"They arrested the bastards, didn't they?"

"Those guys are just hired thugs. What about Crossman?"

"Would you keep your voice down?" Rob darts glances back and forth. "Besides, you're talking about stuff you don't know anything about."

"I know plenty about it. I was there. *You* were there, remember?"

Rob starts to answer, then shrugs. I look at Phillip, exasperated.

"What do you think, Phillip?"

He hesitates for a moment. "I don't know much about making meth, but I'm pretty sure you don't cook it in a microwave."

"Exactly!" I exclaim. "Doesn't it take a bunch of equipment, like barrels of chemicals and stuff? Where was all that?"

"Look, they *caught* the guys," Rob huffs. "Maybe they had their meth gear in the garage, and we never saw it. Maybe they *were* acting on their own. How should I know?"

I gape at him in disbelief. "You can't really believe that."

"I'm saying we *should* believe it," Rob says. "It's time to drop this."

"So that's it? Just forget the whole thing?" I ball my fists up, wishing I had something to hit. "*I* can't drop this. You didn't see how sketchy Ross acted at the station. He's working for Crossman, I know he is. The only reason he arrested those guys was because he needed somebody to take the fall after I called that investor lady and she started asking questions."

Rob's eyebrows shoot all the way up his forehead. "Hold up, you called *who?*"

"Tess sent me her phone number, and... look, the point is, Crossman wanted to stop her and anyone else from poking around, so he threw this story out there to cover things up. Can't you see that?"

"I told you," Rob says. "It's been dealt with. You need to forget this."

"You want me to *forget?*"

We stand there glaring at each other. Then Rob suddenly smirks. "We should go to the football game tonight," he says.

I blink in stunned silence. "What?"

"Why not?"

"Because we've got bigger problems right now."

"No we don't," Rob says. "I'm telling you, now that those assholes are in jail, everything'll work out fine. You'll see. You just need to get your mind off things. A football game's as good a way as any to do that."

"Even if everything around here was fine, why would I want to..." I shake my head. "We've never gone to a game before."

"So now is a good time to start."

I glance over at Phillip. He shrugs. "Why not?" he says.

"I don't know, man." I glance across the hallway, trying to pretend I'm not looking for anyone specific.

"You're wondering if Emily's gonna be there, aren't you?" Rob says. "And who she's going there to watch?"

I don't even bother with a comeback. I find Emily, her hair draped like red silk down her back. She's with Kyle, touching his arm, making doe eyes at him. Her voice is flirty and confident when she talks to him. Kyle spouts off about the big game tonight, how it's going to be epic, there'll be college recruiters there, blah blah blah. And she gushes about it, like a good doting girlfriend. I can't watch anymore and look away.

"Whatever," I say. "Sure, why not go to a stupid game?"

"There you go," Rob says, ignoring my sarcasm. "You in, Phillip?"

"Sure," he answers. "Besides, maybe Kyle will get sacked by some lug."

"God, I hope so," I chuckle.

I look back down the hall at a small figure walking slowly through the crowd, one careful step at a time, never taking her eyes off her phone.

"We should invite Tess," Phillip announces.

"What?" Rob says.

Phillip shrugs. "Sure. She's one of the group, isn't she?"

"Well, yeah," Rob says, "but she's never come to anything like that before. In fact, I don't think I've ever seen her anywhere outside of school."

"Well... why not ask her?" I say.

"I just told you why not."

"Don't be like that for once." I follow Tess outside as she steps through the door. Somehow she knows exactly when to reach out to push the door open, even though she never looks up.

I push through the door myself and feel the warm sun hit my skin.

"Hey, uh, Tess?"

She keeps walking.

"We're gonna go to the football game tonight. Do you want to come with us?"

Her steps slow to a stop, swishing her hair, but she still doesn't look up.

"What do you think, Tess?" I ask.

I'm waiting for her answer when I see a set of long khaki-clad legs stride toward us from the parking lot.

"Tess?" the man says. "Why didn't you wait for me in the office like I told you?" He reaches her in two more strides, hurried and agitated, and takes Tess by the shoulder. "Your mother and I talked to you about this. We don't want you walking out here on your own, getting hurt or wandering off somewhere. I need to talk to Mr. Stokes about having one of your paras walk you out."

He adjusts the black hipster glasses framing his face and sweeps his dark hair out of his eyes. Then he looks at me, noticing me for the first time. "Who're you?"

"Matt. I'm, uh, Tess's friend."

"Friend? I didn't know... Tess had any friends."

"Well, yeah. I eat lunch with her every day. A bunch of us do."

He squints at me through his glasses. "Wait, you're not making fun of her, are you? Stealing her dessert, that sort of thing?"

"What? No, we'd never do that."

"He's my friend, Dad," Tess says.

He glances at her skeptically, still squinting.

"Thanks, Tess," I say. "See? Look, I was wondering actually, we're going to the football game tonight. I thought maybe Tess would like to come with us?"

"Of course not," her dad says immediately.

"Uh… why not?"

"Are you kidding? A football game? Tess can't go to things like that. It's not safe for her."

"*I'd like to go,*" Tess says.

"Wow, Tess, you really want to?" I ask her.

"She doesn't want to go, and she *can't* go," her dad says firmly.

"But she just said—"

"Wait here, Tess," he interrupts. "I'm going to talk to your friend Mike for a second."

"It's Matt, actually…"

He puts his hand on my shoulder and pulls me a few steps away, glancing back at Tess to make sure she doesn't go anywhere. She doesn't, of course; she just keeps tapping.

"Look," he says, "I appreciate you eating lunch with Tess. I didn't think any of the students would want to eat with her."

"You never asked her who she eats with?"

Something between pain and anger flashes across his face. "In case you haven't noticed, I can't have a normal conversation with her."

"I mean, it's a little different talking through her phone, but that doesn't mean you can't—"

"Her mother and I have been down this road," he snaps. "I've had to accept this is the way things are." He glances back toward Tess again. "Don't go anywhere, Tess. I'll be right there."

"Well," I say, "just because she's different doesn't mean she can't do normal high school stuff. Why not let her come? It's just a football game, and we'll make sure she gets home okay."

He shakes his head briskly. "No. You seem like a nice kid, but you can't possibly protect her."

"But I'm not sure she needs anyone to—"

He turns and walks back to Tess, who still hasn't moved an inch. He puts a hand on her shoulder, soft but firm, and guides her toward the car.

Phillip steps up beside me. "I guess she isn't coming to the game, then," he says.

"You heard all that, huh?"

He shrugs.

I watch as the car drives off. Tess has her head down; I can't decide if she looks sad.

25

THE ROAR OF THE CROWD REVERBERATES with a tin echo off the bleachers. The floodlights cut harshly through the night air. The announcer's voice shouts through the speakers, barely understandable, but with such excitement it's hard not to take notice. One of the cheerleaders gets tossed into the air, spinning like a corkscrew before dropping down into a web of arms waiting to catch her.

Still, somehow I'm having a hard time getting into it all.

"Come on, man," Rob prods. "You could at least *pretend* to have a good time."

Phillip nudges my arm. "Might as well have fun."

My foot lands in something sticky, and the stickiness stays with me as my steps clang up the bleachers. I slide in and sit down, the cold metal shocking me through my worn jeans. The announcer yells something else I can't make out. The crowd seems to like whatever it is, but I don't really care. My mind's on other things.

I try not to look for her, I really do, but I can't help it. Emily sits up by the sideline, where the JV players and the other cool kids hang out. The ones who aren't already on the field.

"You're looking for Emily, aren't you?" says Rob.

"No."

"What's your deal, man? Let her go."

"Get off my back about it, will you?"

"I'm just looking out for you," Rob tells me. "You're acting like you lost her, but you never had her in the first place."

That one stings because I know he's right.

I look out at the field. Kyle breaks the huddle and glances at the bleachers. Emily waves at him, but he's not looking at her.

I follow his eyes to three older guys sitting by themselves. Their football jackets are each a different color, none of them Chaplain High blue. One pulls out a pair of binoculars, another scribbles in a little notebook.

College recruiters. Sure, do the dog and pony show for them. Don't pay attention to your doting girlfriend who's way too good for you, and never mind that you snatched her up from people who really do care about her.

Kyle takes the snap and helmets crack together as the two forward lines smash into each other like a bunch of dump trucks. He spirals the ball up and over the brawl to a skinny receiver downfield.

"That's my boy!" I hear a husky voice bellow.

I see the guy two rows in front of us. He just *looks* like Kyle's dad; tall and lean, but with enough lines on his face to tell that it's been a couple decades since he played football himself. But I'm sure he did play, and I'm sure he was just as big a jerk about it.

"Look at the arm on him!" he says, jabbing an elbow at the guy next to him. "Think what he could do if he had some real players to work with, huh? Not these jokes he's stuck with."

"What a prick," I mutter.

"No kidding." Rob gives me a sly grin. "You could take him down a notch, you know."

"What are you talking about?"

He grins some more. "Your magic trick."

I'm about to tell Rob there's no way I'm not going to use it for something petty like that, but then I think... what the hell. If anyone deserves it, it's someone with the last name Draughton. I see a soda cup sitting on the bleacher in front of him, a ginormous one you could use to irrigate a small farm. With a rush of nerves, my hand tingles as I reach for the cup.

It slides toward me, dragging along the metal of the bleacher, and then it drops. Topples off the edge in glorious slow motion. I watch it burst like a dam, spewing out its syrupy, foamy torrents, vomiting all over him.

"What the hell?" Draughton erupts, bolting to his feet. "Hey, buddy! What the hell, huh?"

He shoves the guy in front of him. The guy stands up, with effort. He looks like he used to play football, too, but it looks like he may have *eaten* a few football players since then.

"What's your deal?" rumbles the big guy.

"*My* deal? You're the one who spilled your drink all over me!" Draughton shoves him again.

Then the big guy shoves back, and he's got enough weight on him that Draughton tips backward into the seat behind him.

Normally, I'd love to see what happens next. I'd pay good money to see Kyle's dad get his face punched in. But an urge bubbles up in me that I have to let out.

"I've gotta go," I say. "I want to try something."

"And miss this?" Rob says. He pulls out his phone. "Don't worry, I'll get it on video."

I start to stand up when I feel a tug on my arm. I turn back to see Phillip looking at me intently.

"You sure about whatever it is you're doing?" he asks.

I hesitate for a second, but I have to do this. And if I don't do it now, I'll lose my nerve. "Yeah. Don't worry about it." I turn before he guilt-trips me any more, clanging my way down the bleachers. Right to the railing at the edge, and I glare out at Kyle. I feel the hate building in me. Why does everyone fawn over him for no reason? Even Emily. All because he can throw a damn football.

Well, I can do something too.

Kyle takes the ball and drops back. One of the receivers sprints off down the field. Kyle watches him, casual almost, as the linemen crush against the visiting team, straining to hold them back. He looks toward the stands—not at Emily, as if he cares about her, but at those recruiters. His big moment. We'll see about that.

I reach out my hand, feeling the energy. Kyle plants himself, pulling his arm back. And then, just when it matters, I tug at the ball.

It lingers, hovers there for a moment. Then it rolls right out of his fingers. Kyle brings his hand forward to throw, only then realizing that the ball isn't in it. His eyes go wide, dart to the ball, and watch it drop; and that smug smile finally wipes off his face.

The crowd behind me takes a collective gasp as time stands still for one glorious second. I watch the ball hit the grass. Kyle scrambles for it, losing his mind, but it takes a bounce and jumps away from him. And then, as if on cue, the linemen wrench apart. One of the visiting team bursts through, a burly guy wearing number 23, and two steps later he scoops up the ball and takes off with it. And Kyle just watches, dazed, looking like he might fall over. I find myself laughing while 23 gallops toward the end zone, with a trail of linemen huffing hopelessly after him. He crosses the goal line just as the ref's whistle shrills the end of the game. The college recruiters shake their heads in disgust and struggle their way out of their seats to leave.

I did that.

Kyle totters there at midfield. The other players file past him; some pat him on the back like it's okay, others give him dirty looks. The crowd slowly files out of the stadium, everyone sort of slumped over, a mix of bummed and embarrassed. I take it all in, thinking this must be what Kyle feels like when he actually wins a game.

"What's up with you?" someone asks me.

I turn to see Phillip. He's got genuine concern on his face that almost snaps me out of my gloating.

"Why do you think there's anything up with me?" I push back.

He points up to the bleachers. "*That's* certainly not like you."

Draughton and the big guy are still shouting and shoving each other. A short, sixty-plus-year-old security guard hurries up to pry them apart, failing to make much headway.

"You really think that was a good idea?" Phillip asks. "And don't tell me Kyle dropped that ball on his own."

I don't answer. I'm not even looking at him. My eyes move past him to Emily, who's heading toward the locker rooms to wait for Kyle.

"You and Rob take off without me," I tell him.

"Matt, seriously... you're not gonna do something you'll regret, are you?"

"I'm done having regrets."

I stride off, more confident than I've ever been.

26

"EMILY."

When I say her name, I feel like I'm saying it for the first time. She turns toward me, her hair draping over her shoulder. I feel like I'm looking at her for the first time, too.

"Matt?"

I step up to her, over the last of the fall grass that hasn't died out yet, into the back corner behind the bleachers. A single light casts a dull flicker over everything.

"What a downer tonight, huh?" she says.

I bite my lip to keep from smiling. "I guess so."

We stand there for a moment, the light flickering. The murmur of conversations fades as the crowd makes their way out of the stadium.

"I'm... waiting for Kyle," Emily says.

"I know."

She gives me a look, confused and a little irritated. "So why are you here?"

"You shouldn't be with him." My voice is strong. I barely

recognize it. It feels good.

"Matt, if this is more of what you unloaded on me at the lake, about me ditching you guys at the lunch table, then—"

"I'm not talking about that. I mean you should be with me. *With* me."

Emily cocks her head, like she doesn't know what she's looking at. "What're you talking about?"

"I like you, as more than a friend. I have for a while now."

"Seriously?" she says. "You're serious right now?"

"Yeah, I am." I reach up and brush her hair back. Emily flinches but doesn't pull away. Her hair feels soft and smooth. And she's got earrings now, those are new. "I saw you before all this. Before Kyle even knew who you were."

Her mouth quivers, like she's trying to figure out what to say but nothing comes out.

I take a step closer. I put my hand on her arm. "You should be with *me*."

"What the hell are you doing?" comes a new voice.

I hadn't even noticed Kyle step up beside us. Kyle and the pack of letter jackets with him.

I also hadn't noticed how isolated this corner is, and how the voices of the crowd are pretty far away now.

"We're just talking," Emily says.

"Just talking?" Kyle steps closer. "Looks like you're doing a lot more than that."

"Why don't you mind your own damn business?" I tell him.

Kyle grabs Emily's shoulder, firmly, and pushes her away. "Clint, why don't you walk Emily to my truck?" he says, without looking at her. "I'll be there in a minute."

Clint grabs her and drags her away.

"Don't hurt him, Kyle!" she calls over her shoulder.

"It's okay, Emily," I say. "I can take care of myself."

"Oh, yeah?" Kyle sets his face hard. "You can take care of yourself, huh?"

"Better than you can. Like the way you handled that game-winning pass?"

I watch Kyle's face explode, like a bomb of rage went off under the surface. Good.

Then his fist comes at me.

I watch it, paralyzed. Time stretches out; then his fist connects, and I feel the flesh on my cheek crush against my teeth. A firecracker of pain goes off inside my mouth. I spin awkwardly and my knee buckles, suddenly unable to hold me up. I drop over and my hands catch me. The rough dirt grates into my palms. I taste blood, thick and salty, and spit red onto the ground.

I look up and see Kyle glaring over me, his fists clenched tight. I push myself up and stumble backward, but in two steps my back hits the wall. Kyle stalks toward me. I think about running but there are letter jackets all around him, crowding me in. Besides, my legs are barely holding me up as it is. I press my back further into the cold concrete behind me.

Get yourself together, I tell myself. *You're a superhero, damn it.*

I force myself up straight and hold out my hand, and pull at Kyle's bulky form. My hand burns until it hurts, but of course it doesn't do anything. He's too big for me to move, they all are. Cold fear rushes over me as I realize there's nothing I can do.

Kyle hits me again, crushing my eye like a meat hammer. I drop to the ground, cowering like a scared, pathetic little dog, the cold dirt scratching into my cheek.

27

"MATTHEW? I... didn't think you'd be home so late."

Damn.

I wasn't expecting Dad to still be up. I'd taken the long way home and even doubled back around the block just to make sure he'd be in bed. So much for that.

"Yeah, uh, the game went into overtime," I say.

The living room is dark as I walk in. At least that's lucky. I'm just hoping I can get up the stairs without him seeing my face.

"I've been wanting to talk to you," Dad says. "Why don't you sit down, and we can—"

"I'm really tired, actually."

I take quick strides across the room, as quick as I can without running. The lights come on before I'm halfway across. My hand goes up over my face, even though I know it won't do any good.

"Matthew! What happened to you?"

I drop my hand. No matter how hard I try, I can't help feeling ashamed. I expect Dad to shout at me, ground me, all of that.

But that's not what he does.

"My God, this is my fault!" he exclaims. "It's my fault, it's my fault..."

He reaches up and touches my cheek. It stings, more from shock than pain.

"Are you all right?" Dad asks, pleading almost. "It was him, wasn't it? I knew it. I knew he'd do something like this..."

I look at him, stunned into silence. What scares me more than anything is that I don't have to ask him who he thinks hit me, or even why.

***

THE COLD MORNING AIR stings my cheek while I wait for Rob's hatchback to get here. The pain has mostly sunk down to a dull ache, but I'm still very much aware of it. And it's not like I slept much last night.

Rob pulls up and I get in, holding my hand up to cover my face again. I don't know why, it's not like it's going to fool anyone. Maybe I'm hoping the bruise will magically disappear.

"Dude, what happened to you?"

I guess it didn't.

"I don't want to talk about it," I tell him.

"You okay, man? I've never seen you get beat up before." Then his face changes. "Wait... this was about Emily, wasn't it?"

I stare out the windshield. "Don't go there, man."

"I'm going there because *you* went there," Rob says. "Where's all this stupidity coming from? What did you do, pick a fight with Kyle or something?"

"I said I don't want to talk about it."

"Oh my God, you did, didn't you? *Kyle?* What were you

thinking, Matt?"

There's no way I can answer that question. I keep staring straight ahead.

"You really thought you could get Emily that way?" Rob says. "She's gone, Matt."

I watch a trash wrapper drift across the sidewalk. "Can we just go to school? Please?"

There's a long pause. The car shudders as Rob shoves it into gear, and we head off.

But Rob is the least of my problems. Everyone stares at me as soon as I walk through the door. I just want to forget about last night, forget about the whole week, but now it's branded into my face for everyone to see.

I almost don't care about what anyone thinks. Almost. Then I see Emily. She looks at me, and for an instant, I see concern on her face. Then the expression fades and she looks away, all as if she never saw me.

And suddenly, I'm not depressed or ashamed anymore. I'm mad. Not at Emily, not at any of the other idiots snickering at me right now. At someone else. Someone who got me into all of this.

I march down the hall, feeling the anger pound in each step, to the science room and then burst through the door.

"This is your fault, Plask!" I yell, not even caring that there are other people in the room. "This is all your damned fault!"

Plask stares at me in utter shock. A cluster of girls on the other side of the room moves back a few steps, but they hover there to watch the train wreck I just started.

"What are you talking about?" Plask asks.

"You know damn well."

"What happened to your face?"

"*You* did! You happened! I had this thing repressed, buried down inside, and I *liked* it that way. Maybe it wasn't heroic, but it was *safe*. And then you saw it and dragged it out of me, filled my head with all this stupid talk about finding myself and making a difference. Well, I made a difference, all right! I made an ass of myself!"

Plask's mouth quivers. "Matt, I... I don't know what happened, but—"

"You made me use it. That's what happened."

"Matt, I never meant for you to... are you okay?"

"No, I'm *not* okay! I should've left it alone, left it buried. You made me think it was good for something, but it isn't, is it? *Is it?*"

He struggles to find what to say. I don't wait to hear what it is. I turn and push past the girls who're pretending not to listen to us and storm out the door.

28

A COUPLE OF CROWS CAW OVERHEAD while I trudge down the street. The cold breeze makes the bruise on my cheek burn. How could I be so stupid? I wish I could keep blaming Plask; that would make it easier. But deep down, I know this is my own damn fault. Mom would be ashamed of me.

The crows keep cawing, like they're jeering at me. It's all I can do to push down the shouts of guilt coming from inside my head. My eyes are on the cracks in the sidewalk... until a trail of yellow caution tape slides into my view.

I stop and look up. The charred carcass of the house stands out starkly against everything else. Steph's house.

My lungs itch, remembering the smoke from that night. The image of Stiles's bloody face rushing down the stairs fills my head. It makes every part of me tense... just when a lady rides casually by on a bike, ignoring the crime scene completely, not a care in the world.

Damn it, why will no one pay attention to this? I pull out my phone and snap a pic and post it on my feed, as if anyone will actually see that. I punch out the caption, *"This is all that's left."*

I chew my lip as I think about Chief Ross's ridiculous explanation. Meth lab, my ass. *I* know what happened in there. And I know who's behind it all, no matter what the police or Rob or anyone else tries to tell me.

My phone buzzes, and I look to see the same photo I just posted, but this is from Tess. She texts me one word with the photo—*discouraged?*

I stare at the screen. Yeah, I'm discouraged. How can she have me pegged so well, especially when no one else will even listen to me?

MATT—*guess so. just wish I could do something*

MATT—*thanks, btw*

She sends me a map of town. It's got a red dot stuck a few blocks from here.

MATT—*what's there, Tess?*

TESS—*do something about this*

MATT—*do what?*

I get no response. Tess does cryptic well. I shove the phone away and look back at the house; what's left of it. Well, I said I wanted to do something, didn't I? I start off at a brisk pace, with the crows cawing behind me.

* * *

THE COFFEE SHOP SITS lonely on the corner. This isn't one of those swanky places with the suede lounge chairs and the mood lighting, not even close. It's basically a shed with a hole cut out of the front for a counter, with one pathetic patio table off to the side where you can drink your watered-down latte. I'm wondering why on earth Tess sent me here. She doesn't think a little caffeine will fix all of this, does she? That's a bit shortsighted. I round the side of the building, wondering if maybe I will get a coffee or a muffin since I'm here anyway, when I see the gleam of the SUV parked on the curb. I tense up, looking for Crossman—or worse, Deckert—but then I see a lady in a navy pantsuit standing at the counter.

"I can't believe you don't have soy milk," she huffs.

"Sorry," says Susie behind the counter. She doesn't sound very sorry. "We don't get a lot of call for that around here."

It's Katherine Franc, the investor. How Tess found her, I'll never know.

"And no gluten-free muffins?" she says.

Susie shrugs.

"I suppose I'll just have to wait till I get back to the city, then," Katherine says, and steps away. Toward me.

For a second, I think about letting her walk right past me. She looks a lot more intimidating than in her photo. Then I think about the Suttons' charred house, and I step into her path.

"I need to talk to you," I say.

"I'm in a hurry."

"It's about those guys who got arrested for burning down the Suttons' house."

Katherine stops, and her eyes narrow. "You're the one who called me the other day." She says it decisively, no hint of a question. I find myself flinching a little as she looks me up and down. "Thought you'd be taller," she says. "And it looks like you lost whatever fight you got in."

I force myself to ignore that. "Those guys at the house weren't making a meth lab."

"I don't much care what they were doing. They're in police custody, so whatever it was, it's over."

"They're not the problem, though. They're just taking the fall."

"Implying that someone else sent them," she says.

"Crossman."

She stares me down with her steel blue eyes. I hold her gaze as long as I can, then I switch my focus to the top of her head. She's got a patch of gray coming in there, fading out the brown.

"You don't seem to give up easily," Katherine finally says, "so I'm sure you'll be disappointed to know that I don't share your enthusiasm for this witch hunt." She steps around me.

"You believed me when I talked to you the first time," I call after her. She stops.

"What I believed," she says, her voice clipped, "is that there were loose ends. I don't like loose ends on my investments."

"It made you ask questions, and it got Crossman rattled enough that he—"

"I made inquiries. Once recent events satisfied those inquiries, I moved on."

I glare at her with my mouth open. "You mean you believe him? You're going to let him get away with it?"

Katherine crosses her arms. Her jacket is so stiff it barely moves. "Young man, the police conducted their investigation. They have presented their findings, which explain the events in a way that is perfectly reasonable and satisfactory. And nowhere in their findings is there any room for accusation against Crossman."

"That's because the police are working for him."

"So you say."

"You have to see this is a cover story," I plead. "Please, if you ask Crossman about—"

"Once I get the answer I'm looking for, I stop asking."

Her answer stops me cold. "So that's it. You don't *want* to know the truth. You'd rather believe whatever story will make you the most money."

"I'll choose to ignore your tone," Katherine says. "You're young; when you grow up, you'll learn how things are."

"That doesn't mean it's how they have to be."

When she smiles, it feels condescending. "You keep believing that. See how far it gets you."

She steps past me to her shiny SUV and glides off.

29

I GET TO THE SCHOOL JUST when it's letting out. Everyone piles out through the doors, bitching about flunking the history test or talking about the video they're going to post tonight. I swim upstream through the crowd to get inside. No one even asks me why I'm the only idiot going back in. Doesn't bother me. I don't feel like talking to them, either.

I peek into the science room, half hoping Plask is gone. Not that lucky.

"Matt? What are you doing here?"

I take an awkward step into the room. "I need to... apologize to you," I say.

He looks down. "It's okay."

"No, it's not. I shouldn't have yelled at you like that."

"I shouldn't have pushed you like I did."

"You didn't push me into anything," I say. "You just helped me see what I have. That it matters. That I should use it."

"Thanks," Plask says. "I was afraid I came on too strong. People tell me I do that."

"Maybe a little, but it's okay. You have to be who you are." I glance awkwardly around the room, unsure what to look at. "There's, uh, something else. I was hoping you could—"

"People don't like who I am," he mumbles.

"What?"

He looks down at his hands. "I didn't say anything."

"Yeah, you said… people don't like you?"

Plask shrugs, his eyes still down. "You said I have to be who I am, but people don't like who I am. So where does that leave me?" He clenches his fists, then releases them and looks up. "Sorry. Forget I said that. What were you saying?"

I look at him, suddenly realizing why he's always in this classroom. I don't think he has anywhere else to go, let alone anyone to go there with.

"Why don't we, uh, get something to eat?" I hear myself say.

"What?" He looks at me surprised. "No, you don't want to do that."

"But I really do," I say, almost making myself believe it. "We could go to the diner or something. I mean, I'm really hungry, and it'd be nice to have some company."

Plask hesitates, then smiles, pulling his cheeks into crooked wrinkles.

＊ ＊ ＊

THE DINER IS QUIET. There are a couple of truckers in the back finishing off the last of their early bird specials, but that's it. There's a comfortable feel in here; not just because the place hasn't changed since I was five, but because it's the picture everyone has in their head when you say "small town diner." Even has the typical black-and-white checkered floor, though it's gotten pretty scuffed over the years.

We sit down on the bar stools, and I feel the worn padding of the seat smush underneath me. The waitress sits at the far end scribbling at a crossword puzzle, and looks up over her glasses at us. She slides off her stool and lazily strolls over, pulling a pad out of her apron and a pencil out of her hair.

"What'll ya have?" she croaks, with a hoarse voice that I'm guessing cigarettes had something to do with.

Plask fumbles with the menu. "I'll have the, uh, ham sandwich. And a salad."

She turns to me and taps the pencil.

"Cheeseburger," I say.

She strolls around behind the counter and slaps the order down, calls, "Order up!" and then drops onto her stool to go back to her crossword.

"Thanks," I tell Plask. "For, uh, bringing me along."

"Oh, sure, sure," he says.

We share an awkward look. I suddenly realize I have no idea what we're supposed to talk about.

"Were you really going to work on the space program?" I ask him.

Plask immediately looks down, and I feel like I stepped in something I shouldn't have.

"You, uh, don't need to tell me, if..."

"I was at MIT," he says, surprising me. His voice is different now, sort of far away. "I was working on it with Dave, one of the other students. It started small, a research paper for some conference or other. And then it just... happened. I saw it. That one little idea stuck there in the jumble."

I see his eyes sparkle with something. Pride. That sort of hesitant pride I've started to feel myself lately.

"We were working with gyroscopes," Plask says. "You know what those are, right? Sort of like old-fashioned tops." He fumbles with his hands, trying to demonstrate. "They spin, and they always point the same direction. Do you know why they do that? It's… well, that's not important. Anyway, I saw something new. Something no one had tried before. And then Dave, he saw that it could work on the space shuttle."

His voice breaks quietly. I hear the waitress's pencil tapping on her crossword.

"Dave was the big thinker," he says. "I'd never thought like that, never dreamed. I mean, I'd always wanted to do something big with my life, with science, but… to actually *do* it? I didn't have that in me. But Dave did. He saw the opportunity, and he knew how to make it happen."

I jump when the waitress drops our plates in front of us. My burger's got that strong, greasy smell like they haven't cleaned the grill for a while. The waitress looks at me over her glasses. "Ketchup's over there," she croaks, casually strolling away.

"Dave knew how to connect with people, how to track down who we needed," Plask says, barely aware of her. "He started making calls, and before I knew what was happening, we had a meeting at NASA. We had *lots* of meetings. All these important people with all these titles and letters after their names. Colonel this and technical consultant that. I was so far out of my league. And every time I talked to them, I'd get that look."

His neck suddenly twitches, and he rubs it as if to calm it down.

"Dave asked me if I was nervous. Of course I was nervous! These weren't the kind of people I normally talked to. But it was just science. That's all I had to do, right? Explain the science." Plask's face tenses up. "But it wasn't about the science. It was about *me*. They kept giving me that look. Because I talked too fast, or I didn't make enough eye contact, or… I don't even know why. The harder I tried, the more they looked at me like I was some freak that didn't belong." His throat spasms. "Because I was *weird*. God damn it, I was doing the best I knew how."

I sit there silent. One of the truckers in back starts coughing. The waitress walks over to refill his water.

"So Dave started cutting me off in the meetings," Plask says. "Jumping in to fix things, to smooth things over with the important people. To apologize for me. And I started hearing him saying things about me when he thought I wasn't listening." There's a long pause. "And then he stopped inviting me to the meetings altogether."

I watch Plask's face, wondering what I should say.

"I'm sorry," I say. It's all I come up with. I don't think he even hears me.

"Dave told me it was no big deal, that he just wanted to free me up to handle the research. He said the meetings were boring anyway, all politics and fundraising. No need to trouble myself with those. I told him it was fine; told myself it was fine. It saved me some stress, and Dave would email me whatever happened, so it was fine. But then the emails stopped, and Dave wouldn't return my calls." His mouth tightens. "A few months later, I found out. I had to read about it in a freaking journal because my partner cut me out of the project. Dave implemented the idea—*my* idea—under his name. He *stole* it from me."

Plask comes out of his story like he's broken a trance, realizing for the first time that he's got his food sitting in front of him. He grabs his sandwich up and shoves it in his mouth, as if to keep himself from saying something he'd regret. I take a bite of my burger too, crunching on the charred edges.

Mom was right. People don't understand things that are different.

30

"YOU OKAY?" Phillip asks. He looks at me with concern from under his hoodie, where he sits across the lunch table.

"*He doesn't seem okay,*" says Tess.

"Matt's fine," Rob says, picking at his taco casserole. "He's still just pissed about Kyle popping him in the jaw."

I involuntarily rub my cheek and feel the sting. Damn, I'd almost managed to forget about that. "I just have a lot on my mind, and it has nothing to do with my jaw."

"If you say so."

"Look, Rob," I huff, "I know you told me to accept Chief Ross's story about the Suttons' house, but I can't do that."

Rob gives me a firm look. "I'm just trying to look out for you, Matt."

"You were there, too! You know what happened. Those guys only got arrested to take the fall so everyone would stop asking questions."

"Do we really know that?" Rob says.

"Better question is," Phillip says, "did their plan work?"

"*Matt's still asking questions,*" Tess says.

"Damn straight," Rob chimes in.

"Yeah, but no one listens to me," I mutter.

"What about that investor you talked to?" Phillip asks. "Maybe she's smart enough to see through this."

I blow out a disgruntled sigh. "She's plenty smart. She just doesn't *want* to see."

"Oh really?" Rob says. "And how do you know what she thinks?"

"I went to talk to her."

"You *what?*"

"Gutsy," Phillip says. "How'd you find her?"

"She must've been in town to see Crossman. I, uh…" I glance over at Tess. "…happened to run into her at the coffee shop."

"You 'happened to,' " Rob says. "Uh-huh. So what'd you two talk about?"

"The truth. I tried to get her to keep asking questions, because she might actually be able to get somewhere."

"But I'm guessing she didn't go for it," Rob says.

"Yeah," I sigh. "All she cares about is her investment. She heard what she wanted to hear, so she's pretending to believe it."

"Okay then," Rob says. "The police are satisfied. The investor is satisfied. That's it, end of story."

"End of story?"

"I told you, everything's going to work out. Can we please drop this now?"

"God damn it, *NO!*" I slam my fist down on the table, sending the trays clattering. "I don't care if I'm the only one who thinks it! I don't care if I'm the only one who wants to do anything about it! Crossman *is* behind all this, and I'm going to keep digging until I can prove it."

Rob leans forward, a seriousness in his eyes. "Matt, I appreciate what you're saying, what you're feeling. I really do. But for all the digging you've done so far, what's it gotten you? I'm telling you, for your own sake, you need to let this go."

I look at him as silence settles over us. I feel the weight of his words tug at me.

"Maybe we're digging from the wrong end," Phillip says.

Rob throws up his hands. "Really, Phillip?"

"What do you mean, the wrong end?" I ask.

Phillip scratches at a clump of his spiky black hair. "Maybe we haven't gone far enough back. We've been looking at what happened after Mr. Sutton's funeral, right? Steph's mom made a scene about how his death was Crossman's fault. I figured she meant because it was one of Crossman's trucks that hit him, but what if it's more than that? What if Crossman was actually behind Sutton getting killed in the first place?"

The realization sends a cold shudder all through me.

"That's ridiculous," Rob says.

"No, it's not," I say, my voice thin. "Of course Crossman killed him. I don't know why I didn't see it before."

"But why?" Rob asks. "Why would Crossman want to run Sutton over?"

"Well," says Phillip, "what was Sutton's job at the factory?"

I let out a whistle. "Good thinking, Phillip."

"Okay, sure, but how're you gonna find that out?" Rob says. "I mean, without tipping off even more people that you're up to something."

He's got a point about that. But there's someone sitting right here who may be able to help with that. "Tess? Do you know what Mr. Sutton's job was?"

There's no sign of recognition on her face. But a moment later, my phone buzzes, and I pull up the message she sent me.

"Carl Sutton, head of safety compliance," I read off my screen.

"Nice work, Tess," Phillip says.

"Hold on—safety compliance?" My thoughts spin, trying to catch up. "That's what the investors were worked up about! They said something about the brake pads not passing one of the tests."

Even Rob looks interested at that. "So Crossman offs his safety guy for that? Wow, that's a little harsh."

"This isn't the mafia," I say. "If the guy messes up, you fire him. You don't have him whacked."

Tess turns her phone around and hands it to me. I take it from her slowly.

"What is it?" asks Phillip.

"It's somebody's email account," I answer. "Somebody from the factory. Wait, this is Carl Sutton's email!"

"Seriously, Tess, how do you find this stuff?" Rob says.

I scan the page as quickly as I can. "There's only one message in here, one he sent to someone. Wait... no, this is his draft folder. He hadn't sent it yet."

"Who's it to?" Phillip asks.

"Someone at the... some initials, the NHTSA... it says he has something he wants to discuss and wants to set up a meeting. And... that's it." I look up. "What's the NHTSA?"

"National Highway Traffic and Safety Administration," Rob mumbles.

I stare at him. "How the hell do you know that?"

"I know how to use the internet," he says, holding up his phone.

The dots start to connect in my head. "Okay... okay, so Mr. Sutton starts an email to somebody at the National Highway...

uh…"

"Traffic and Safety Administration," Rob finishes.

"Yeah, whatever… and he says he has something important to show them. But it's a draft, so he never actually sent it."

"So whatever he was going to show them, he didn't," Phillip says.

I dart glances back and forth between them. "You realize what this means?"

"I'm guessing you have a theory," Rob says.

"Isn't it obvious? Sutton was on to something Crossman was covering up, something about the new brake pads, and he was about to blow the whistle. That's why Crossman killed him."

"That's an awfully big jump," Rob says.

"Come on, you've gotta admit it makes sense! And what about Mrs. Sutton? She said her husband told her stuff. Maybe she knew about the cover-up too, and that's why she and Steph… why their house…" My mind flashes back to that night, and I trail off.

"Uh, guys?" Phillip holds up his phone. "I'm not as good as Tess at finding stuff, but look what's live streaming on Channel 4."

My eyes lock onto the screen. It's Crossman, standing in front of the factory.

"That's what the investor was here for," I say. "Getting ready for that press conference."

Phillip turns up the volume and Crossman's voice fades in. "…and I'm pleased to announce that we've completed safety testing for the new brake pads, and they've performed admirably in all areas. We'll begin production very soon. This is an exciting time for Crossman Industries and everyone in Chaplain. This is…"

"See?" I cut in. "He faked the safety results."

"How the hell do you figure that?" Rob says.

"Look, we know the pads didn't pass one of the first tests. Then, while Crossman's scrambling to fix that, Carl Sutton says he found something; and then *after* he ends up dead, the brake pads suddenly pass. You do the math."

"Well... how do you know they didn't just fix the brake pads?"

"At that investor meeting, Crossman said the testing is self-regulated. Meaning it would be super easy to fake the results."

Phillip nods. "Unless an honest guy like Carl Sutton wouldn't roll over for that."

"Exactly," I say.

"You don't *know* that," Rob says. "It's all guesses and pipe dreams."

"But it fits!" I exclaim.

"I feel you, man, but who you gonna report it to? You've got no proof."

I lean back in a huff, knowing he's right. Then my eyes dart back to the image of Crossman on Phillip's phone. "Maybe so, but I'll bet there's someone on the other side of that camera who can help with that."

***

THE HATCHBACK COUGHS AN extra-loud pop when we pull into the factory's parking lot. I scan the lot and immediately see the smug, oversized face plastered on the side of a white van up front.

"There!" I jab a finger at it. "He's still here."

"I was kinda hoping he'd be gone," Rob says. "I guess we're doing this, then." He steers us toward the van.

"Shit, it's Crossman!" I blurt out.

I drop down in my seat, wishing I could dissolve right into it. Crossman stands next to a black SUV that's polished to a sheen. Deckert opens the door for him, scanning everywhere behind his dark glasses.

"Rob, get down!" I grab his shoulder to pull him down with me and pray they don't see either of us.

"Damn it, I'm trying to drive!" Rob snaps, craning his neck to see over the steering wheel.

I glance up as well to find we're headed straight for a parked rusty pickup truck. Rob cranks the wheel, throwing me into a heap against the door, and we barely swerve around it.

I sneak a glance through the window to see Deckert looking our way, and I hold my breath. I feel his eyes narrow at us through those glasses; but he shuts the door on Crossman, then crams himself into the front seat, and their SUV creeps off.

Rob pops back up in his seat and we shudder to a stop next to the news van, a giant 4 filling the windshield. I throw my door open and jump out.

Antonio Rivera stands there, chest puffed out, hair exceptionally slicked back today. "For crying out loud, Tom," he barks, "hurry up with that equipment so we can get out of here!"

The dumpy cameraman wipes his forehead with his sleeve as he wrangles a pile of cables.

"Mr. Rivera?" I say, though I don't know why it's a question. With his giant face on the side of the van, it's pretty clear I have the right guy.

"I'm busy here, kids," Antonio says, though it doesn't look like he's doing much of anything. "No autographs right now."

Rob laughs. "Why the hell would I want your—"

"We, uh, need to talk to you," I cut in, giving Rob a glare.

"Like I said, I'm busy," says Antonio.

"Look, it's important. We need your help investigating a story."

He chuckles at me. "Seriously? I don't look for lost bikes, kid. I do big news." He strikes a pose with a canned smile straight off one of his billboards. "Channel 4, keeping you in the know!"

"This *is* big news," I insist. "It's about Crossman and those new brake pads."

Antonio breaks his smile and his eyes narrow. "What could you possibly know about those? We just finished the live stream for the announcement five minutes ago."

"We know plenty." I make sure I'm standing up straight. "The pads didn't pass safety tests, and Crossman's covering it up."

Antonio stares at me until I slouch again. Then he laughs so hard he almost falls over. "Okay, you got me! Who put you up to this? Marcus? Sandra? It has to be Sandra! I knew she'd try to get me back for that thing with the coffee!"

"Can't put anything past you, sir," Rob says. "We'll tell Sandra you didn't fall for it."

I jab Rob with my elbow. "Nobody sent us, and we're not joking. We know what Crossman is doing—what he's already done—and I'm not going to keep quiet about it."

Antonio's laughter trails off with a hint of disappointment. He glances back to the cameraman. "Tom, let's go already."

Tom hefts up the rolls of cables and takes a step toward the van, when suddenly he trips and goes down hard. The cables drop into a pile of spaghetti. Antonio huffs out a frustrated exhale. "Fine. You have until my colleague gets his stuff together. Go."

I take a deep breath. "Okay. Did you hear about the guy who got killed here when one of Crossman's semi-trucks plowed into him? Carl Sutton?"

Antonio makes a flippant wave of his hand. "Maybe that's big news around here, but in the city, people get hit by trucks every day of the week. Makes a nice little intro to hook the viewers, then we forget all about it."

Rob's nostrils flare. "You son of a—"

"Look," I jump in again, "Carl Sutton was Crossman's chief safety compliance guy, or, uh, officer. Right before he got killed, he started an email to the National Roadway… uh, Highway…"

"The NHTSA," Rob says. "Seriously, you can't remember a few letters?"

"Anyway," I push on, shooting Rob a look, "his email said he had something important to show them, so he could blow the whistle on what Crossman was hiding."

"How in the hell would you know about something like that?" Antonio says.

"The point is we do. And it means Crossman killed Carl Sutton to keep him quiet."

Antonio glances at Tom, still struggling with the cables, and sighs. "All right, you've got me curious enough to take the bait. I've been itching for a good cover-up story. But you're going to have to fill in the gaps for me because I have a *lot* of questions. Exactly *what* do you think Crossman did to this Sutton guy?"

"Not just him," I say. "His wife and daughter too. They disappeared right after the funeral."

"So the police conducted a search for missing persons?" Antonio probes.

"Uh, no… they said the Suttons moved to Michigan."

Antonio laughs. "Well, that does sound nefarious."

"They didn't move! We went to their house, and all the furniture was still there, and there was a big bloodstain on the carpet! And while we were there, two guys broke in and burned the place down to cover it up!"

Antonio pulls out a vape pen and takes a long, slow draw from it as he looks me over. "You're really serious about this, aren't you?"

"*Yes!*"

He ignores my enthusiasm and turns to Rob. "He's not blowing smoke? You saw this stuff too?"

Rob hesitates for a second, then he nods. "Yeah. Except I told him we don't have any evidence."

"Well, that would be a problem." Antonio takes another puff on the vape pen. "The bloodstain is no good if the house is burned now. You say this guy, Sutton, drafted an email to blow the whistle on Crossman? What did it say he found?"

I look down at a crack in the pavement. "It, uh, didn't say."

"Mm-hmm. So what *did* it say?"

"That he had something to show them."

Antonio chuckles. "That's all?"

"That's plenty! What could he be talking about except a cover-up?"

"Okay, let me get this straight." Antonio counts off on his fingers. "This guy drafts an email saying he has 'something' to show somebody, then he dies in an accident, and then his house burns down. That all you got?"

"Well... no! I've got this!" I pull Deckert's cufflink out of my pocket. "This was at the Suttons' house. It belongs to Deckert, Crossman's thug."

"You mean his associate," Antonio says. "And that cufflink could belong to anyone."

"It belongs to *him!* I saw him wearing these!"

Antonio rolls his eyes. "Even if it does belong to him, there's no proof it was in the house."

"We *found* it there!"

"Says you. And I'm guessing you didn't exactly have a legitimate reason for being in the house when you found it, did you?"

I open my mouth to respond, then shake my head.

"So at the end of it, you've got nothing," Antonio says.

"Well... so far, yeah. But that's where you come in, right? To investigate, to get evidence. Isn't that what you do?"

Antonio blows out a long wispy puff. "Nope."

"Told you," Rob says.

I give him a jab. "Why not?"

"To get evidence, I gotta start asking questions," Antonio says. "Awkward, accusatory kinda questions. Crossman'll hear about that, and he's not gonna like it."

"I don't care if he likes it," I mutter through gritted teeth.

Antonio chuckles. "I'll bet you don't. Bet you've been asking some questions yourself already, haven't you? How's that working out for you?"

"Police chief thinks he's up to something," Rob says. "Which he is."

"So Crossman's got the police in his pocket," Antonio says matter-of-factly. "That's about right."

"That's why we need *you!*" I shout at him.

"The point is, you don't start slandering a guy like Crossman unless you have some *hard* evidence in your pocket already. Otherwise, he'll sue the pants off you, or worse."

I feel the anger burning my face. "So that's it? You're just going to let him get away with this?"

"It's not up to me, kid," Antonio says flippantly. "He *will* get away with it. There are plenty of ways for Crossman to squirm his way out of this. Powerful people do it all the time."

"But he *shouldn't* get away with it!"

He smiles. "That's nice. Idealism is so cute these days."

"For Christ's sake, please!" I plead with him. "You've got to be able to dig around and find something that will prove—"

Antonio holds up his hand. "You don't want me to do that."

Rob clears his throat. "I thought we were being pretty clear that we *do* want that. Or *he* does, anyway."

"No, you don't," Antonio says, looking at Rob. "I'm guessing your dad works at the factory?"

"Well, yeah."

He looks at me. "And yours too?"

I hesitate, then nod.

"Crossman employs half of this pathetic town," Antonio says. "And the tax revenue from the factory pays for most of your school, the fire department, and the old ladies' water aerobics at the rec center. Not to mention whatever other donations Crossman makes out of his... generosity. Do you know what all that means? Crossman *owns* this town."

"No one should own a town," I say. "Not like that."

"You don't get it, do you? It's not just the money. It's what the money buys. You can't go asking questions about a guy like that without consequences."

"I don't *care,*" I mutter through gritted teeth.

"Well, you should."

I stare bullets at him. "So that's it? You're done?"

Antonio takes a long, slow drag on his vape pen. "That's what I'm saying, kid."

"God damn it!" I clench my fists. "Everyone we've talked to is either scared to death of Crossman, or they're working for him."

"Sounds about right," he says. "You need to get it in your head, kid. If you keep poking Crossman, he'll chew you up and spit you out in the gutter. If he spits you out at all."

THE WALK TO THE OLDER SIDE of town gives me time to think. The trees get bigger, more gnarled up along the way. Everything feels darker. It could be shadows from the trees, but it's probably just the thoughts churning in my head.

Phillip was right. Crossman had Mr. Sutton killed, I know it. Which means I need to go right to the source—the guy driving the truck that hit him. Don't know why I didn't think of that before, but I've got plenty of questions for him now. Maybe he can actually give me something that will get that reporter Antonio off his ass to do some digging. The good news is, I've got someone else who's good at digging, even if she doesn't say much. Tess found me the truck driver's name and address in five minutes flat.

I step over a tree root bulging through a crack in the sidewalk and check the number on the mailbox at the corner—213, the label peeling off at the end. The house is gray, halfway faded to a dirty, ghostly white. I take a breath and step up the uneven stones of the walk. A crack runs down the paint on the front door, the white flaking off to let out a layer of black underneath. I knock on the door with a hollow echo.

A dog barks inside. Not an aggressive growl or some energetic yippy thing, it's a long, low, pathetic sound like the dog hasn't gotten up in a month. A crow caws from the half-dead tree in the yard as I stand there, shifting from one foot to the other.

The door swings open. "Yeah?"

Her voice is a croak. A cigarette bobs in her mouth, and she blows a mouthful of smoke in my face. I sputter a cough. She impatiently scratches at her cheek, which sags like a loose sack.

"I'm, uh, looking for Ralph Kurtz," I cough.

"He owe you money?" she croaks.

"Uh, no."

She adjusts the bulky glasses on her face and looks me up and down. "Good, 'cuz you look kinda young to be one of his bookies."

I shift to my other foot, not really sure how to respond to that.

"He didn't give you that shiner, did he?" she says, pointing to my face.

Damn it, I'll be glad when that thing goes away. "No, the black eye is from someone else."

"So what ya want with Ralph, then?"

"I need to talk to him about his truck," I say. "The day he was driving it, when… well, the accident."

Lines crease around her sagging mouth. "Lawyer told me not to talk about that. Said you can take it up with th' insurance comp'ny."

She starts to push the door shut. I shove my hand against it to hold it open. "It's not about that. I just need to…" My mind races with what to say. "That accident must've been hard for you, too."

She glares at me through her glasses, pushing against me on the door. The cracked paint bites into my hand. After a long moment, she releases. The door swings inward.

"You want a beer?" she says.

"I'm, uh, not old enough."

"Suit yourself."

She turns and walks inside. I hover on the doorstep for a moment, not a hundred percent sure if she's inviting me in. I decide it doesn't matter, and step in after her.

Curtains block out most of the light inside, and the cigarette stench reeks through everything. I stifle a sneeze. The floorboards creak underneath me with each step. I trip over something and look back to see it was the dog. A fat, saggy, black and white mutt. He shoots me a grumpy look, then rolls over and goes back to sleep.

"Neighbors used to just bitch at me," she says, " 'bout stupid shit like leaving my garbage cans out. Now, they do their best to pretend I ain't even here."

"They blame you for what happened?" I ask.

"Nah. They've always hated me, they wuz just looking for an excuse to make it official." She opens the fridge door with a clink of glass and pulls out a beer bottle. "Well, the joke's on them. 'Cuz I hate all of them, too."

"People can be pretty awful sometimes," I say. "I'm sorry."

"No, you ain't." She jams the bottle against an opener on the fridge door and pops the cap off with a flourish. "But you're more polite than most of the folk that come botherin' me."

I wave off a cloud of cigarette smoke as I wait for her to go on. She doesn't. "So, uh... can I talk to Ralph?" I ask her. "I mean, Mr. Kurtz?"

"Be my guest, if you can find him."

I stop short. "You don't know where he is? Oh my God... have you talked to the police?" My mind whirls, wondering what good the police would even do. They're probably in on it. But she just laughs, deep and throaty.

"Don't get yourself all worked up, kid," she chuckles. "Sometimes he's here, and sometimes he ain't. He don't tell me his schedule."

"Well, can you get in touch with him? Can you find out where he is?"

"You act like I'd want to." She takes a chug from her bottle.

"Look, I really need to find him. Is he driving a route somewhere?"

She shrugs. "Or on his way to a casino or a horse track. Or..." She picks at her yellowed teeth. "Shackin' up with some bimbo. He's real good at droppin' outta sight for a while to have a good time. He'll show up sooner or later when his luck and his money run out."

"You don't understand," I urge. "This isn't like those other times. I think something happened to him."

She blows a long, slow puff of smoke at me. "Why d'ya think that?"

"It's... about the accident."

She rolls her eyes. "What, you think he got all weepy about what happened? Ralph ain't the weepy type."

"That's not what I mean." I struggle with how much I should tell her. "I think there's something behind him being gone. I think... someone wanted it."

She squints at me through a smudge on her glasses. "Boy, you really are nuts."

"Look, did anything weird happen right before the accident? Was he acting strange?"

"How the hell should I know?"

"Well... he's your husband, isn't he?"

She takes a drag on her cigarette and shrugs.

"Did he get a lot of money right before the accident?" I ask. "Or right after?"

She laughs again, which turns into a hacking cough. "You think if he got a chunk of money, that I'd see any of it?"

"Please," I plead with her. "I have to know what happened to him."

"Look, kid, you act like there's some big reason why Ralph's gone. I'm sure he'll come waltzin' back sooner or later, acting like he never left. And if he don't... well, maybe I'd be better off. Ain't that right, Spike?"

The dog rolls over with a grunt, giving me a look that makes me wonder what I'm still doing here.

"I'm sure you're right," I lie. "I'm sure Ralph is just fine, and... you'll be just fine."

The floor squeaks as I step back out the door.

THE SUN CHANGES FROM YELLOW TO orange to red as it travels down toward the lonely horizon. At least the sun knows where it's going. Me... not so much. I just wander until the sky finally fades to dark. But I can't wander forever. Eventually I end up back at home like I always do and push through the front door with a sigh.

The first thing I see is my dad hunched over on the couch, head down, cradling the bottle of scotch. He tips his head back to look at me, his eyes drooped half closed.

"Matt... Matthew?"

I slam the door. "How long you been at it this time?" I don't bother trying to hide the disgust in my voice.

"It's not... not like before," he slurs. "Just... work's been stressful, lately..."

"Forget it." I move toward the stairs, but as I pass him, Dad grabs my arm.

"I'm sorry," he says.

"I said forget it." I jerk my arm away and take another step toward the stairs; but then the anger overheats. I spin around and glare daggers at him. "Damn it, is this all you're going to do? Drink yourself into a stupor and shove your head up your ass? You *have* to see what's going on out there."

"What's… going on?"

"*Damn* it!"

Fire ignites in my hand and the bottle of scotch flies out of his grip, dropping and smashing to the floor. He looks down at his hand, as if he's trying to decide if he really saw that.

"You really don't see what Crossman has done?" I yell. "Everyone in this God damn town is pretending everything's fine. You're all too scared or too stupid to do anything about it!"

"Matt, I—"

"Forget it. Just sit here and drink until it all goes away. That worked after Mom, didn't it? God, you don't even want any of her stuff around! You've left it all to rot in that storage unit, hoping you can forget she ever existed."

I feel the barbs in those words as they come out, and watch Dad's face sink as they lance into him. I turn and run up the stairs before he can say anything else, before my anger can cool. By the time I slam the door to my room, I'm shaking, fighting the tears pooling in my eyes.

I jolt when my phone buzzes. I pull it out to see a video call request from Phillip. The hell if he's going to see me cry. I furiously wipe at my eyes before swiping the screen to accept.

"Hey, Phillip, this isn't a good time—"

He holds his finger up to his lips to shush me. I'm about to ask him what he's on about when I catch a glimpse of something behind him that makes me stop. It's a dark room, but I see something familiar on the wall—the Crossman Industries logo.

"Are you in the factory?" I ask him. "What're you doing there?"

He jams his finger tighter on his lips and starts walking out of the lobby down a hallway. A patch of yellow light glows somewhere up ahead of him. I hear men's voices, but I can't make them out. The glow gets brighter until Phillip slips inside the doorframe of an office, crouching down behind a desk.

He turns the phone around. From around the desk, I get a glimpse of the men—and my heart stops as I recognize them. Crossman and Deckert. I clap my hand over my mouth. They don't see Phillip, yet, but if they catch him, he's dead. Phillip swings the phone back on himself and smirks. I frantically wave my hands and mouth the words *GET OUT!* but he just puts his finger to his lips again and turns the phone back around. I gasp for air and watch, the only thing I can do.

"I can't believe how much trouble Sutton caused," Crossman says, his voice both agitated and fatigued. "Even now, we're still cleaning it up."

"I told you," comes Deckert's deeper voice. "If you'd let me deal with this sooner, we wouldn't be in this mess."

"I'm still not sure I like the way you deal with things."

"I did what was necessary."

"Without consulting me!" Crossman yells.

"Waiting for your permission was what got us into this mess in the first place," Deckert says. "It needed to be done whether you liked it or not."

My heart thuds like a battering ram against my chest. I know he's talking about killing Carl Sutton.

"Damn it, Deckert," Crossman says. "Do you work for me or is it the other way around?"

"I never interfere with your business. But I run this side of things. And speaking of *your* side of things, we need those originals. You sure you can't find them?"

Originals—the safety test results, it has to be. Which means they did fake the results.

Crossman roughs at his hair, the curls all tussling together. "I told you, I checked all the servers. All electronic copies were purged."

"That means he has a hard copy," Deckert says.

Who's 'he'? It can't be Sutton, he's dead.

"I won't see the project go down like this," Crossman says. "This is my father's legacy."

"I don't give two shits about that," Deckert mutters. "You know what your dad's legacy is? He was an asshole."

Crossman grabs a mug off the desk and hurls it at the wall—right where Phillip crouches. The camera swings around and I see Phillip hunch down as the mug shatters against the wall above him. I hold my breath, expecting the next thing I see to be Deckert dragging him up by the throat. But Phillip pans the camera back to the two men, glaring at each other, still oblivious to him.

"How dare you talk about my father that way!" Crossman shouts.

"Don't get me wrong," Deckert says. "I like assholes. Your dad knew how to do what was necessary. He had focus."

"And you're saying I don't?"

"I'm saying you've been awful soft in dealing with this, considering how much money's riding on it."

"I told you, it's not about the money," Crossman says. "My father entrusted this to me, and I have to finish it."

Deckert grunts. "You sure you don't care about the money? You've never had a problem spending it. You never asked your dad what he did to get it."

"I said don't *talk* about him like that!"

"Fine. But if you're really concerned about this legacy shit, we need to deal with this."

"And I *will* deal with it," Crossman says. "Do whatever the hell you want. But first, find the originals. That's the real problem."

Deckert's mouth spreads in a wry smile. "Good. You're finally thinking with focus."

"Why, thank you, Deckert," Crossman says harshly. "Don't worry about me. I know what I'm doing. We just need to be ready for tomorrow night."

Tomorrow night? What's happening then? And who's the 'he' they keep talking about? But my questions are interrupted as Crossman starts toward the door—toward Phillip. My heart slams into my chest again. The camera jostles as Phillip ducks down, but they're going to see him, I know they are. I hold my breath, but with the camera pointed at the floor now, I can't see anything. A shadow drapes into view, and I know it's all over; then it moves away, and another shadow moves past. The light switches off, dropping the screen into darkness. My head is about to explode when the camera finally swings up, revealing a barely visible Phillip, smiling and giving a thumbs up in the dark. Crossman and Deckert's footsteps fade away down the hall.

I want to say something to him, tell him how I can't believe what just happened, tell him he's brave or just plain stupid, but I'm breathing too fast to say anything at all. Phillip turns the video off, and I drop onto my bed, still gasping for breath.

33

THE MINUTE I GET INSIDE THE school and find Phillip, I punch him in the arm.

"Hey, what gives?" he says.

"Dude," Rob says beside me. "What's up with you? You're all amped up about something on the way in here but you won't tell me what it is, and then you slug Phillip?"

"I'm still pissed about what you did last night," I tell Phillip. "Do you have any idea how dangerous that was?"

"Seriously, what are you talking about?" Rob says.

"They never knew I was there," Phillip answers me.

"Maybe so," I say, "but if they had, you'd have gotten yourself killed. Don't get me wrong, I'm also super impressed." I glance at his shoulder. "I didn't hurt you, did I?"

He tries to hide a smirk. "You don't hit that hard."

"Is somebody going to fill me in already?" Rob huffs.

"Sorry, yeah," I say. "Phillip did something brave and stupid last night that blew the lid off this Crossman thing. You want to tell him, Phillip?"

He opens his mouth to answer when a portly figure waddles into our personal space.

"Don't you boys have somewhere to be right now?" Principal Stokes asks.

"Not that I know of," Rob says, with just a hint of sarcasm.

"Sorry, we're in the middle of something," I say. "And the bell hasn't rung yet."

Stokes glances at his watch, then points up at the overhead speakers with a satisfied smile just as the metallic ringing echoes down.

Rob shrugs. "Fair enough." He turns to leave. I grab his arm.

"We're in the *middle* of something," I mutter to him.

"Your conspiracy theory can wait until after class," Stokes says.

"It's not a—"

"*After* class."

I look to Phillip for some support, only to find he's disappeared already. "Fine," I grumble. I amble off down the hall, not in a hurry and not really caring that Stokes stands there tapping his foot the whole time. Rob heads off in the other direction, I think he's got English this period.

Mr. Warren's voice carries into the hall before I even open the door. The man loves to hear himself talk. I slip inside and he barely notices me plop into a seat in the back row. Cindy Ferguson gives me a disinterested glance before she goes back to drawing a wanna-be tattoo on her forearm.

"So members of the House of Representatives are elected for a two-year term, senators for a six-year term." Warren pauses, dramatically fussing with his hair. What he has left of it. "Have I mentioned I helped call potential voters for Senator Campbell's re-election bid last year?"

"Only every chance you get," I mutter to myself. I lean back in my chair, preparing myself for his eighteenth retelling of how he single-handedly got the dude elected when my phone buzzes. I whip it out under the desk, knowing Warren will be way too caught up with himself to notice.

"Holy—" I have to clap my hand over my mouth to stop myself. It's a text from Phillip in our group chat—with a video of everything he overheard last night. I dart glances around to see if anyone heard me; Warren doesn't even take a breath. Cindy gives me an eye roll and goes back to her drawing as I text back.

MATT—u recorded it???

Phillip replies with a wink.

MATT—this is awesome! we finally have proof! don't tell me its a conspiracy theory anymore, Rob

ROB—slow down, bro. i'm still tryin 2 watch this w/ Mrs H talking about adverbs

I tap my foot, impatiently waiting for Rob to catch up.

"You may think it's TV ads that decide an election," Warren prattles on, "but it's those calls, those *individual* connections that really…"

I glance around the room, looking for someone other than Warren to keep me occupied. I try to figure out what Cindy's drawing on her arm; I think it's supposed to be a skull, but it's kind of lopsided. My eyes land on Scott over on the far side. He's slumped down in his chair, that dark swoop of hair hanging limp over his face. He's not wearing that cocky smile anymore without Emily around. It isn't just that she's in math class this period. She dumped him. And as much as I want to gloat about that, I almost can't help feeling sorry for Scott. At the end of the day, he's just one more guy that Kyle Draughton stepped on.

My phone buzzes again.

ROB—holy shit

MATT—I know, right??? now u know what I'm talking about

ROB—Phillip, u have some balls on u

PHILLIP—thx bro

MATT—important question is what do we do with it?

ROB—u kidding? nothing

MATT—WTF????????????????????????

ROB—do u have any idea what crssman wld do if he knew we had this?

MATT—thats the point. we finally have him

PHILLIP—Rob may be right, Crossman's dangerous. Need 2b careful

MATT—I'm done being careful, this will finally put the bastard in jail!

ROB—hate 2 break it 2u, but it won't

My face gets hot and I use a lot more force than necessary to pound out another *WTF*

ROB—they didnt say anythng specific

MATT—they said they killed Sutton!!

ROB—no they didn't

MATT—but they said

MATT—...

PHILLIP—guess they didnt actually say that

MATT—ok, maybe they didnt ACTUALLY say it, but isnt it obvious?

ROB—u can't convict a guy on obvious

MATT—look, what about the original safety results they'r looking 4? It means they faked them!

ROB—they didnt say that either. just said they want the 'originals'. could mean anything

MATT—damn it, dont tell me u can't see whats going on

ROB—course I do. but u dont think crossman's lawyers can

poke holes all through this & get him off?

PHILLIP—so what do we do?

ROB—like I said, nothing. dump the video & hope he never finds out we had it

I shove the phone back in my pocket, smoldering because Rob's right. The video is enough to piss Crossman off but not enough to land him in jail. Damn it, I thought this was our ticket. But I'm not done yet.

***

MY MASHED POTATOES SPLATTER as I slam my lunch tray down on the table.

"So you're still in your mood, then," Rob says, wiping a blob of gravy off his sleeve.

"I just can't accept that there's nothing we can do with that video," I grumble. "We're so close."

"Rob's right," Phillip says. "I went over it a few more times. They don't admit to anything in there. *We* know what they're talking about, but that's not enough."

"We could still post it to the internet," I say. "It may not prove anything, but it would make a hell of a scene."

Rob puts his hand on my shoulder. "Matt, remember the bloodstain at Steph's house. I don't want to think about what would happen if we make a scene. Not without real proof to back it up."

I lock eyes with him for a minute, then look down at my slop of potatoes. I nod.

"One thing still bothers me," Phillip says. "Who's the 'he' they said has a copy of the originals?"

"Hell if I know," I say. "And hell if I know how to find out."

"Well, Crossman sure wants those originals back," Phillip

says. "And he said they had to be ready for tomorrow night. Which I guess is tonight. So what do they have to be ready for?"

"I don't know, and I don't *want* to know," Rob says. "It's time to leave well enough alone."

"Yeah," I say, slumping down in my seat.

Rob raises his eyebrow at me. "Really? You're actually dropping this?"

I shrug. "Doesn't matter. There's no way for us to figure it out before tonight. It's not like we're gonna get another chance to eavesdrop on Crossman."

"I could always sneak into the factory again," Phillip says.

"You're not doing that," I tell him.

"Good, finally," Rob says. "We all agree we're done, right?"

I catch a movement out of the corner of my eye and look over to where Tess sits at the end of the table. She makes a motion with her hand.

"*Crossman's voicemail,*" she says.

"What're you talking about?" I ask her.

She taps her phone. A man's voice comes over it.

"*Crossman, you'll want to listen real close. This is Tim Draughton.*"

"Draughton… Kyle's dad?" I sputter. "That prick from the football game?"

"*I found that thing Sutton was working on,*" Draughton says. "*Real interesting. I'm guessing you'll want this back. Oh, don't worry, I won't go spouting off to anybody. I'm not looking to rock the boat. I just want my cut. A big cut. After that, you'll never see me again and you can do whatever the hell you want. Meet me at the factory tomorrow night, 10:00, and we can talk terms. Otherwise… I'd hate to see what would happen if I gave this to someone else.*"

The recording goes silent and we stare at each other in disbelief.

"Now *that's* got to be enough proof," I say.

Rob shakes his head. "He still doesn't say anything specific."

"But he said—"

He holds up his hand. "All he says is he has something Crossman wants."

"But it means Draughton *does* have the proof," Phillip says.

"*Phillip's right,*" Tess says. "*I was just going to say that.*"

"Still doesn't do us much good," Rob says.

" 'Us'?" I say. "I thought you wanted to drop this?"

His cheeks burn red against the brown. "I just mean, all Draughton wants to use those records for is blackmail."

"You're right," I admit. "Blackmailing Crossman doesn't change anything. We need to convince Draughton to turn those records over to…" I trail off with an ironic chuckle. "Who am I kidding? All Draughton cares about is himself."

"That's one thing we can agree on," says Rob.

"So close," I mutter. "Of all people, why'd it have to be him?"

I glance across the room and see Kyle, a smug look on his face, listening to himself talk, relishing the attention everyone lavishes on him. Emily sits beside him. Her bright red lipstick is spread in a smile, but I can tell it's forced. Her eyes are empty when she looks at Kyle. She touches his arm, and he ignores her.

"He doesn't even appreciate her," I say.

"What?" Rob says.

"Nothing." I shake myself out of my trance. "I just mean, of all people to find those records, why'd it have to be Kyle's dad? He'll hand them over, get his money, and then split, leaving the rest of us to deal with the mess."

"If he gets the money at all," Phillip says. "Crossman will

probably kill him as soon as he gets those records back."

"Damn," Rob says. "Hate to agree with you, Phillip, but I'm guessing you're right."

I look back at Kyle, feeling a momentary splash of satisfaction before mentally slapping myself. "I can't let that happen. Not even to Kyle's dad."

"Look, Matt," Rob says, "I don't wish the guy dead either. But what do you plan to do about it?"

"We need to get those records from him before the meeting tonight."

"Hold up, you want to do *what?*"

"We steal the records," I tell him. "It's the only way to end this."

"Why's it *our* job to end it?"

"Because no one else will."

"That's not a reason," Rob says.

Phillip leans forward and pulls back his hoodie. "Where do you think Draughton would hide them?"

I look at Phillip, and I can tell by his face that he's with me. I smile, then turn to Tess. "Hey, Tess, does Draughton have a safety deposit box in town? Or maybe a storage unit somewhere?"

Her fingers flurry over her phone, reflected colors splashing across her eyes. After a moment, she shakes her head.

"Then they must be in his house," Phillip says. "Let's go."

"Damn it," Rob huffs, "we're not breaking into another house! We already did that once, look what happened with that!"

"I can do it alone," Phillip says. "In and out, no problem."

"No," I say. "I'm not letting you take the risk by yourself. We're in this far together; we finish it together." I look to Rob. "Right?"

"Not in a million years," he says.

"Rob, please. You were there when Carl Sutton's car blew up. We watched him die in front of us. Can you really stand by and let that happen to someone else?"

"Right now, I'm worried about that happening to one of *us*."

"You know I have to do this," I say, "and I can't do it without you."

He stares at me for a long time before finally letting out a breath. "Fine. What's the worst that can happen?"

"Thanks," I say. "You're a good friend."

"You can remember that when we're buried next to each other."

I try not to think about his comment and push myself up from the table. "Let's go."

"What, you mean right now?" Rob says.

"Yeah. While Kyle's here, and his dad's at work."

"What about his mom?"

I think about that for a second, when Tess turns her phone toward me.

"What's she got there?" Phillip asks.

"It's a map of downtown," I say. "There's a red dot at the corner of... Elm and Third."

"Nail salon," Rob says. Phillip and I stare at him. "What? My mom goes there a lot."

"Why are you showing us the nail salon, Tess?" I ask her. I squint at the screen. "Wait, this is a GPS locator for a car... registered to..."

"Don't bother reading it," Rob sighs. "We all know it's gotta be Kyle's mom. Crying out loud, Tess, do you track my car, too?"

For just a second, I think I see her smirk as she turns her phone back around.

"Good work, Tess," I say. "So Kyle's house is empty. We go now."

"*Let's go,*" Tess says.

"See?" I say. "Even Tess agrees." I start off, with Rob and Phillip scrambling after me.

"*We're in this together,*" Tess says from behind us.

"You're right, Tess," I call back to her. "Don't worry, we'll tell you everything when we get back."

I think I hear her say something else, but I don't catch it as we get to the front hallway. That's where we run into Principal Stokes.

"Going somewhere, boys?" he says, eyeing us suspiciously. "I didn't think lunch period was over yet."

Rob flashes a grin. "We were just getting our history books. Wanted to study up while we eat."

"That's interesting. Because last I checked, your lockers are that way."

"See, Rob, I told you," I say, slapping him on the shoulder. "Gosh, you'd think we'd know our way around this place by now, huh?"

I turn back the other way, giving Rob and Phillip a look to do the same. Stokes watches us walk a few steps. I glance over my shoulder at the clock on the wall. My hand tingles, and the clock drops, clattering to the floor.

"What the blazes?" Stokes blurts out, spinning around.

I grab Rob and Phillip and we hustle out the door.

34

"I THOUGHT YOU SAID YOU COULD open the lock," Rob mutters behind me.

"Don't rush me. This isn't as easy as it looks."

I can feel the deadbolt behind the door. My hand tingles and the bolt jerks back and forth, but it won't quite line up right.

"Almost... there..."

It clicks. I turn the knob and pull the door open.

"Okay, that is pretty impressive," Rob admits.

Phillip gives me a thumbs-up.

I step through into the laundry room and get my bearings. "Okay, so where would Draughton hide the records?"

"Underwear drawer," Rob says. "That's where guys hide all their important stuff, isn't it?"

"File cabinet," Phillip says.

"Okay, you guys go check those out," I say. "I'll poke around and see what else I come up with."

Phillip disappears immediately, and Rob hurries off down

the hall. I start where I am in the laundry room and pull open cabinet doors and drawers. All I find is batteries, a pile of mismatched buttons, and screwdrivers. With all the clattering in the drawers, it takes me a second to hear the other sound— low, deep growls.

My hair stands on end, and I spin around to see a German shepherd the size of a pony. He rounds the corner through the door and bares his teeth. The growl vibrates through every bone I have.

"Uh, guys..."

I make a move toward the door, but I'm not fast enough. The dog blocks me, pushing in to pin me into the corner. I feel a cold sweat bead on my forehead.

"Guys..."

I watch a drop of saliva drip off his fangs and I'm about to piss myself when I see a box sitting on top of the dryer across the room. Dog biscuits. *God, I hope this works...*

My hand tingles as I yank at the box. It falls and scatters biscuits across the floor. The dog stops growling and glances at them. With one last glare at me, he darts to the biscuits with a look like *I'll eat these first but you're next*. He snaps them up three at a time and crunches them with a sound like gravel in the garbage disposal.

I rush toward the door in two strides, reaching for the doorknob on my way out; but my hand misses, and I trip. I'm falling, watching as the dog chomps the last bite and comes charging at me. Another second and he'll be through the door. I desperately reach for the knob with my invisible grip. My hand burns and the door slams shut, with one last glimpse of the dog's teeth, just as I fall in a heap on the kitchen floor.

"What the hell are you on about in here?" Rob says, stepping into view.

"D-dog," I stutter, out of breath, and point to the door.

"You're making all that fuss over a little fluffball?"

A growl erupts from the laundry room and the door shudders as the dog thuds into it. Rob tries to hide a flinch.

"Okay, maybe not so fluffy," he says.

"Keep looking." I drag myself up off the floor. "We need to find those records and get out of here."

Rob darts back down the hall. I start ransacking the kitchen. I throw open the cabinets, making sure to check under the sink—just bleach and cockroach traps. I think I have a clever idea when I pull open the oven door, but it's empty. I'm about to check the freezer when my phone buzzes with a text.

TESS—911

I squint at it, confused.

MATT—what's wrong? u want me to call 911?

TESS—neighbor called them

Cold fear drenches me as I stare at the words. I bolt through the living room, down the hall, and burst into the back bedroom.

"Rob, we've gotta go!" I yell.

He sticks his head up from where he's hunched over the dresser. "What is it now? You run into another puppy?"

"Neighbor called the cops," I wheeze. "Must've seen us come in."

"How the hell would you know that?"

"Tess texted me."

Rob pauses. "Okay, give me one second. I just found the underwear drawer."

"Hurry up..." I dart across the hall to the office. "Phillip! Where are you?"

I jump out of my skin when Phillip suddenly appears beside me.

"What's wrong?" he asks.

"You've gotta stop sneaking up on me like that!"

"Sorry," Phillip says. "I heard what you said about the cops. I can't find a file cabinet, a safe, or anything." He starts toward the door, then stops. "You know if we leave, we won't get another chance at this, right?"

I hesitate, feeling a swallow catch in my throat. "We don't have a choice." I start back toward the living room, with Phillip behind me. "Rob, come on!"

"I said give me a second!" he yells back.

"I mean it, Rob, I'm not going to watch while you—"

I step into the living room and get a glimpse out the wide picture window, when I frantically dive to the floor, knocking the wind out of myself. A dark-blue uniform fills the window. The officer stares off to the side, before turning his gaze in toward us. I slide myself in underneath the window, praying I'm out of sight.

A hazy view of the cop reflects off the coffee table. I hold my breath as I watch him stare with his narrow eyes; I swear he looks straight at Phillip, but it's like he looks right through him. The cop turns away and starts walking toward the corner of the house. I let out my breath... then I hear Rob's footsteps pounding much too loud toward us.

"Okay, you wusses," Rob says. "If you can't take the heat, then—"

"*Shhh!*" I wave at him frantically, and his eyes pop wide open when he sees the uniform in the window. He throws himself on top of me on the floor. I stifle a grunt as he squeezes up against the wall.

The reflection of the cop spins around and steps back up to the window, staring in. Seconds tick by on the clock. The cop says something into his radio; I can't make it out.

Phillip pulls out his phone and taps something on it, and then I feel mine buzz. I struggle against Rob's belly squished against me to pull my phone out.

PHILLIP—I'll distract him so u can get out

I glare at Phillip and type back.

MATT—no way, we're in this together

PHILLIP—dont worry about me

Phillip smiles and stands up. I wave at him to get down again, but he scurries out of the room.

"What's he doing?" Rob whispers.

I show him Phillip's text. Rob nods. "He can handle it," he says. "We need to slip out, back the way we came in."

"Not that way," I whisper back. "Fido's in there."

Rob grimaces. He nods toward the bedrooms. "That way."

I glance back to the coffee table, looking for the cop's reflection. He's gone. I scramble up and run down the hall to the bedroom. Rob beats me there. He throws open the window. "Come on, through here," he says.

I want to look for Phillip to make sure he's okay, but there's no time and nothing I can do about it anyway. I climb through the window and drop like a rock into the bushes on the other side, scratching up my hands. Rob starts to climb out too when I see a blue jacket emerge from around the corner. I wave for Rob to wait, but he's already halfway out. Another step and the cop will see him. I look around frantically, when I see a green-yellow lump on the far side of the lawn; a tennis ball, what's left of one after Fido chewed on it. I reach for it and my hand tingles, the ball pops up off the ground and flies toward the cop. I hold my breath.

It misses. My aim isn't that good.

The ball whizzes a foot past his head, but thankfully close enough for him to notice. He spins around to figure out where that came from, giving Rob time to drop into the bushes beside me.

I crouch there, my knees tight and burning, watching the cop dart glances back and forth. It still won't be long before he sees the open window, then us.

Then I see something at the other corner of the house. Just a dark shadow; I think it's Phillip's hoodie. He swings the door open—to the laundry room.

The German shepherd charges out, all teeth and growls and bristling fur, straight for the cop.

"Whoa!" the officer shouts. "Down, boy! Oh, shit…"

He turns and runs with the dog on his heels. Rob and I dart the other way and take off. I fight for breath and keep running, with Phillip's words lodged in my head.

We won't get another chance at this.

35

THE BENCH CREAKS UNDERNEATH ME WHEN I drop my weight into it, and I plant my forehead on the table. It's not much of a table, really, just what passes for the dining area at the Jiffy Mart. Right between the snack cakes and the motor oil. The fluorescent lights buzz overhead, and it smells like cheap disinfectant. Seems pretty fitting right now.

"Epic fail," I mutter into the table. I smell something else, a mix of stale burned meat and salt, and look up. Rob slides in across from me with an armful of three hot dogs and a tray of nachos.

"Seriously?" I say. "You're gonna stuff your face at a time like this?"

"Breaking and entering makes me hungry."

The front door slides open with a squeak, and Phillip slips in.

"Glad you guys made it out okay," he says.

"Thanks to you," I tell him. "I still don't know how you got outside without being spotted."

"I can't believe you thought letting that dog out was a good idea," Rob says, or at least I think that's what he says with a mound of hotdog in his mouth.

"How'd you keep the dog from biting your face off?" I ask.

Phillip shrugs. "Dogs like me."

"More like they ignore you," Rob says with a swallow. "Like everybody else does. I just never knew you could turn that into a superpower."

"The point is, it worked," I say. "Thanks, Phillip."

He nods, and I think I catch a faint smile. Then his smile's gone. "Too bad we didn't get those safety records," he says.

"Yeah," I sigh. "It's gonna be a lot harder now."

Rob coughs on his hotdog. "Harder? You mean you're not done yet? I'm sorry, but did I miss something? We took our shot, pretty bold and noble if I do say so myself, and it didn't work. You win some, you lose some. Nothin' else to do."

"There's got to be something else we can do," I insist.

"For Christ's sake, let it go, Matt! Draughton's meeting Crossman tonight. *Tonight*. You think we can break into the same house, the one we just broke into, a couple hours later? Hell, you think Draughton would even leave the records there after that? He probably thinks we were Crossman's goons coming to get those back. He'll be sitting on those things tight until the meeting, making sure he gets his money."

"Crossman won't just pay him and let him walk away," I say. "He has to tie up loose ends. He'll kill him."

"Not our fault," Rob says.

"It doesn't matter whose fault it is. We need to do something to stop it."

Rob rubs his forehead. "I thought we went over this. There's nothing else we *can* do."

"Yes, there is. We go to the factory tonight. Get the records from Draughton, and stop Crossman from killing anyone else."

"Are you *serious?*" Rob exclaims.

Even Phillip looks at me like I'm crazy. Maybe I am, but I don't care anymore.

"Someone has to do something," I say.

"Yeah, someone," Rob says. "Not us."

"Well, we've tried talking to everyone who *should* do something, and none of them will."

"Exactly. We've tried talking to people, then tried jumping in like idiots ourselves, and it didn't pan out. Sometimes the bad guy wins."

"Not like this," I say. "Not because everyone just lays down and lets it happen. I'm done lying down."

"You're really serious about this, aren't you?" Phillip asks.

"Yeah, I am."

Rob flails his arms. "Why? Why you?"

"Because *someone* has to do something," I answer. "To say enough is enough. And if no one else will stand up, then I guess that leaves me."

"Us," Phillip says. He nods at me.

"Great, now you're *both* crazy," Rob says. "You know we can't take those guys, right? They'll kill us. I mean, literally, *kill* us."

Maybe. Probably. I'm trying not to think about it.

"That's why I need you guys," I say. "I have my... thing, but I need your help."

"You think your magic trick's going to make any difference with them?" Rob says.

"I know, Rob, that's why—"

"Damn it, no! I'm done listening to this!" Rob shoves up from the table, sending the rest of his food toppling, and storms out. The door squeaks shut after him.

I turn to Phillip. "Thanks for not walking out too, man."

He nods.

"Are you really up for this?" I ask Phillip. "I mean… Rob's right. About some of it, at least. What we're up against. I don't know if we can—"

"That's why we'll do it together," Phillip says. "Someone needs to stand up. I want to be one of the people who did."

I smile at him, even though I'm still fighting off a wave of fear. "Thanks."

"Don't need to thank me." He glances back at the door. "You want me to talk to Rob?"

"No, it should be me. I'm the one that got us into all this."

I stand up and step out the door to look for him. I don't have to look far. He sits slumped on the curb by the tire pump that's always broken. I walk over and slowly ease myself down next to him.

"Sorry," I say. "Look, I know this is nuts. I know it probably won't work. It's not fair to ask you to go in there with me."

"That's not it." Rob glances toward me, but he doesn't quite make eye contact. "You're right, okay? Of course I want to do something about Crossman. I want to stand up for what's right, not put my head down like everyone else."

"Oh… okay, thanks. But if you feel that way, then why did you—"

"Because I'm not like you guys."

"What?"

"Matt, you act like your magic trick is nothing, but it's sure as hell something nobody else can do. Phillip has his stealth ninja mode. Even Tess… I was a jerk and never gave her credit before, but it turns out she can hack into the Pentagon. You guys are like your own band of misfit superheroes. Me…" Rob shakes his head. "I don't have anything."

I look at him in disbelief. "You think you don't have anything?"

"Nothing that matters."

"Rob, you think you need some special ability to matter? That's not what this is about. I used to think it was, that being a hero meant flying or punching through steel or something big like that, but it's not. Being a hero means standing up anyway, with whatever you have."

"If you say so." He doesn't sound convinced.

"Look, so you're not a superhero," I tell him. "That doesn't matter. You're... their mild-mannered alter ego."

Rob chuckles. "Dude, I'm anything but mild-mannered."

"The point is, those guys can do plenty of good without putting on a cape, and so can you."

"Don't pretend I'm important just to keep from hurting my feelings," Rob says.

"I'm not. Look, there are plenty of times you're an ass, and when you are, I'll tell you. But you're also the most loyal friend a guy can ask for, and there's no one else I'd rather go into a fight with."

Rob looks at me for a long moment, then nods. "All right then. So we're really gonna do this?"

"Yeah," I say. "But there's one more person we need to get on board first."

***

THE BELL RINGS, SENDING birds flapping up from the trees. Everyone starts pouring out the school doors. Chatting, texting, laughing; just going on, like everything's fine. All oblivious to what's happening. Part of me wishes I could be like them and ignore all of this. But I've already made my choice.

I feel Phillip's hand on my shoulder. "You want to tell Emily?" he asks me.

I hadn't realized I was staring at her. Of course I want to tell her, but I can't do that. I shake my head and look away.

"I can't drag her into this," I say.

"Didn't stop you from dragging us into it," Rob says. "And speaking of dragging people in..."

He points to where Tess emerges from the doors. I hurry up to her, with Rob and Phillip behind me.

"Tess?" I say. "We, uh, we're going to do something tonight. We're going to..." I begin to trail off because saying it out loud makes it feel nuts. Here goes. "We're going to sneak into the factory tonight and end this. We're going to get the records and keep Crossman from killing anyone else. But we need your help."

"We're in this together," she says.

"Good. Great! We need you to get us ready. You can get us all the info we need, like... uh, a layout of the factory, so we don't get lost in there."

"I can do that."

"Perfect. And we'll probably need some info on the machines in there. Maybe we could use those for something."

"Sure, but I can do more once we get there."

My stomach clenches. She wants to come? I suddenly realize that's what she was trying to tell me earlier today, too— she wanted to go with us to Draughton's house. I glance at Rob.

"She can't come," he says. "You know that, right?"

I clear my throat nervously. "Uh, thanks, Tess, but you don't need to worry about coming with us. We just need you to—"

"I want to come," she says.

"I know, Tess, but this is dangerous. Really dangerous. We might not... might not make it back."

"Do you think I don't understand that?"

"Of course you do. It's just..." I look at Rob in desperation.

"No way," he says.

"I know, but what if—"

"No!" Rob yells. "Christ, has everyone but me lost their ever-loving minds? Look, Tess, I'm sorry. I really am. I used to think you weren't even paying attention to us, and I was an ass for thinking that, and I'm sorry. I know you can take care of yourself just fine around here, and you're way smarter on your phone than I'll ever be. But what we're doing tonight is nuts. You'll just have to stay out of it, and you can read about it in our obituaries tomorrow."

"I'm going," she says.

He throws his hands up.

"I don't know, Rob," I say, "maybe she comes, and we keep her behind us? We can protect her—"

"Are you *kidding?* You act like this is a game of capture the flag. It's stupid enough we're going ourselves."

I glance back and forth between Rob and Phillip, feeling my shoulders slump. "Look, Tess, you're... brave, really brave, to want to come. But we each have our own part in this, and your part is to get us ready. And we'll tell you everything, the whole story, I promise. I'm... I'm sorry."

I turn to step away when Tess grabs my arm. And I mean *grabs.* Her fingers clamp tight and squeeze into my skin with no sign of letting go. She yanks me back toward her. Her face lifts up, swishing her hair back, and then—just for a second—she looks me in the eye. I freeze, staring back at her. Then she drops her eyes and lets go of my arm, and her fingers flurry over her phone faster than I've ever seen.

"*Everyone assumes I need protection,*" she says. "*But I don't need you to protect me. I just need you to be my friend and let me be myself.*"

I glance at Rob and Phillip. They're as shocked as I am.

"*Of course I know this is dangerous. I don't care. I want to make a difference too.*" Her face is set hard as she keeps typing. "*I can make my own decision, and I'm going.*"

We stand there for a moment in stunned silence as the waves of students flow past us.

I let out a guilty sigh. "You're right, Tess."

I share a look with Rob; even he doesn't have a comeback for that.

"It's your decision," I say. "Not ours. I guess I was a jerk about that, huh?"

She smiles. "*It's okay. Friends mess up sometimes.*"

"You've already proven yourself, Tess," Phillip says. "You're a lot more than people think."

Rob sighs. "Great. Now we can all get killed together. Touching."

Then Phillip nudges me. "Uh, guys... we might have a problem."

I follow his eyes toward the street. Tess's dad steps out of his car, eyeing us.

"See?" Rob says. "It doesn't matter what we think. Her dad's never going to let her out of his sight."

"So we sneak her out of her house," I say without thinking.

"Are you *serious?*" Rob yells.

"Just shut up, okay? Go with me on this." I turn to Tess and talk quick before her dad can get to us. "We'll come for you tonight, okay? 9:30. You'll need to be ready."

She nods. Then her dad steps up.

"Tess, I told you to wait for me in the office," he snaps at her.

"Are your... friends playing nice with you?"

"*You have no idea,*" she says, and I think I see her snicker.

His forehead scrunches up in a confused look, then he shakes his head. He grabs Tess by the hand and leads her off to the car. We stand there, watching her go.

"You *still* sure about this?" Rob says.

"Yeah," I say. I'm surprised at how confident my voice sounds.

***

THE SCHOOL HALLWAY IS quiet, save for my footsteps and a few scattered voices around the corner somewhere. It's amazing how little time it takes for everyone to clear out of here. I reach the science room and glance inside.

"Mr. Plask? You still here?"

Of course he's still here. He looks up from his papers.

"Matt? Hi. I, uh, wanted to thank you for the other night, at the diner. You didn't have to come with me. That was... nice."

"Yeah, it was," I say. "Look, I wish I was just here to talk as a friend, but that has to wait. There's something important going on. Something life or death."

I tell him all of it. Crossman, Deckert, Sutton's email, the fire at the Sutton house, and the meeting with Draughton tonight. Plask listens, his eyes widening with increasing disbelief until I finish. Then he sits there, stunned.

"I... I don't..." he sputters. "You're sure about this?"

"Positive."

"But you can't really know Crossman killed Mr. Sutton. That was just an accident, right?"

"It wasn't an accident, and I do know."

"Well, you don't know he's going to kill anyone else tonight,"

Plask insists.

"I do, though. I may not have proof, but I don't need proof to know."

Plask roughs at his hair. "Okay... okay, so have you told the police?"

"Weren't you listening? The police chief is obviously protecting Crossman. Probably on his payroll."

"Well, even if Crossman is paying off the chief, he can't have *all* the police on his payroll. Matt, this is exactly what the police are for!"

I shake my head. "I can't trust them. If I go to the police, I'll probably get arrested. Or worse."

"Okay, but what about—"

"I've been through all the options already. I have to stop this myself."

"Yourself?" Plask says, his voice rising. "Matt, you're just a kid!"

I don't feel like a kid. Not today. "I have an Ability," I say. "You taught me that. You taught me to use it."

"To charge in and take on a bunch of criminals? Jesus, Matt..." He wipes at his forehead, jostling his glasses. "When I told you to use it, this isn't what I meant!"

"Then what *did* you mean?" I step toward him. "That I should use it, but only if it's easy and convenient? Rescue kittens out of trees, that sort of thing? Is that what you meant?"

Plask stares at me desperately. "I... I don't know, okay? I just know you can't do this."

"I can," I say. "I have an Ability. Maybe this is why I have it."

"Why *you?*"

"Because someone has to."

"But you can't do this by yourself!"

"I'm not," I say. "I'm bringing my friends with me. And I'd like you to come, too. If you're willing."

There's a hint of hesitation in him, debating; then Plask shakes his head. "No. No! I can't do this with you. In fact… I can't let you go, either."

"I already told you, I'm going."

"No, you're not!" He stands up and starts around his desk toward me.

I step backward. "What are you going to do? Lock me in the closet?"

"If that's what it takes to keep you safe." Plask's face tightens with a forced determination.

"Sorry, but I can't let you do that."

I pull at his glasses with a tingle of my fingers. They fly off his face, across the room, and into my hand. Plask falters, flailing with his arms, and bumps into one of the desks.

"I'm going," I say. "With or without you."

Plask tries to shuffle toward me, feeling his way along. "You can't do this, Matt. You can't stop them, not even with your Ability."

"I just stopped you," I say.

"That's different!"

"Maybe it's not." I set the glasses on the desk furthest from him. "This is my choice, to use what I have. Because someone has to and no one else will."

"Matt, listen to me. I… I won't be able to live with myself, if…"

"Your glasses are on the desk over here. You'll find them eventually." I turn to leave. "Either way, I still want to thank you. For showing me what I can do."

I walk out, trying hard to ignore Plask's desperate pleas behind me.

36

"THIS IS A BAD IDEA," I say. "I should be going in there with him."

"Chill, man," Rob says. "You don't see me freaking out."

"Easy for you to say. I'm the one who talked Phillip into this. What if he gets caught?"

"You talked *me* into this too, you know."

"You're not helping."

"Look," Rob says, "this is what Phillip does, remember? He'll be in and out of there like a ghost. You, you'd probably trip over your own feet and alert half the neighborhood."

He's right about that, but it doesn't make me feel any better. I don't like the idea of sending someone else to take a risk for me.

And this is still the easy part.

I look out the car window at the house across the street. Tess's house. The moon shines down through the haze of clouds in the sky, but not much of that light gets through the trees.

I catch sight of Phillip's shadow, swimming through all the other shadows, moving toward the side window. Rob's right, Phillip is a ghost. I have to squint to see him slide the window open and climb through; if I didn't know he was there, I wouldn't see him at all. Then I keep watching the shadows shift around as the breeze blows through the trees, waiting for one of those shadows to be Phillip coming back out.

"What's taking him so long?" I ask.

"I told you to relax," says Rob.

"He should be out by now. It doesn't take that long to climb out a window." I reach for the door handle. "I've got to get in there."

Rob grabs my shoulder and pulls me back. "Wait!"

"Wait for what?"

"Someone's coming out the door!"

I shrink into my seat as the front door opens. Light streams out, then a shadow emerges—no, two shadows. It has to be her parents. Damn it, Phillip got caught. How are we going to talk our way out of this? They'll have us arrested. Can they do that? Charge us with trespassing, or kidnapping, or—

"Dude, it's Phillip and Tess," Rob says.

I let out a breath. A long one. The door closes, shutting the light behind it, and then the two shadows drift across the lawn and then the street toward us. Phillip opens the car door for Tess, then slips around to the other side.

I swing around and stare at him. "You just walked out the front door?"

"Tess didn't want to climb out the window."

"Are you telling me," Rob says, "that you walked right past her parents?"

Phillip shrugs. "Yeah."

I keep staring at him. "And?"

"They never knew I was there."

Rob shakes his head. "Unbelievable."

I look at Tess. She's working her phone like always, but... she rocks back and forth.

"You okay, Tess?" I ask.

She doesn't answer. She keeps rocking.

"What's the matter with her?" Rob asks.

"I don't know," I say. "I think she's stimming."

"She's what now?"

"Stimming. I looked it up on the internet. Autistic people do it sometimes when they're happy, or scared, or—"

"Or freaked the hell out," Rob butts in. "So at least one of us is reacting like they should be right now."

I ignore him. "She's done it before, remember? When her mom came to school and surprised her with that cake on her birthday?"

"Oh, yeah," Phillip says. "She really liked that."

I watch her keep rocking. "It's just that..."

"What?" Rob says.

"I've never seen her this intense about it."

"What we're doing tonight is pretty intense," Phillip says.

I lean toward her, trying to keep my voice calm. "It's okay, Tess. We're freaked out too, but we're in this together. We'll all keep each other safe."

"Safe?" Rob scoffs. "This is *not*—"

I punch him in the arm.

"What we're doing is important, Tess," I say. "We need your help to do it, or people will get hurt. But it has to be your choice."

Her rocking slows, then stops. Her fingers keep moving.

"*I'm okay,*" she says. "*Let's go.*"

"Are you sure?" I ask her. "You still want to do this?"

"*I can do this. You need me.*"

I let out a breath. "Yeah. We do need you." I look at Phillip and Rob. "I need all you guys."

"Well, don't get all mushy on us," says Rob. "We're just getting to the interesting part."

Rob throws the car in gear, driving us off into the night.

37

STARS PIERCE THROUGH THE DARK AS we pull up to the hill overlooking the factory. Rob is careful to idle in slowly to keep the noise down, and fortunately the hatchback doesn't backfire this time. Although I'm pretty sure my heart does.

We get out of the car, and the cool air makes me shiver. Or maybe it's just my nerves.

"You guys ready to do this?" I say.

Phillip nods, and Tess does too.

"Sure," Rob says. "We're in this far. Might as well do this."

"Tess, did you find a map of the factory?" I ask.

I barely finish the sentence before my phone buzzes and there's a complete blueprint of the building on the screen.

"Okay," I say, firming my voice up. "Remember what we're here to do. Keep Draughton from getting killed, and get those safety records to prove what Crossman did."

"And get back out in one piece," says Rob. "Don't forget that part."

I'm trying not to.

"Let's go," I say. "We'll go in the back door to avoid a welcoming party."

"At least that's one smart thing you've said," Rob quips.

I start down the hill toward the building, quickly, my heart beating a dull thud with each step. We make it to the door without hearing another sound. I glance at the others, making sure they're still with me.

I put my hand on the door handle. It's cold, sharply cold. I take a long breath and close my eyes. Once I open this door, we're committed. I start to pull.

"*Wait*," Tess says.

I open my eyes. "What?"

"*Alarm*," she says.

Phillip motions above the door. I look up. A small light glows a dull red.

Rob looks at Tess. "You, uh, can't do anything about that, can you?"

Tess's fingers keep flying. A second later, the light fades out.

Phillip whistles. "Not bad."

"Not bad at all, Tess." I pull at the door, only to have it stick shut. Locked.

"Well," Rob says, "Tess did her magic trick. I'm guessing this is where you do yours?"

I nod. I pull at the deadbolt, my hand tingling, until it clicks. I feel a wave of confidence as I swing the door open. I try to hold onto that as I step inside, because I'm going to need all the confidence I can get.

The others slip inside behind me, and I slide the door closed. The click it makes cracks ominously off the walls. I squint down the long hallway, dark except for the red glow of exit signs. Machines hum faintly in the distance. The air smells of rust and chemical solvents. I glance back and forth, trying to figure out where we are.

"The machines are running," Phillip says. "Means that's probably where we need to go."

"Good thinking." I pull up the map on my phone. "Looks like we can cut through here."

I hurry down the hallway, the others quick behind me. The patter of our steps echoes off the lockers that line the walls. We round the corner and I see the dark window of the conference room and the bulletin board on the wall—the one I almost pulled down on top of Deckert the last time I was here. I slow to a stop, my stomach suddenly twisting with doubt. I couldn't do it then; can I do it now? I'm almost ready to tell the others to abort, to get the hell out of here, when I hear hard boots on the floor ahead. Lots of boots.

I dive for an open office door, grabbing Tess and Phillip by the shoulder on the way in. Rob scurries in beside us and we shove into the dark room. I bump into a box sitting by the door, knocking my elbow on the corner. I wince and rub my funny bone, then jolt when I see the glow of Tess's phone. They'll see that. I frantically shove myself in front of her to hide the light.

"You can't arrest us!" comes a strained voice from down the hall. "Arrest *them!* They're the ones breaking the law!"

"I already told you," answers a deeper voice. A familiar one. "The open carrying of firearms in this building is prohibited. We can't allow anarchy like that in this town, can we?"

I inch my head out the doorframe to see Chief Ross standing in the lobby, arms folded. Half a dozen officers stand with him, holding three men in cuffs. Draughton, and two guys I don't recognize. I get a glimpse of Deckert and Crossman behind all of them.

"All we were doin' was protecting ourselves," Draughton argues. "What about him? He's got his gun out, too!"

Deckert casually closes his jacket over the gun in his belt, and flashes a look at Ross.

"I don't see a gun," Ross says.

Draughton lurches forward. "Why you little..." He doesn't get far, as the officer tugs on his cuffs and he flinches. "Are you really tucked that deep in Crossman's pocket, Ross?"

Ross steps toward him. "I don't like your tone. Time for you to go." He waves his hand, and the officers drag the three men toward the front door.

"Not so fast," Deckert says. He grabs Draughton by the shoulder and pulls him back. "We need to have a chat with this one first."

"What my associate *meant* to say," Crossman says, stepping up, "is how grateful we are for you officers responding so quickly. Far be it from us to impede you as you administer justice, but—"

"Justice, my ass," Draughton scoffs.

"...but we'd like to have a private discussion with Mr. Draughton here," Crossman says with a glare. "Before you take him away."

The officers shift uneasily.

"I'll handle this myself," Ross tells his officers. "Take the other two, and the rest of you wait outside."

The officers march the two guys to the door, casting anxious glances behind them on the way out. The thud of the door closing echoes through the whole room.

"Have your chat already," Ross says. "I'd like to wrap this up."

Deckert chuckles. "You really want to see this? I get pretty intense when I 'chat.' "

"Stop fooling around and take him to the machine room," Crossman says.

"You can't let them take me back there, Ross!" Draughton yells. "I'll never come back out, and you know it!"

Ross hesitates. "Is that really necessary?" he asks. "Perhaps we could—"

Crossman steps up to him and gives him a long look. I can't see it from here, but I can *feel* it. Ross straightens up.

"Very well," Ross says. "I don't interfere in civil matters. Have your discussion."

"You asshole!" Draughton shouts. He could mean any of them, but I'm pretty sure he's talking to Ross. "You know what you've just done to me? Are you such a coward that you can't—"

"That's enough," Deckert snaps, clamping his hand on Draughton's shoulder and pulling him away.

Crossman adjusts his shirt cuffs. "I appreciate your discretion, Ross. You and your officers do Chaplain proud."

Deckert drags Draughton to the doors to the factory floor, and glances back. "Your job isn't over yet, Ross. Keep an eye on the perimeter in case any more of Draughton's friends show up." He pushes through the doors, and they swing shut behind them.

"Happy to help," Ross says with awkward hesitation.

Crossman nods at Ross, then disappears through the doors behind Deckert.

Ross grabs his radio from his belt. "Get back in here," he barks into it.

I startle when Rob grabs my arm and pulls me back into the room. "What're we gonna do?" he hisses. "I wasn't planning on taking on a bunch of cops."

"It's not a bunch. It's just Chief Ross," I say. I glance back out the door and catch sight of a couple of the officers walking back in. "And, uh, two more."

"You're not helping."

"Look, I know what we're up against, but we have to go on," I say. "I can't let this happen. Can you?"

"I'm with you," Phillip says. "But what's our plan for those cops?"

I'm about to say I have no idea when I hear a burst of static from the lobby.

"*Alarm has been triggered at the bank,*" comes a voice over Ross's radio. "*We need unit four to check it out.*"

The two officers turn to leave, when Ross grabs them by their jackets and pulls them back. He barks into his radio, "Unit four is with me. Send someone else."

"*All other units are occupied, sir.*"

Ross glances toward the factory doors. "Fine," he says, a hint of hesitation in his voice. "You two go. I'll hold here."

The officers cast one last glance at Ross, then shuffle out.

"Well, that's convenient," Rob whispers beside me. "How often do we have a bank robbery around here?"

"Something tells me we didn't," I say. "You have something to do with that alarm, Tess?"

She nods.

"Good thinking."

I peek out the door toward the lobby, where Ross stands alone. He starts walking this way. I slide back into the room, but I knock over the box beside me.

A gush of things spill out—hundreds of them, small, cold, and round. They pour over my leg and skitter across the floor. Ball bearings, probably, but I could care less what they are. What I care about is all the noise. I frantically swipe at them with my arm, trying to contain them, but they rush on past.

Ross's footsteps quicken toward us. I press myself up against the wall, praying that I'm out of sight. But I won't be out of sight for long.

Focus, Matt. I reach out with my mind to feel what's out there. The hallway feels empty. Ross's steps get closer. Come on… there. A picture frame on a desk, a couple offices down. Ross reaches our doorway and his flashlight cuts through the room to the far wall. Rob darts to the side to stay out of the beam. The tingle in my hand sparks, forcing the picture down the hall to drop to the floor with a crack.

The light swings out of the room, and Ross's steps move away. I let out a breath. Just for good measure, I reach out for something at the far end of the hall; I feel something in one of the lockers, kind of hazy because it's so far away. I pull at it and hear a faint scrape. Ross's steps fade as he follows the sound around the corner.

"Now's our chance," I whisper. "Let's go."

I push myself up and hurry out the door, but I only make it four steps.

"Stop right there!" Ross booms.

Shit.

I quicken my pace, darting a glance back to see Ross galloping toward me. I wave my arm at Rob and Tess to get out of here, and they hurry on ahead. I don't see Phillip anywhere. Ross is only a few steps from me now.

The tingling in my hands burns like mad as I reach out. I've never moved this many things at once before. The ball bearings swarm out of the doorway, rolling across the floor like a pool of steel. Ross reaches them at a sprint. His foot comes down and skids out from under him. His head smacks against the floor and scatters the ball bearings everywhere.

Rob hurries over. "Nice job. You didn't kill him, did you?"

I bend over the chief. "He's dazed, but he'll be fine. Help me get him into this office." We drag him through the doorway, when Phillip appears again.

"I got these off of him," he says. He hands me a radio and something else—something cold and hard, with a long barrel. I choke down a swallow.

"I still don't know how you do that, Phillip," Rob says.

I stare at the gun in my hands.

"What are you going to do with it?" Phillip asks.

I hesitate, wondering for just a second if it would be smart to keep it. Then I shake my head. "We don't use guns." I step into the next office and lower it—slowly—into the trash can. The radio drops in beside it.

"You guys okay?" I ask.

"Aside from the fact we just assaulted the police chief, fine and dandy," Rob says.

"I know, this just got real. If you want to leave, I won't stop you."

"I'm in," Phillip says. "You know that."

"*Me too*," Tess says.

"Thanks, guys," I respond.

Rob shakes his head. "If you're stupid enough to keep going, I'm sure as hell not gonna let you go without me. Let's finish this."

38

THE METALLIC GROWL OF THE MACHINES rushes over me as soon as I push the door open. Rumbling, rattling, and thick smells of dust and oil. At least the lights are on in here. We scurry in through the side door Tess found for us and crouch in a shadow by one of the machines.

I peer out and find Draughton just in time to see Deckert's fist pound into his face. Draughton recoils with a grunt.

"Had enough yet?" Deckert growls.

Draughton spits blood in his face, earning him another punch from Deckert.

Crossman stands to the side, his face passive. "I really don't enjoy this, Draughton."

"Could've fooled me," Draughton mutters.

"You don't understand. This launch is bigger than any of us. I can't let anything jeopardize my father's legacy."

"I told you," Draughton says. "I don't give a shit about your legacy, and I'm not here to stop the launch. I just wanted my cut."

Deckert pulls a handkerchief from his pocket and wipes the blood and spit off his face. "How's that working for you? You thought bringing a couple guns and your worthless friends would protect you?"

"The point is," Crossman says, "I have to be sure this is put to rest permanently. I need those records."

"The records are the only reason I'm still alive," Draughton says.

Deckert throttles him by the collar. "I'd be happy to change that."

"Easy, Deckert." Crossman takes a long breath. "Perhaps we're approaching this the wrong way. I told you, I can't let this fail. I'll do whatever is necessary, even if it's... unpleasant." He turns to Deckert. "Find his wife and son."

"What? No!" Draughton tries to lunge at Crossman, only to have Deckert choke him back. "You bastard! You wouldn't dare!"

"I'll be glad to track them down," Deckert says with a smirk. "Didn't think *you* had it in you, though."

"If it's what is necessary," Crossman says, with just a hint of reluctance on his face.

"So what's it gonna be?" Deckert says to Draughton. "You want to watch me cut your boy's nose off? Or your wife's?" He laughs, like he's enjoying himself. "Of course, there are other things I could do to your wife, too."

Draughton's anger fades to a smolder. "Okay. Okay, the records are... here. In the stockroom."

"More specific," Deckert growls.

Draughton chews his lip, until the last bit of resolve drains from his face. "Shelf D7."

"There." Crossman adjusts his collar. "That wasn't so hard, was it? I'll retrieve them. Deckert..." His face betrays doubt, for just a moment. Then he wipes it away. "Finish up in here."

Deckert smiles. "With pleasure."

"You're not man enough to watch, Crossman?" Draughton scoffs.

Crossman glares at him but says nothing. Probably because he knows Draughton's right. He turns and walks crisply out.

"All right, Draughton," Deckert says. "Time to say goodbye." He drags him toward one of the machines, a conveyor belt leading into a long metal box.

"The curing oven?" Draughton shrieks.

"Don't worry. It may take a while, but it'll take care of you just fine after it heats up to five hundred degrees."

Draughton tugs against him. "You're too lazy to just shoot me?"

"Bullets lead to questions. Besides, you know how dangerous this place is. Accidents happen all the time."

Deckert pushes him down onto the conveyor belt and shoves him through, like luggage going through the x-ray machine at the airport. As Deckert clangs a door shut to block him in, those words repeat in my head—*five hundred degrees.*

I turn to the others. "We need to get him out of there before it cooks him," I whisper. "Tess, can you shut it down from your phone?"

Her fingers tap; then she shakes her head. She angles her screen over to me.

She's got a diagram of the machine pulled up. I scan it quickly. "All right," I say. "We need to get across the room to that red knob, the emergency stop, and crank it to the right."

"Isn't that what we have you for?" Rob says. "Can't your magic trick do that from here?"

I shake my head. "I can't control it like that. I can pull stuff in a straight line, but I can't turn a knob."

Tess tilts her phone to me again. *Internal temperature 120 degrees and rising,* it says.

I swallow. "How hot can it get before he…"

"250 degrees," Tess answers.

"We don't have much time. Rob, see if you can… wait, where's Phillip?" I dart glances back and forth, then get a sinking feeling because I'm pretty sure I know where he is. I look toward the machine, where I see a shadow creeping along behind Deckert. "Damn it, Phillip," I whisper to myself.

His shadow reaches the controls. The machine shudders to a stop.

"What the hell?" Deckert spins and bumps into Phillip, knocking him into the light. Phillip's eyes surge wide open. Deckert grabs him by the hoodie and drags him close.

"He's going to kill him," I say with a shudder.

Rob leaps up and races toward them. "Not if I can help it."

"Damn it, wait for me!" I jump up from my crouch. "Uh, stay here, Tess," I say, then sprint after Rob.

Deckert throttles Phillip with one hand. He jabs at the machine with the other, and it rumbles to life again. "Where'd you come from, you little shit?" he yells. "Now I'm gonna kill you, too."

Rob reaches him and throws a punch that thuds into Deckert's jaw. Deckert snaps his head right back, drops Phillip, and throws his fist like a hammer at Rob. It pounds into Rob's temple, dropping him instantly. Deckert turns his eyes toward me as I close the last few steps to him.

He pulls his gun, the metal glinting in the light. "You kids really are something. You think bringing a couple of your little friends will change anything?"

I skid to a stop and stare at the gun barrel. Rob rolls over on the ground and makes a quick motion toward Deckert. "Trick," he mumbles.

The energy builds in my hand, reaching for the gun. It jerks. Deckert throws a confused look at his hand, grips it tighter, and tugs back. My hand burns, my eyes water from pain as the gun shakes, until I can't take it anymore and release it. "I can't get the gun out," I gasp.

Deckert hardens his eyes, steadies his hand, and levels the barrel at me. I hold my breath, waiting for it to happen.

Suddenly a shriek pierces everything. I flinch and cover my ears. Deckert does too but then clutches at his hip like he's got bees in his pocket.

"Come on!" I grab Rob and drag him away. Phillip scurries off in the other direction. I can't see Tess, and have to hope she's okay.

I glance back to see Deckert pull out his phone, fumbling it as it shakes violently and shrieks keep screaming out of it. He jabs at the screen with no result. Finally he drops it on the ground and smashes his foot into it, silencing it with a crack.

Nice work, Tess, I think as I pull Rob behind one of the machines. "You okay, man?" I ask him.

"I'll have a hell of a headache tomorrow."

Deckert's gun goes off, cracking through the room like thunder. The shot pings off of the metal shielding us.

"Split up," I tell Rob, shoving him right as I go left. Deckert fires again while I race across the room and slide into a new hiding spot.

"You think you can stop this?" Deckert shouts. "You all are nothing."

"It doesn't matter who we are," I call back. "We're not going to lay down and let you hurt anyone else."

Deckert laughs. Long, cold, and hard. "Hang onto your

idealism, kid. You'll need it after I get through with you."

I force off the cold shiver that washes over me. My phone buzzes with a text.

TESS—150 degrees and rising

Damn it, we need to get back to that machine. I hear a noise across from me, probably Rob. Deckert hears it too and spins around, starting toward him. I frantically look for something I can use. A chain sits coiled on the floor, one end latched to a pillar. I let the energy surge through my hand and watch the chain unfurl, stretching itself into a tight line a foot off the ground—right in front of Deckert's shins.

He reaches the chain at a run and catches his foot. He thuds hard on the concrete, and I hear the scrape of metal when his gun hits the floor. His grip on it loosens just enough, and I pull at the gun. I dart out from my hiding spot as it slides to me, grab it up, and dash off before Deckert can lay a hand on me.

"I got his gun, guys!" I slide behind a bin full of black powder. I drop the gun inside and bury it as deep as I can.

"You thank that matters?" Deckert yells. His voice is harder than ever. "I don't need a gun to kill you. Now it'll just be slower and more painful."

As I try not to think about how he's right, the main doors burst open and in rushes Chief Ross. The dark lines of his face shine under the harsh light. I cringe to see he's holding a shotgun.

"About time, Ross," Deckert growls. "You were supposed to watch the perimeter."

"I'm here now, aren't I?" Ross snaps back. "What's going on?"

"Some little punks broke in. They got my gun. You'll need to use yours."

I scamper around the bin to get out of Ross's sightline. The curing machine shudders to a stop again. I steal a glance to see Phillip at the controls, then he disappears.

"Damn it!" Deckert shouts. "Ross, turn that machine back on!"

Ross hurries over and scans the controls. A moan comes from inside. Ross stares at it. "There's someone in here!"

"Of course there is, you idiot!" Deckert shouts. "Now turn it on!"

Ross stands motionless. He reaches slowly toward the controls, but his hand hovers just above them.

"What the hell are you waiting for?" Deckert lumbers up to the machine and punches the controls himself. The machine hums back to life, with a muffled yell from Draughton inside.

Ross stifles a shudder. "This isn't what I signed up for. You do what you want, and I don't ask questions. That was the deal."

"I don't have time to bicker over details," Deckert snaps. "Just shut up and do what we pay you for."

The lines on Ross's face quiver for a second. "Fine, but this gets me another ten percent."

"Whatever. Now help me deal with this."

Deckert goes left. Ross goes right, with one last hesitation. I realize he's coming toward me, and I duck around a conveyor belt. I catch a glimpse of Rob slipping out of Deckert's path and around a corner when my phone buzzes again.

TESS—170 degrees and rising.

Damn it. I sneak a glance at the curing machine. The coast is clear. I jump up and make a run for it, when two dark holes and a long barrel block my view.

I jolt backward as Ross levels his shotgun at me.

"You're under arrest!" he orders.

"Under arrest?" Deckert yells. "*Shoot* him, Ross!"

Ross creases his forehead tight, staring at me. I'm paralyzed, not seeing anything but the holes in that gun barrel. Then the barrel lowers.

"I'm not killing a kid, Deckert," Ross shouts back.

I stand there stunned for another second, then dash for cover before he can change his mind.

Deckert storms over to him. "You're backing out now, Ross?"

"I'm not backing out of anything," Ross says. "*This* was never part of the deal."

"This was always the deal, and you know it."

I duck behind a shelf and then sneak a glance around to see Deckert looming over Ross.

"I don't kill innocent people," Ross says.

"Don't play dumb with me," Deckert growls back. "You knew what you were getting into. What exactly did you think we've been doing while you looked the other way?"

Ross glares at him until his resolution fades. "All right, maybe I did know, or I should have... but it's over. I'm not letting you cook Draughton in this thing. I'm shutting it down."

"No, you're not," Deckert barks.

"Yes, I *am*. Crossman may be the money in this town, but I'm the police."

Ross reaches for the controls... but in one swift motion, Deckert snatches the shotgun from him, swings it around, and pulls the trigger.

The blast bursts into Ross's chest and kicks him backward. I clap my hand over my mouth and watch Ross slump to the floor, a red hole gaping in his jacket. His eyes stare toward me, hollow and empty; somehow I can't look away.

"All right, you little shits!" Deckert shouts. He fires a blast into the rafters, pellets clanging off the metal. "This ends *now*."

He lumbers around the curing machine, and another shot rings out as Rob dives out of the way. Rob trips and goes down. Deckert pumps a new round into the shotgun. Rob tries to crawl away, but I know he'll never make it in time. Suddenly Phillip darts into view and into the line of fire. Deckert turns the gun away from Rob and toward Phillip. Another shot explodes, but it misses, and Phillip disappears. Rob scrambles up and darts to safety as Deckert fires again. I breathe a momentary sigh of relief when I get another text.

TESS—200 degrees and rising.

"You think you're going to make any difference here?" Deckert shouts. He comes around the corner and levels the gun at me. I run and the shot pings into the panel behind me. He pumps the shotgun again. I don't have anywhere to hide before he can pull the trigger. I see a box on a shelf and surge the energy in my hand to pull it over as I sprint past, spewing a mess of screws across the floor behind me. I hear the metallic scrape of Deckert's foot coming down on the screws and his foot slides out from under him. The gun blasts again, making me flinch, but the shot pings into the rafters, right before Deckert's body thuds against the concrete floor. I slip around a shelf for cover while Deckert slowly pries himself back up. I glance back and cringe to see a screw impaled in his cheek.

I run toward the curing machine, flinching as Deckert pulls the trigger again but it clicks against an empty chamber. He growls and hurls the shotgun across the room. It thuds against a wall, and I hear a yelp—a female voice. It jerks me to a stop and makes my stomach twist into a knot.

Tess.

"Well, what did I find here?" Deckert says with cold pleasure. He lumbers to where Tess crouches, grabs her arm, and drags her up. She jerks against his grip but she's not going anywhere. Then she releases one hand from her phone, pulls her arm back, whips it forward, and slaps Deckert right across the face. The smack echoes like a blow from a prizefighter, and I swear I see her handprint on his cheek.

"Oh, you're a feisty one, aren't you?" Deckert laughs. "I'm gonna have fun with you."

If Tess is scared, there's no trace of it on her face, but I'm oozing cold sweat as I sprint toward her.

Rob gets there first. He pulls Tess away from him and slugs Deckert in the nose. Deckert's dark glasses shatter. He flings the broken frames away, finally revealing his eyes, and they are *pissed*. He clamps his hand around Rob's throat. Rob's eyes pop wide and his hands go to Deckert's arm, trying to pry loose but getting nowhere. His face pales to a chalky gray color.

A shadow appears beside Deckert. It's Phillip, holding a long pipe. He swings it at Deckert's head, but Deckert blocks it with his arm and the blow glances off. Deckert drops Rob, who wheezes and crumples to the ground. Deckert grabs the other end of the pipe. Phillip tugs to get it back, but Deckert pries it from him and lets loose with it, cracking Phillip across the face. The life empties from Phillip's eyes and he goes down. Deckert squares himself over his limp body and raises the pipe again.

"Hang on, guys!" I'm still ten steps away when I see a stack of brake pads on a shelf. My hand burns, and I pull at them. One flies off and clocks Deckert in the temple. He shakes it off when I hit him with another, and another, until he looks away from Phillip toward me.

Deckert's eyes squint at me in confusion. "What the f—"

One more brake pad hits him square in the jaw before he

lunges at me. I turn and run, making sure he's clear of the others before I duck for cover.

My phone buzzes, and I look to see a pic from Tess—a winch hanging from the ceiling. I look up and see it above us, with a cable dangling down to the floor. A light bulb flashes on in my head. Then a text message pops on top of the photo

TESS—*220 degrees and rising*

I send the pic to Rob with the words *hoist him*. I catch sight of him across the room and see the idea register on his face. He hurries across to grab the cable.

"You kids have some guts," Deckert grunts, picking the bloody screw out of his cheek. He's got a limp in his right leg. "I don't know how you're pulling those tricks, but I'm going to enjoy making you pay for those in a minute."

Deckert turns and looks back at Phillip and Tess with a cold smile. Rob's still pulling the cable down; I have to keep Deckert where he is. I see the metal panel of an access door on the machine next to his head. It looks heavy. My hand tingles as I reach for it—it *is* heavy. The door rattles but gets caught on a latch. Deckert takes a step but stops, trying to figure out where that sound is coming from. I pull harder at the door. My hand burns red hot. Then the latch gives way and the door bursts open and whips around, just as Deckert turns to look.

The crack it makes against his nose is surprisingly satisfying.

TESS—*230 degrees and rising*

Rob's on top of Deckert now with the winch cable and gets it around his legs. Deckert's stunned from his face plant, but he swings his arm and grabs hold of Rob's jacket. "This time," he barks, "I'm gonna squeeze your throat until it cracks."

Rob's eyes get wide. "Matt..."

I see the winch panel across the room, and I can feel the

lever from here. "Here's one more magic trick," I say, surging the energy to pull at the lever.

The lever snaps toward me and the motor whines. The slack of the cable slithers itself up until it sweeps Deckert's legs out from under him. He claws at Rob's jacket but the cable drags him away, across the floor, and then up. The motor whines to a stop with Deckert dangling upside down, screaming obscenities and flailing his arms.

I stand there with a rush of self-satisfaction, but only for a second. I look at my phone.

TESS—240 degrees and rising

My eyes dart to the curing machine, clear on the other side of the room. A long, unearthly shriek echoes from inside. I run toward it, stumbling awkwardly with each step. I'm too far away. Rob's too far away. Phillip's knocked out. I don't think we're going to make it.

Then I see Tess in front of me, walking with slow even steps toward the machine. She takes the last step and reaches out, grasps the shutoff, and slowly, smoothly, turns the knob. The machine's hum stops with a shudder.

I skid to a stop, feeling my chest heave as I try to catch up with my breath. Draughton quiets down to a whimper inside.

"Thanks for that, Tess," I wheeze. "Are you okay?"

Her hands go back to her phone. *"I'm okay. Check on Phillip."*

I run to where he's slumped on the floor. His eyes are dazed, but he raises his head to look at me and gives me a thumbs up.

Rob struggles his way to us, wheezing himself.

"Rob, take care of Phillip," I tell him. "Tess, you help him. Look up what to do after someone gets whacked in the head, will you?"

"Already on it," she says.

I look up to where Deckert dangles overhead, glaring at me. "Make sure that asshole stays up there," I say, jumping up and taking off running. "Oh, and get Draughton out of that machine."

"Where are you going?" Rob calls after me.

"I've got to stop Crossman!"

39

THE HALLWAY STRETCHES AHEAD OF ME. The dim lights cast disjointed shadows on the floor, shaking up and down because I'm sprinting and I don't sprint very well. I sneak a glance at the map on my phone, hang a left, and pound up to the stock room.

I slip inside, trying to control my breathing. Like I said, I don't sprint well. I look around—shelves everywhere. Rows and rows, two stories high. They block out the overhead lights like trees in a forest.

I dart my eyes back and forth, looking for Crossman. Damn it, he must be gone already... that fight with Deckert took too long. Then I hear it. A soft whirring from the far side of the room. I scurry toward it, keeping myself low and silent. I duck my head around the corner.

Crossman sits in a forklift. The box it's lowering reaches the ground, and the whirring stops.

He slides out of the seat and steps quickly to the box. He lifts the lid and pulls out a handful of papers. "Finally," he says.

He turns and strides off, through the shelves that tower on either side. I scurry after him, careful to keep my steps quiet on the hard floor. Time to act. All I need is those papers. My hand tingles as I reach for them.

Nothing happens.

I crease my forehead and pull harder. My hand starts to burn. Still nothing. What the hell? I can barely even feel them...

Suddenly it dawns on me. My mind goes back to Kyle's cheat sheet, and to my comic book when I was a kid. *I can't move paper.* Which means I'll have to get those papers away from Crossman the same way anyone else would. Phillip could do it easy, but he's in no condition for that right now.

With my thoughts whirling, it takes me a second to realize that Crossman has stopped walking. He hesitates for a moment, then he turns around.

I freeze. We stare at each other for what seems like a long time.

"This isn't worth killing for," I say.

I see his face flinch, like something cracked through the surface. He forces it back down. "What do you know about any of this?" Crossman snaps. "And who the hell are you?"

"Someone who's not looking the other way while you do this. Who wants to do the right thing." I swallow. "Someone who thinks *you* might want to do that, too."

I can see the thoughts churning in his eyes. Then he pulls a gun out of his jacket.

The dark barrel stares at me, startling me back a step. It quivers. Crossman's hand shakes, but he keeps it leveled at me.

"I have to do this," he says. "For my father."

I can't take my eyes off the gun. It won't stop shaking, but it's still just as deadly. I force myself to look up at Crossman's face. His eyes are wide with doubt… then they narrow. His finger tenses around the trigger.

I frantically surge energy into my hand and pull at a box behind him. It drops to the floor and echoes through the room. Crossman's eyes go wide again, and he spins toward the sound. His back is only to me for a second, but that's all I need to dart behind the next shelf.

A shot goes off behind me, like dynamite in my skull. I skitter to the corner and duck down. Thick silence settles as the echo dies out. I huddle in the shadow, breathing hard.

"You think I like doing this?" he yells. "I'm doing what needs to be done."

I can hear the conflict in his voice. "I know you didn't want to kill Draughton," I call back.

"That… that wasn't for me," he says. "That was to protect my father."

I hear his footsteps, hard and fast, coming toward me. Crossman appears around the corner. Before I can jump out of my crouch, he raises the gun and fires. My heart stops, but the shot goes wide, puncturing a box to my left. I thank my luck and scramble away. He's not comfortable with the gun like Deckert was, but I can't count on him to miss every time.

"I remember you now," Crossman says. "You're Pine's boy, aren't you? Don't you remember what I said to you? About looking up to your father?"

"You think this is what your father wanted?" I yell back, ducking behind another shelf. "For Carl Sutton to die?"

"I didn't want Sutton to die either! But he…he stuck his nose where it didn't belong. So I had to deal with him. I *had* to. But that wasn't enough, damn it, because then his wife stuck her nose in, too!"

I taste bile in the back of my throat. "You did kill her too, didn't you? And...and Steph?"

"It was *necessary!*" Crossman shouts, a forced resolution to his voice. "Deckert... helped me see what was necessary. They were going to ruin everything!"

He appears around the corner again. I scramble up and run. A shot goes off, and I see the spark of a ricochet off the shelf up ahead. Crossman's steps are gaining behind me. I hold my hands out as I run, feeling them burn, and pull. Boxes come tumbling off the shelves on either side. I turn the corner, leaving Crossman blocked by a barricade of cardboard.

I collapse into another shadow, my thoughts spinning. I have to keep talking to him, but every time that I talk he can hear where I am.

I pull out my phone and text Tess—*can u patch my phone into the PA system?*

I'm wondering if this place even has a P.A. system when my screen morphs like I just answered a call. I hold it up to my ear, confused. "Hello?"

My voice echoes down from the ceiling.

Good job, Tess.

I take a breath to compose myself. "You need to think about what you're doing," I say, my words ringing through the room.

"I know what I'm doing," Crossman calls out. "It's you who can't see it. You, and Sutton, and Draughton... you're all trying to ruin this! Can't you see how important this factory is? Can't you see what this new product will do for Chaplain?"

"Steph was part of Chaplain, too. She had...people who cared about her." My voice chokes as I remember seeing Emily crying. "And you killed her and her parents, just for a better paycheck for everyone else!"

"They should have minded their damn business! It's their

fault, not mine." Crossman fires off a shot, this time toward the other side of the room. "Where are you, damn it? Come out here!"

"You don't really believe that," I say. "That's just what Deckert's been feeding you."

"This isn't about Deckert! I'm doing this for my father. This launch was everything to him. I won't let you rip it away."

I hear his footsteps, back and forth, searching for me.

"You have to accept the truth about your father," I say.

"My father was brilliant! He wasn't clouded by emotion and sympathy. He did what was necessary. I can... I can do that too. I can do what he wanted."

"But what do *you* want?"

"It doesn't matter what I want!" Crossman screams. "Don't you get it? He planned my life out from the moment I was born. I never had any say in this."

His footsteps get closer. I pull tighter into the shadow. "You do have a choice. You can stop this. You can make sure no one else gets hurt."

"You don't know what it's like," he says. "To claw and fight just to meet the expectations set for you, everyone wanting you to fail. You think I have control over this?"

"It's not about control or power," I say. "It's a choice. To take what we have, whatever it is, and stand up to do what's right. Your father may have started you on this path, but you don't have to follow it. You can..."

My words stop, and the echo from the speakers dies out. Crossman stands three feet from me, holding the gun level at my head. I stand up, slowly.

"You're right," he says. "I don't want this. But I'm in too deep to turn back."

I stand there paralyzed, preparing myself for what's about

to happen.

Suddenly a new voice breaks the silence, shouting, "Matt, duck!"

My eyes dart to see a figure across the room, the outline of a man standing in shadow. Then I see something whizzing toward me. A bottle? I register to duck just in time. It whips over my head and smashes into the shelf, then—*BANG!*

The bottle erupts in a blinding flash, bursting with smoke. Crossman staggers backward. I sprawl on the ground, wondering what the hell just happened. I look up in a haze of confusion and see Crossman flailing for his gun. My thoughts aren't focused enough to pull the gun away from him. I hear a whoosh as another bottle hurtles in and smashes by Crossman's feet. I cringe, waiting for the bang, but instead a froth of foam pours out of it, mushrooming to smother Crossman's legs. He tries to crawl forward to grab the gun, but the foam sticks him to the floor just out of reach. I shake off my haze and stretch out my hand, just starting to feel the tingle when Crossman makes a lunge, tearing away from the foam, and gets his hand on the gun. I pull at it, but he pulls back. He raises the barrel at me and steadies his hand, his face hardening. My eyes dart everywhere, looking for anything else I can use. There—a crate hanging over the shelf above us, jostled by the explosion. I reach for it and my hands begin to burn. It's off balance, but heavy. I pull with everything I have, the burn searing, my teeth gritting, just *pull*—

The crate shifts just enough, topples over the edge, and plummets down, slamming onto Crossman's arm. It forces a shriek out of him, pinning his arm and the gun to the floor.

I let out an exhausted breath, and cough at the smoke lingering in the air. I glance back at the shadow across the room, where I catch a brief glimpse of the figure hurrying away. All I can make out is some tufts of hair sticking up before he disappears.

My body aches as I pry myself off the floor. Crossman lays there dazed, tugging at his arm pinned under the crate.

"You can't stop this," he says.

"I just did," I answer. "You may have made your choice, but I've made mine, too."

I take the papers from him and walk away.

40

IT WAS TESS'S IDEA TO CALL 911 from a landline at the factory. Anonymous tip, then we got out of there. We didn't stick around to see what happened when the cops showed up, but even for Crossman, a dead police chief is hard to talk your way out of. That should land him in jail at least for the night while they sort everything out. His lawyers will come barking to get him released tomorrow, but we've got a plan for that.

By the time we sneak Tess back into her room and drop off Phillip, it's almost morning when I drag myself through my front door. My body's so drained from exhaustion and adrenaline overload that I can barely think straight. I shuffle into the living room, not really registering that the light is already on.

"Matthew?" My dad hurries into the room. "Do you have any idea what time it is? Where have you been?"

I try to rub away the tension in my temple. "You wouldn't believe me if I told you. Look, I don't have the energy for a lecture right now. Can we do this later?"

"I don't know who you are lately, Matt. Coming in at all hours, that bruise on your face—"

"I don't know who you are, either," I argue back. "Because you won't say two words to me."

"There's no point in talking if you won't listen," he snaps.

"*I* won't listen? For God's sake, you might actually have a clue about what's going on around here if you just paid attention for once!"

"It's not that easy," Dad says. "You don't know what kind of pressure I've been under."

"I know a lot more than you think, and if you'd get your head out of your—"

"*Stop!*" he yells, cutting me off. "I don't want to fight. I want to talk to you, *really* talk to you for once. I just didn't expect it to be so damn late."

"I know it's late, Dad, I was—"

"It doesn't matter. Just let me get this out. I have to get this out." He roughs at his hair and forces in a labored breath. "You were right, okay? There *is* something going on at the factory."

I fight off an ironic laugh. "I know, Dad. It's okay."

"It's not okay, and just listen! I saw some emails from Carl Sutton, written before he died in that accident. I don't... really *know* anything, not for sure, but I think Crossman fudged some numbers on the new brake pads. And I think Carl was trying to say something about it." He paces the floor, agitated. "Crossman's been pressuring me, pressuring everyone, to look the other way. To roll over and forget what we saw. And... I did roll over."

"It doesn't matter anymore, Dad."

"I did it for you." He looks me in the eye, startling me.

"For me?"

"I did it to protect you. At least that's what I told myself. Hell,

Crossman and his muscle showed up here! I didn't know what he'd do if I spoke up. And I didn't even know what I'd be speaking up about, not for sure. So I just kept my head down and didn't ask questions. Just like everyone else."

I almost shoot an angry comment back at him—sure he's kept his head down, he's done that ever since Mom died. He's a drunk, he's a coward. But as I look at him, I feel… sympathy. My words melt away.

"I can't ignore this anymore," Dad says. "Someone has to stand up for what's right, and I can't keep waiting for it to be someone else." He looks at me, then drops his eyes. "The truth is I'm scared, Matt. I'm so God damned scared. But I'm going to do it anyway. I'm going to stand up to Crossman, because it's what's right. I don't know what's going to happen to me. But I can't do this anymore. I can't… disappoint you anymore."

I step forward and put my arms around him. I can't remember the last time I did that. When I was a kid, when he was still my hero? He puts his arms around me, too, and I remember how they used to feel so strong back then. Now they just feel tired. But they feel real.

"I love you, Dad."

As I say those words, his arms jerk tight around me. Like a reflex, like he's been waiting for years to hear me say that. And I realize I've been waiting for years to say it, too. And there's something else I've wanted to say, that I've needed to say, but I've been too proud and angry and scared.

"Mom dying wasn't your fault."

When the tears fall on my shoulder, I'm not sure if they're his or mine.

41

I SET MY LUNCH TRAY DOWN next to Rob and Phillip and Tess, like every other day. Only this isn't like every other day.

"I just wanted to say… thanks," I tell them. "I couldn't have done that without you."

"Damn straight you couldn't," Rob says, but he smiles.

Phillip nods. "Glad we could be there."

"*We were in it together,*" Tess says.

"You know, Phillip," Rob says, "that black eye you got makes you look pretty badass."

Phillip tries to hide a smirk. Yeah, he does look pretty badass, the black and blue standing out starkly against his pale skin. He's also not wearing his hoodie, for the first time I can remember. And as for Tess, her eyes don't have that preoccupied look anymore.

"We were all pretty tough last night," I say. "I don't know how, but we did it. We made a difference."

"You're not gonna get all sappy on us, are you?" Rob asks. Then a flurry of excited conversation from the cool table draws a glance from him. "Hey, what do you think they're talking about over there?"

I look over. Funny… I hadn't even given them a thought today. Or I should say I hadn't given *her* a thought. Emily's there, looking beautiful as ever. But somehow, it doesn't hurt to look at her now.

"They're on about something big," Phillip says.

Ben the skateboarder wanders by on his way to the soda machine. Phillip motions him over. "What's the gossip?" he asks him.

"Something went down at the factory last night," Ben says. "I guess there was a big cover-up with the new brake pads, but somebody busted 'em up. Must'a been awesome."

I have to forcibly keep my eyes from popping wide open. I share a look with Rob—*how the hell do they know about that already?* I make a hard swallow.

"Do you know, um, *who* busted them up?" I ask, trying not to sound too interested.

Ben shrugs and sweeps his hair out of his face. "Nope. But whoever it was posted this."

He pulls out his phone and taps the screen, and I see a video of a shockingly familiar image from last night—Crossman telling Deckert to "finish up," and then Deckert shoving Draughton into the curing machine. I'm still gaping when Ben walks off.

"Did you put that up there?" Rob asks me.

"Of course not!" I exclaim. "I was too busy trying not to get killed to even think about recording anything, much less post it. All I did was email the safety records to those investors this morning, and the NT… uh, NHT…"

"If you can't remember the letters, just say highway safety people," Rob says. "But that doesn't answer the question of who put that video up there."

We share a glance, then swivel to look at Tess.

"*Insurance,*" she says.

"She's right," Phillip says. "No way Crossman can squirm his way out of that."

She keeps typing, when I think I see her smirk for a second. "*We busted him up,*" she says.

Phillip breaks out in a laugh. A real, full laugh.

I shake my head and get up to get a soda, walking past all the other kids who have no idea what really happened last night. Then I bump into someone, and realize it's Emily.

"Oh... hey, Matt," she says, barely masking the awkwardness in her voice. "Pretty crazy. With the factory, I mean."

"Uh, yeah."

We stand there for a minute, avoiding direct eye contact. I try to convince myself to tell her everything, what *really* went down last night. I want to tell her about...what happened to Steph. But maybe it's best she doesn't know that.

Emily looks down. "Look, Matt, there's something I need to talk to you about." She brushes her hair back. She's wearing earrings again and a pale green eye shadow. It looks strangely normal on her now. "I've been doing some thinking," she says. "About what you said at the lake. About me being too good for you guys now."

I feel my face get warm. "Look, Emily, I was—"

"No, you were right," she says. "I guess I got excited when people started noticing me. It's just... nice to be noticed, you know?"

"I guess it would be. There's nothing wrong with that."

"The funny thing is," Emily says, "I found out I actually like these people. Well, some of them. But I shouldn't have ignored you. You've been my friend for a long time, and I don't want to lose that."

I nod, and smile faintly. "I don't want to lose that either."

"Oh, and about Kyle... you were right, he is a jackass. I guess I went with him because I thought it would make me cooler or something." She looks down. "That wasn't a very good reason. In fact, I was kind of a jackass, too. Scott was the one who noticed me when no one else did, and then I dumped him."

I almost speak up to say that *I* noticed her when no one else did; but I suddenly realize I don't need to say that anymore.

"I told Scott I was stupid for doing that," Emily says. "And you know what? He's such a great guy, he doesn't hate me for it. He actually cares about me." She blushes. "I'm going to see where it goes with him."

"That's great," I say, surprising the hell out of me. A week ago, I would've thought I'd be crazy to say that. Now... it feels okay.

"I'd better get back," she says. "But I'll see you around, okay? Really."

I watch Emily walk back to the cool table, back to Scott. She slides in next to him, stroking his shoulder. Part of me still wishes that was me there with her, I'm not gonna lie. Part of me wishes she knew what I did last night; maybe that would be enough to win her over. But that's not the way I want to do it.

I know what I did, and that's enough.

42

THE FADED ORANGE ROLL-UP DOOR covered with a black stencil of *Unit 68* fills my view as I stare out from Rob's parked hatchback. I've been staring for a while. So far, I've gotten as far as rolling the down the window. I'm working myself up to opening the car door. Two women hunch over the bed of a trailer a couple doors down, before carrying another load of empty flowerpots through their own orange door into Unit 66. The pots clink as they set them down, then they go back for more. The sound's sort of rhythmic, calming almost. That helps a little, but I still can't get myself to open the door.

"We're here for you, man," Phillip says from the back seat. "We can hang out here as long as you need."

Even Rob doesn't make any snarky comments. He nods beside me. The ladies clink some more flowerpots.

"Thanks for coming, guys," I say. "I wasn't expecting it to be this hard."

For all the crap I'd given Dad about abandoning this storage unit for years, there's a reason I haven't come here either. It was just easier using him as an excuse.

"You don't have to do this today, you know," Rob says. "Could always come back later."

"No, I do. It's time for me to deal with what's in there."

I finally shove the hatchback's door open with a squeak and force myself to step out. The sun hits my back with a faint warmth, trying to force its way through the breeze. I dig in my pocket for the key and reach for the padlock, fighting the jitters in my hand. The metal pinches my fingers when I jab the key into the lock and turn. One of the ladies at Unit 66 gives me a polite nod as I stand there holding the door for an awkwardly long time; finally I pull, ratcheting the door up.

A flurry of moths swoosh past me as it opens, carrying with them the musty smell of decaying cardboard. The sunlight only makes it a few feet through the door, where a folded-up treadmill at the front throws shadows on all the boxes piled behind it.

Rob scrunches his nose as he steps up beside me. "Smells pretty stale in there."

"This stuff's been abandoned a long time," I say. "I think my folks stuck it in here when I was born, emptying out the spare room so they could turn it into the nursery. Then when the house burned... the only stuff left from my mom will be in here."

Rob slaps my back. "Well, let's dig in, then."

I give him a half-smile, appreciating his attempt to lighten my mood. As I step inside, the shadow drapes over me, and my nose tickles at the thickness of the air. I hear another clink of flowerpots, this time muffled through the walls.

"Do you even know what's in here?" Phillip asks.

"Not really. Just stuff they didn't have room for." I step around the treadmill and knock into something leaning against the wall, catching a pair of snow skis before they topple over. "Huh. My dad always said he wanted to get back to skiing."

"He ever teach you?" Phillip asks.

I shake my head. "No. I think he stopped doing it himself, too. Guess he never got back around to it."

"Forget the skis, man. Look at this!" Rob pulls off a box lid and sends up a fresh cloud of dust. "It's one of those tiny pool tables for your desk. Hey, Phillip, rack 'em up!"

I shake my head at him and lift up a plastic tarp to find a set of encyclopedias. When I pull the first one out, the cover falls off.

"Matt," Phillip says. "You'll want to see this."

He zips open a garment bag, letting loose a flow of white silk.

"Wow," I gasp.

I step over slowly and rub my fingers over the lace at the edge, the texture both soft and rough. I try to tell myself it's the dust making my eyes water.

"Your mom must have looked beautiful in this," Phillip says.

"Yeah."

Rob comes up and pats my shoulder. "You ever see pictures of her in it? Of your folks' wedding?"

I nod slowly. "Once, a long time ago. Before she died. I was too young to really know what a wedding was, but I knew she looked beautiful." I remember how the light shone on her dark hair, all curled and tucked up on her head... and her smile. She looked so happy in that picture.

Phillip delicately closes the bag over the dress and sets it aside.

"Here's something," Rob says. "This box here says 'Susan kid stuff.' "

I step over and lift the flaps open. I dig through some stuffed animals, a coloring book; further down are high school yearbooks and cassette tapes of some boy band from way before my time. I'm about to open one of the yearbooks, trying to picture my mom doodling in math class or dancing away at a concert, when I uncover the bottom of the box and my heart stops.

The small plastic figure has black hair that drapes beautifully over her shoulders, but she wasn't meant for playing dress-up. Her arms are strong, and the emblem on her red and gold breastplate is unmistakable.

"Oh my God…"

Rob leans in over my shoulder. "What? It's a doll."

"She's a superhero," I whisper.

"Well, yeah. But girls play superheroes sometimes, don't they?"

"Not my mom. She didn't want anything to do with them."

"Why not?" Phillip asks.

"I don't know. She told me heroes don't work like that, with bright costumes, but… there was something more she wouldn't tell me."

I gently pick up the doll, running my fingers over the muscles in her arms. I try to picture my mom with this, saving the world in her room like I did. Did she really do that?

"There's something else down here," Rob says. "Looks like an old newspaper clipping."

He pulls it out, handing me the yellowed scrap of paper. It feels thin and dry in my fingers.

"Look at the date," Phillip points out. "Your mom would've been, what? Like our age?"

I nod. Rob and Phillip crowd in beside me as I begin to scan the faded black of the text.

Local Woman Miraculously Recovers Wedding Ring

It started as a simple outing to the salon for Peggy Hawthorn. She'd just gotten her hair done—and was quite pleased with it, too—when the unimaginable happened.

"My wedding ring fell off my finger!" Hawthorn frantically explained. "I was so proud of myself for losing some weight, but it made my ring loose and slip right off, right down the storm drain!"

Hawthorn could see the ring glistening at the bottom of the drain, but it was well out of reach. As she was desperately staring through the grate, a teenage girl walked by and asked her what was wrong. Hawthorn didn't get the girl's name, but she said she was kind enough to listen to her whole story— how her husband passed away last year, and she couldn't bear the thought of losing the ring he'd given her.

Intent on calling the fire department and begging them to help, Hawthorn turned to hurry back to the salon. But before she could get inside, the girl she'd been talking to tapped her on the shoulder... and handed her the wedding ring.

Hawthorne grabbed her up in a hug and asked how she could possibly have gotten the ring out of the depths of the storm drain, but the girl gave no explanation and began to back away. Wanting to give her some money as a token of thanks, Hawthorn looked down for just a moment to dig in her purse; when she looked back up, the girl was gone.

"I didn't mean to scare her away," Hawthorn says. "I just wanted to thank her and give her a reward. It was a miracle! The only way she could've gotten that ring out is if she got it to float up through the grate..."

"Oh my God!" I stop reading and stagger back, knock into

the treadmill and lean on it for support. "Oh my God, oh my God..."

"What's wrong with you?" Rob asks.

"Did you see that?" I say. "The ring *floated up through the grate!*"

"Come on, there's gotta be a simpler explanation than that." Then he hesitates. "Right?"

Phillip raises an eyebrow. "You think that girl was your mom?"

I stare at my hand, feeling the energy inside it, then look at the doll. "I don't understand it. My mom spent my whole childhood telling me to get rid of my superhero toys, and then I find out she had one herself? And this story... but I never saw her do anything like that. She never caught a falling coffee mug, or..."

Then the memory finds me. The lost secret jumping out of the haze of my subconscious. The blue of the sky; the grinding sound of my tricycle wheels against the concrete as I pumped my four-year-old legs on the pedals. Mom and Dad were behind me, by the house. I got to the edge of the driveway and Mom shouted to stop, but of course I kept going. All I could see was the sky; my dad's car was parked on the curb, I remember that now, that's why I couldn't see the street. I kept pedaling and Mom screamed, and that's when I heard the truck engine. More like the growl of a monster. It was a garbage truck, I think, but all I saw was that steel grill coming straight at me when I darted into the street. The engine roared, shuddering my skin. In my nightmares, that's when I'd always wake up.

But the memory doesn't stop this time. As the truck charged with me frozen in its path, the tricycle jerked itself backward underneath me. Violently, like someone grabbed on and pulled. The pedals whipped around, knocking into my feet. Then it skidded sideways, still pulling me back, until it grated to a stop and the truck rumbled past. I slumped there trying to breathe, until a second later when my mom grabbed me up in the tightest hug I'd ever had. As she crushed me in her arms, I saw my dad across the lawn, staring at me with a look of...

Holy shit. *That's* where I'd seen that look before. From that day with the action figures, when Dad saw what I'd done. Finally, I understood what that look meant. It wasn't just about what he saw me do. It was what he'd seen *her* do.

The thick air of the storage unit wheezes in my lungs and I jerk back into the present, trying to stay upright. "I got my Ability from my mom," I choke out. "She had it too!"

"Are you sure?" Phillip asks.

"Hey, man," Rob says, "That newspaper story does sound kinda like your magic trick, but I don't get how that doll means—"

"It all came back to me," I say. "That day when I was four, when that truck almost hit me. I didn't backpedal myself out of the way. The tricycle jerked backward on its own. My mom pulled me, *pulled* me, like I can do."

"Wow." Phillip puts his hand on my shoulder, steadying me. "You okay?"

I don't know. There are tears in my eyes, but my mouth is smiling. "Now I know why she told me people wouldn't understand," I say. "Because they didn't understand her either. Not even my dad."

"What do you mean, not your dad?" Rob asks.

"He saw what she did that day with the truck. The way he looked at her... and then he gave me that same look the day I showed him what I could do. When he pretended not to see."

"Wait, what? I don't follow," Rob says. "Does your dad know what you can do, or not?"

"He knows. But he doesn't understand, or he doesn't want to, so we pretend it's not there. We haven't talked about it, ever."

Phillip gives me a probing look. "Maybe it's time to change that."

I shake my head. "I don't think he'll ever understand, but that's okay. Now I have something better. I have a connection with my mom, like... almost like I have her back. I wish I could have shared it with her while she was still here; I wish I could tell her what we did last night. But this is enough."

I squeeze my mom's doll tight, knowing I'll keep her close with me for a long time.

43

I FEEL AN UNUSUAL SENSE OF calm as I make my way down the hallway. Ben flies past me on his skateboard, and I even throw him a wave. He gives me a thumbs up. I hear Principal Stokes yell at him from the other side of the hall, and I laugh.

When I reach the science room, Plask looks up from his desk. His eyes don't pop wide open like they usually do. He almost looks like he was expecting me.

"Hi, Mr. Plask."

He makes a gesture toward the back of the room. "Tiffany's helping me get set up for tomorrow's lab," he says.

I glance back and see her setting out bottles and test tubes. She looks at me for a second, then goes to work again. There's a rhythmic clinking of glass.

"I heard there was some fuss at the factory last night," Plask says calmly.

I nod. "Yeah, there was."

"So you went through with your choice, then."

I watch his face, looking for anger or disappointment. "I

didn't think you agreed with my choice."

"I was concerned about the consequences," he says. "You were working with elements that were unpredictable."

The voices of two cheerleaders drift past the door as I try to get a read on Plask's face.

"Do you think I made the right choice?" I ask.

He smiles. "Do you?"

The clinking stops for a moment. Tiffany moves to the closet to get more bottles.

"Yes," I say.

"Well, that's what matters," Plask says. "And how did the experiment work out?"

"It wasn't easy."

"But that didn't stop you, did it?"

I shake my head. "No. But I did need help."

"What kind of help did you get?"

"Some others like me," I say. "Not big, or flashy. But with their own... elements to add."

The clinking starts again behind me.

"You still haven't told me what you think about it," I say.

"About the experiment?" Plask says. "Well... I would've approached it differently. But it's not my choice. It's yours. You taught me that."

I look down for a moment, listening to the glass clacking. "You know," I say, "there was another element that showed up last night. An unexpected one."

Plask raises an eyebrow. "Oh?"

"It was pretty flashy," I say. "Kind of... explosive, even."

His expression doesn't break.

"You're sure you don't know anything about that?" I ask.

He scratches his cheek. "Well, I just thought... what's the point in having a closet full of chemicals if you can't have some fun with them once in a while?"

We share a look. "So you made a choice, too?"

Plask nods. "I suppose I did."

The rhythm of the bottles continues on.

"Thanks," I say.

He shakes his head. "Don't thank me. I didn't do it for that. Make sure you're not doing it for that, either. Because not everyone will thank you, or even notice what you did."

"I guess not," I say. "Doesn't work like it does in the comic books, does it?"

"Afraid not. No cape, no key to the city." He probes me with his eyes. "Are you going to keep doing it anyway?"

"Yeah. But not because I have to. It's a choice, and I've made mine."

Plask nods. "You think you can make a difference?"

"Maybe," I say, a faint smile on my face. "But I'm not a hero."

THANK YOU FOR READING
BUT I'M NOT A HERO

GO TO 5310PUBLISHING.COM
FOR MORE GREAT BOOKS YOU CAN READ TODAY!

IF YOU ENJOYED THIS BOOK, PLEASE REVIEW IT.

5310
PUBLISHING

Connect with us on social media!
@5310publishing on Twitter and Instagram

Subscribe to our mailing list to get exclusive
offers, news, updates, and discounts for our
future book releases and our authors!

BONUS CONTENT!

SUE'S STORY (1st Edition) - EBOOK ISBN: 9781998839032

Author: Eric Demarest | Editor: Alex Williams | Design: Eric Williams

THE HIDDEN ABILITIES UNIVERSE

SUE'S STORY

ERIC DEMAREST

ONE

"*THIS IS WHERE YOU BELONG,*" the cute boys sang through her headphones.

The drums beat over the static, along with the energetic synthesizer rhythm and a repeated chorus of *"uh-huh"* and *"baby."*

Sue rubbed the goosebumps on her arm as she listened. That song lyric always did something to her—*where you belong.* She told herself it was just because of how hot those boys looked dancing to it in the video, but she knew it was something else.

Her eyes panned over the Laurel High School library. The books sat spread out on the shelves, trying to pretend that the shelves weren't quite full; and half of those books were either outdated or completely falling apart, or both. It didn't really matter, though, because most of the students only pretended to read them anyway. Sue's eyes turned to the carpet, which was somewhere between an orange or a brown; she could never quite tell which it was or figure out why anyone would have chosen either of those colors. Her nose tickled with the musty smell that always seemed to float around in here, though she could never tell where it was coming from.

Sue tapped her pencil on the scuffed finish of the study table, in rhythm with the beat of the song those cute boys in her headphones kept singing. She didn't have to worry about bothering anyone with her tapping, since no one was sitting with her. The table across the way had a whole cluster of kids circled around, chatting, laughing. Ryan and Sam sat on the edge of the table, its legs straining to hold them up. Peggy pretended to read one of the falling-apart books.

"*This is where you belong,*" the song echoed again, and as Sue looked at the group around that table, it looked like they *did* belong. She kept tapping her pencil on her own empty table, her own little island. It wasn't like they'd banished her over here, she could walk right over and they'd make room for her, no problem. Ryan and Peggy waved at her, and she waved back, but she didn't get up. It wasn't them keeping her away, it was her; a feeling she could never quite put her finger on, that deep down, she was...

The drum beat suddenly ramped up double speed, and the chorus of "*uh-huh, oh yeah*" morphed into chipmunk voices. Sue popped the cassette player open and the unraveled tape piled out like loose spaghetti. She yanked the cassette out.

Peggy wandered over, her freckles popping especially bright today. "I hate it when that happens," she said, gesturing for the cassette. "Here, let me. I've got this down to a science." Peggy stuck her pencil into the spool and spun it with practiced efficiency, cranking the loose tape back inside. She glanced at the label on the cassette. "Ooh, I love these guys! They're so much better in concert, aren't they?"

Sue glanced down at the table. "I, uh, wouldn't know. It's not like they'd ever come here, and my dad wouldn't leave Laurel for... well, anything."

"Not even so you could see some killer dance moves in person?"

"Afraid not. But, you know, they're almost as good on TV."

Peggy gave her a look that said otherwise. She motioned with her head to the cluster of kids across the way. "Why don't you come and hang out with us?"

Sue hesitated. That feeling was beginning to gnaw at her again. "Thanks, but... you look like you're having fun on your own."

Peggy gave her a sideways look, then shrugged. "Well, come on over if you change your mind." She slapped the cassette down on the corner of the table and skipped back to rejoin the group. Sue wanted to listen to that song one more time and reached for the cassette, but it was just out of reach and she didn't feel like getting up. She knew the song well enough to replay it in her head anyway.

Sue looked back at the group to see Peggy waving at Tanya to join them. Tanya strode over to their table, her long dark hair flowing in waves over her tan skin and her jean jacket, and slid herself right in the middle of them, effortlessly. Sue chewed the inside of her cheek as she watched her. It wasn't that she was jealous; Tanya had never excluded her from anything. In fact, she was usually the one trying to pull Sue along with her. Ever since the first day of third grade when Tanya had plopped herself down across from Sue at the lunch table, out of the blue, and by the end of the lunch period had announced they were best friends. And Tanya *was* a great friend. But Tanya fit with everyone here without even trying, and Sue...

"You know, Sue," Tanya said, striding over to her, "you could come join everyone."

Sue ran her hand through her hair—it was dark and full and wavy like Tanya's, but it took a *lot* of hairspray to get it that way. "I know. Peggy already invited me. But I don't fit like everyone else does."

"What're you talking about? They all like you fine."

"I know, and I like them too. It's just... I don't really *belong*."

Tanya cocked her head. "Are you quoting that song again? I don't think it's as deep as you think it is."

The metallic ring of the bell echoed through the room, and everyone immediately started collecting their stuff to get out of there as fast as they could.

"You want a ride home?" Tanya asked.

"Could you take me to the fire station instead? I need to give my dad something."

"Sure," Tanya said with a smirk. "I never mind getting a chance to get a look at cute firefighters."

"You're terrible," Sue laughed. "Let me just get my—"

She brought her hand down, and it landed on her cassette tape. That shouldn't have been there; the tape was directly in front of her now, three feet closer than it had been a minute ago. Her hand tingled as she wrapped her fingers around the cassette. She stared bullets at it, her forehead creasing.

"Something wrong?" Tanya asked.

"N-nothing. I just thought this tape was all the way over..." Sue trailed off and then shook her head. "Never mind. Let's go."

But this was getting harder to ignore.

TWO

THE SUN SHONE BRIGHT AND WARM as Tanya's rusty coupe sped them out of the school parking lot. Tanya waved at half a dozen guys on the way out, and they all waved back. They waved at Sue, too, but it was different with Tanya. It was just... different. Sue rolled her window down and let the wind play through her hair, as much as it could with all that hairspray, breathing in the fresh air as they rumbled over the cracked pavement of Laurel's main thoroughfare. Not that it was much of a thoroughfare.

They passed the little two-pump gas station with the faded red overhang that was pointless because it leaked when it rained. Then the antique store with the front window piled full of rickety old chairs, cracked vases, mismatched dishes, and the other junk Mrs. Swanson tried to pass off as "collectibles." Then the video rental store with its window plastered with posters of recent releases, which weren't recent at all because none of the posters had changed for at least a year. Everything was familiar here, and nothing ever changed. She supposed that was comforting, in a way; everyone and everything had their place here. Everyone except...

The deep rumble of the diesel horn interrupted her thoughts. Sue glanced over to see the train the next block over, clattering its way alongside them. Without thinking, she smiled and waved. "I wonder where you're going today?" Sue mumbled to herself.

"What'd you say?" Tanya asked.

"Hmm? Oh..." Sue blushed. "Never mind. It's silly, just something I used to think about when I was little."

"Come on, now you *have* to tell me."

Sue scratched at her neck. "Okay, it's just... you've lived in Laurel your whole life, right? And so have I, ever since... well, you know. And you know how it is here; you can walk from one side of town to the other in an hour, and you keep seeing the same things and running into the same people. There's nowhere new to go here, nowhere else to go to find your place. But the train, it could take you anywhere. Carry you away from here, to the other side of the country if you wanted. All you'd have to do is hop on and find out where it's going."

"Huh," Tanya said. "That's deep. You really think about all that?"

"I don't know," Sue said, trying to play it off. "Haven't you ever thought about leaving?"

Tanya shrugged, arching the shoulders of her jean jacket. "I dunno. I like it here."

"Yeah, but you belong here."

"Are you quoting that stupid song *again?*"

The train rushed on its way, wherever it was escaping to, until it passed them by. Sue watched until it disappeared from sight and the clattering of the wheels faded away. A longing tugged at her insides somewhere, but before she could think more about it, they had reached the fire station. Given the size of Laurel, it didn't take long. The brakes squeaked them to a stop in front of the faded brick building.

"Thanks for the lift," Sue said, climbing out.

Tanya strained to get a look in the firehouse windows. "Hold up," she said. "I'm trying to see if the cute one is in there."

"Who's the cute one?"

"Depends on what mood I'm in," Tanya said with a wink. "Hey, maybe I should come in there with you? You know, just to make sure you get in okay…"

"Seriously?" Sue laughed.

"Oh, fine," Tanya huffed in mock annoyance. "But you'd better do enough flirting for both of us!" She gave Sue another wink, then blasted the radio and sped the coupe away.

Sue turned and stepped inside through the door that squeaked like it always did, into the main engine bay. The smell of grease tickled her nose. A husky, dark-skinned guy not much older than her was loading some gear into the truck with a metallic clang. She hadn't seen him here before, and although she'd never admit it to Tanya, he was kinda cute.

"Is my, uh," she started, then stuttered when he turned toward her and she saw his piercing blue eyes. "Is Chuck here?" she finished, her voice cracking just a little.

He looked her over with an air of suspicion. "The chief is busy, miss. And we can't have visitors in here, so—"

"For crying out loud, new guy," came a strong female voice. Rachel stepped out from around the corner of the truck. "Don't you know who this is?"

The new guy grimaced. "Uh, sorry, I don't—"

"Just go get the chief, will you?" Rachel scolded him.

He scurried off sheepishly, and Rachel stepped over and patted Sue on the shoulder with her deceptively strong arm.

"How've you been, Sue?" she asked.

"Good, thanks. Things good around here?"

"Oh, I'm sure you hear how it is. Not much ever changes."

Sue glanced toward the office door to see a familiar tall form emerge. The gray hair was impossible to hide anymore, and his eyes wrinkled when he smiled, but his arms and shoulders looked as strong as ever. "Susie!" he said in his deep, warm voice.

"Hey, Chief," Rachel called to him. "New guy doesn't know who Sue is."

Mike and Russ emerged, with the new guy following them reluctantly. "He doesn't know who Sue is?" Mike said. "I think he needs to hear the story."

"Now, now," Chuck said. "Everyone's heard the story."

Sue laughed awkwardly. "Yeah, I mean, we don't need to go over that again, do we?"

"I don't know," Russ said, playfully scratching his head. "I'm a little fuzzy on the details. What about you, Mike?"

"Oh, me too," Mike agreed. "Where was it you found her again? Was it in the cab of the truck?"

"No, I think she was sitting in his office," Russ said. "And she was wearing a blue ribbon in her hair, right?"

"All right, all right," Chuck said with a laugh. "I'm not going to let you knuckleheads butcher it like that. No, I first met my little Susie right by the front door over there."

Sue blushed and looked down at the floor, but she knew there was no getting around this.

"There was a knock on the door," Chuck said. "It was a—"

"Tuesday morning," Mike, Russ, and Rachel said in unison.

Chuck ignored them and went on. "I opened up the door to find this tiny, sweet little girl who was all of three or four years old. And it was a *pink* ribbon in her hair," he added, shooting a wink at Mike. "She was standing there all by herself, one little tear running down her cheek, but there was—"

"...a determination in her eyes," everyone finished for him.

Sue blushed some more.

"Her parents left her here?" the new guy asked. Sue was going to have to get his actual name sooner or later.

"I don't know how anyone could leave a girl like that," Chuck said. "A girl like *this.*" He put his arm around Sue, and she couldn't help but smile a little.

"Oh, right, I remember now," Russ said playfully. "You'd always wanted a little girl of your own, hadn't you?"

"Oh, of course he did," Mike chimed in with a smirk. "He'd always dreamed of braiding her hair and picking out little pink dresses. It's all he talked about, those little pink dresses."

Chuck shook his head and laughed. "I *had* thought about having a kid, you know, back when I was with Carol... but I'd only ever pictured a boy. I figured I'd play ball with him, teach him to shave. Make a man out of him, you know. The thought of having a girl, well, scared the pants off me. What the hell would *I* do with a little girl?" His eyes winced, then softened. "But when I saw that sweet, strong girl with the pink ribbon in her hair and that look in her eyes, I knew right then that she was going to be my daughter."

"So *that*, new guy," Rachel said, clapping him on the back, "is who Sue is. She's the closest thing this firehouse has to royalty."

The new guy glanced at Sue sheepishly. "Pleased to meet you, miss."

"All right, everybody," Sue laughed, "you've embarrassed me enough. I need to talk to my dad now, okay?"

"You heard her," Rachel said. "Besides, it's time you losers cleaned up the kitchen." She herded the guys off down the hall.

"So, what brings you down here, Susie?" Chuck asked.

"Dad, you know you're the only one who still calls me that, right?"

"I don't care. You'll always be Susie to me."

Sue shook her head and pulled a pill bottle out of her backpack. "All right, I guess I'll never talk you out of that. Look, the reason I came down is that you forgot to take your blood pressure medicine. *Again*."

Chuck rolled his eyes. "Susie, I told you, I don't need that."

"Dr. Phillips seems to think you do."

"Oh, you know how doctors are."

"Come on, Dad." Sue pushed the pills into his big, rough hand. "Promise me you'll take care of yourself, okay?"

"I always do," he said, smiling.

Sue knew what that meant, but decided she'd pushed enough already. She glanced down the hall after the others. "So, you have a new guy, huh? Something actually changed around here for once. What's his name?"

"Brian." He shook his head. "Nice guy, but he's an idiot. It'll take me a year to get him up to snuff."

"I'm sure you'll have him in perfect shape in no time. You always do." Sue kissed his cheek. "I'll see you at home, okay?"

"Okay, sweetie," he said. "Be careful."

"This is Laurel, Dad. What trouble could I get in around here?"

THREE

SUE STEPPED INTO HER BEDROOM AFTER the walk home from the fire station. The blue walls greeted her like they always did. She knew every scuff on those walls. This was a *good* kind of familiar; if there was any place in Laurel where she felt like she fit, it was here. The walls had been boring old white when Chuck had first brought her here, but like most four-year-old girls, she'd wanted them pink. She'd only had to ask him once before he'd painted them the brightest shade of pink he could find. Seeing that big, strong man getting pink paint smears all over his rough skin, all for her—in her mind, that was when he'd really become her dad. And a couple years later, when she changed her mind and wanted yellow instead, he painted the walls again without a single grumble. The most recent change to blue had taken a little longer for him since his back had been starting to act up, but he still did it with a smile.

She dropped her backpack onto the floor, by the faded remnant of the stain from where she'd spilled her grape soda on it back when she was nine. Her math book came tumbling out of the backpack, along with that boy band cassette tape.

Her eyes caught on the tape for a long moment. That tape *had* been on the other side of the study table, then it was right under her hand. That sort of thing was happening more often lately. She kept telling herself it was her imagination, a coincidence, or whatever other story she could make herself believe, but there was that whisper in her mind she couldn't silence. That voice telling her it was something else, something more, something...

Slowly, she held her hand out over the cassette. Her fingers trembled as she watched the tape for any flicker of movement, as she wondered if she really could—

No. She pulled her hand back. This was silly. She couldn't do things like that, *no one* could do things like that. She reached down and grabbed up the cassette, and walked to her closet to shove it all the way in the back—she'd been listening to that stupid song too much anyway—when her hand knocked into something. She dropped the cassette, and her fingers closed around a plastic figure, flooding memories into her head.

She pulled out the doll, running her fingers over the long, silky hair. But this wasn't just any doll, not one with a pretty dress or a tiara. The plastic limbs were curved with muscle, and the light glinted off the red and gold in her breastplate.

Even now, she wondered... of all the dolls she could've picked, why was it a superhero?

She remembered that day. She was probably six or seven, with her hair in pigtails and the too-big shoes she hadn't grown into yet. Her dad had opened the door for her, like a gentleman, and she'd barreled straight in. He'd called after her to slow down, but come on, it was a toy store.

He said she could get any doll she wanted. She knew he meant it, too; he'd barely just signed the adoption papers to be her real dad, but she already had him wrapped around her little finger. She ran through the aisle past so many dolls—in dresses and high heels, in jeans and T-shirts, doctors and zookeepers and roller skaters. She pulled half a dozen of them off the shelves, she even thought about ripping the boxes open right there in the store, but then Sue saw *her*.

This one wasn't like the others. She was tall, and strong. She wasn't dressed for a party or a royal ball. Not that she wasn't pretty, but she was dressed for battle, and looked like she could win. She was... special.

"I want this one, Daddy," Sue had said, with a tone of wonder in her voice.

"That one?" Chuck strode over and scratched his hair with a rough hand. "What about this one over here? Her dress is all sparkly. You like sparkles, don't you?"

"I did. I mean, I do, Daddy, but this one's... like me."

"Like you?" he asked. "How are you like her?"

"I don't know. But I will be."

She looked at the doll now in her sixteen-year-old hand in her blue bedroom, staring at the red and gold breastplate and the gold boots, wondering again why she'd picked her all those years ago. What had made her think she'd ever be like a superhero?

In the back of her mind, the memories tugged at her again. Not just the cassette tape, it had happened with other things too; a bracelet, a watch; never anything big, but they'd been out of reach and then suddenly... they weren't... but that was ridiculous. She shook her head.

She set the doll down and stepped away, taking one last glance at the superhero emblem on the breastplate.

FOUR

THE RUSTY COUPE SPED THEM ALONG toward the school, back past the same trees, gas station, and video rental store. Tanya pushed them just fast enough above the speed limit to let the wind flow through the open windows, but not quite fast enough to attract the attention of Officer Wilson, who was surveying traffic from his patrol car parked in its usual spot at the corner. The sun flickered through the leaves of the trees, and Sue's preoccupations about superhero dolls and boy band song lyrics faded, at least enough for her to smile a little bit.

"Thanks for the lift to school," she said.

"Don't mention it," Tanya said. "It's not like it's out of my way."

Sue chuckled. "It's not like *anything* is out of the way around here."

"Hey, what's going on over there?" Tanya pointed to the construction site for a new fast food place, where a steel frame rose up over the uneven beginnings of a brick wall. A bunch of guys in hard hats rushed back and forth with a frantic intensity, yelling and shouting.

"Boy, they don't look happy," Tanya said. "Somebody must've screwed up big time."

"I don't think they're mad. It's more like… oh my gosh, look!"

A giant steel beam lay fallen, wedged at an angle on top of one of the workers. He writhed against the concrete, his leg caught. The other guys pulled and shoved on the beam, but it wouldn't budge an inch and the man underneath kept writhing.

"Oh shit!" Tanya yelped.

"Where's a phone around here?" Sue exclaimed. "We need to call 911!"

"I think someone already did—isn't that your dad's truck?"

Sue's eyes darted to the corner where she saw the familiar blue truck with the faded paint, then she looked back to the pinned construction worker. Just over the top of the fallen beam, she could see a head of graying hair.

"Stop the car!" Sue blurted out.

"What?"

"That *is* my dad back there, and he's going to hurt himself! I have to make sure he's okay!"

Tanya jerked the wheel to the right and hit the brakes. The tires bounced against the curb just as they screeched to a stop, and Sue was already jumping out.

"I'll go to the fire station and get the rest of them!" Tanya yelled, and drove off with a squeal of tires.

Sue made a run for the scene. Her dad's face edged up over the beam. He heaved against it, his face dripping with sweat and flushing red as an overripe cherry. Sue pumped her legs faster, feeling the sweat on her own forehead, just as a siren blared and the fire engine roared past. Rachel was the first one out of the truck and beat Sue to the edge of the construction site, holding her hand up to bring Sue to a grinding halt.

"Stay back, Sue," Rachel said firmly.

"But," Sue panted, "my dad's going to hurt himself trying to lift that."

The rest of the firefighters hurried past in their gear. Sue took a step to follow them, but Rachel pushed her back.

"We'll handle this," Rachel said.

"Please," Sue pleaded. "He's not as young as he thinks he is, and his blood pressure—"

"I said we'll handle it." Her voice softened slightly. "Don't worry, all right?"

That didn't help much.

Sue watched as Mike, Russ, and the new guy Brian rushed up to the trapped worker. Mike asked his name, soliciting a scream of "*Clint!*" from the pinned guy.

"It's gonna be okay, Clint," Russ said with a practiced reassurance that Sue didn't quite believe. "We're gonna get this off you."

Chuck gave another shove at the beam, letting out a grunt like he was passing a kidney stone. Mike glanced at him and grimaced. "There's no way we can lift this manually. Brian, get the winch. We'll need to rig a pulley system—"

"Forget that," Chuck barked. "We don't have time for a pulley system, and we don't need one." He forced himself upright, the stiffness in his back clear as day on his face. He wiped the sweat off his forehead. "All we need is for everyone to lift at once. You fellows, too," he said, pointing to the construction workers.

They all scrambled to crowd around, nearly falling over each other. Everyone grabbed the beam and held tight with their work gloves.

Chuck glanced back and forth at the group. "Okay then, everyone ready?"

"Hold up, Chief," Rachel cut in. "I can take your spot."

Chuck's face suddenly got a lot redder. "What the hell are you talking about?"

"Well, sir, uh, someone's got to pull him out once we lift it anyway, so why don't you—"

"I can pull my weight around here," he snapped. "*You* pull him out."

"Dad, listen to her!" Sue shouted through cupped hands. "You're going to hurt yourself!"

"Sue?" Chuck's eyes darted toward her, and another bead of sweat rolled down his forehead. "What are you doing here? This is dangerous. Get the hell out of here!"

"But Dad—"

The rest of it got lost as Clint gave another yelp under the beam.

"Damn it, we don't have time to mess around!" Chuck yelled. "Everybody, grab on! Ready? One, two, *three!*"

Everyone heaved, straining, groaning, grunting. Sue held her breath along with them, watching their faces contort, every muscle tense—theirs, and hers. Just when she couldn't take it anymore, she heard a metallic screech as something shifted, and Rachel yanked Clint's leg out from under the beam. Everyone exhaled at once, releasing the beam to drop with a thud.

Rachel was already examining Clint's leg as Mike, Russ, and Brian dropped to a knee, breathing hard. Chuck stood swaying on his legs.

"Dad?" Sue called. "Are you okay?"

He hovered uneasily, bent halfway over the beam. His eyes

stared straight ahead, glazed and dilated.

"Chief?" Mike asked. "Are you sure you're—"

It was a long, slow, time-stopping motion as he tipped backward and fell to a heap on the ground.

"*DAD!*" Sue shrieked. She took off at a sprint, leaping over toolboxes and power saws and piles of bricks, her focus completely on him.

The crowd herded in around Chuck, blocking her out. Rachel shoved through them, pushing them back. "Give him room, you idiots! Let him breathe!"

His face was red and dazed. His hand fumbled awkwardly in his shirt pocket; when he yanked his hand out, his fingers were clenched around the bottle of blood pressure pills. He jerked it toward his mouth when his hand spasmed and the bottle dropped.

"Grab that bottle!" Sue yelled.

It dropped in the middle of the crowd, bouncing off one work boot and then another like a pinball machine. Sue tried to push a scruffy-faced worker out of the way, but it only made him stumble forward and kick it. The bottle skittered away and she lost sight of it completely.

"*No!*" she screamed. "He needs those!"

"What? What does he need?" Rachel asked.

"His blood pressure pills! Where'd they go?" Sue darted her head in every direction, but there were too many people and tools and bricks lying around for her to find it in all the mess.

"Don't... don't worry about those," Rachel said, but her voice faltered. "We can handle this. Brian, get the oxygen from the truck. I'll get the med kit. Mike and Russ, you take care of Clint's leg. The rest of you, for God's sake, get back!"

The ensuing rush was chaos. Sue pushed her way through the mass of bodies to get to her dad, and no one even bothered to stop her. She dropped to her knees beside him.

"It's okay, Dad," she said, even as tears found their way down her cheeks. "It's going to be okay."

He fought to say something but his breath caught in his throat. He jerked his arm out. Sue tried to grab his hand, but he flailed his arm away from her, reaching to the side.

"What is it, Dad?"

His arm kept flailing, and his eyes stared wildly in the same direction. Sue followed his stare to a cement mixer in the corner—wedged under that, huddled in a shadow, was the pill bottle.

Her hand stretched toward it instinctively. It was twenty feet away and too far back under the mixer to even get to it, but she reached toward it anyway, all her thoughts trained on it, and just as she was about to push herself up to make a desperate dash for it... she didn't have to. The bottle jerked toward her.

It jumped half a foot, shaking and trembling on the concrete. She froze in place, her mind trying to perceive what was happening, her arm still stretched toward the bottle. A tingle rushed through her hand like a million pinpricks, surging through her fingers, her palm. And then the bottle launched itself toward her.

It hurled at her like a fastball from an all-star pitcher, out from under the mixer, through the air, straight as an arrow to Sue's hand. It slapped there with a rattle of the pills inside. Her fingers clenched tight around it as the tingle faded from her skin. She stared at the bottle like she'd caught a grenade.

The chaos continued around her, everyone rushing in a different direction, everyone unaware of what she'd done. Her eyes went to her dad's face. He couldn't speak, but his eyes bugged out, wild, almost animal.

He'd seen.

Rachel rushed up and pulled Sue back. "You can't be here, Sue. You need to let us take care of him! Brian, where's that oxygen??"

Sue's mouth sputtered. "He... I... *pills!*"

"What?"

Sue held up the bottle, her hand clenched around it tight enough to burst.

"Oh my God, Sue, you're a savior! How'd you get those back?"

Sue looked back at her dad, still red and breathless. He stared at her with an intensity that terrified her.

"J-just... give them to him," Sue stammered.

Rachel pried the bottle from Sue's fingers and tore the cap off, already forcing pills into Chuck's mouth. "Get him some water!" Rachel shouted. "And someone get Sue out of here!"

Sue felt a hand close gently around her arm and guide her toward the street. She didn't hear the frantic shouts around her; she didn't even see who was pulling her away. Her eyes stayed locked on her dad, who was staring at her as if she were a stranger... more than that, as if she weren't human at all.

FIVE

SUE STUMBLED THE LAST STEP INTO her bedroom. Her lungs burned after running—sprinting—all the way home from the construction site. She hadn't looked back once, but she'd felt like there were eyes locked on her the whole time. She'd just kept running. She slammed the door, desperate to shut out everyone and everything. Except she couldn't run from herself.

She stared down at her hand. It was that tingling feeling. She'd always ignored it before, told herself it was just her hand falling asleep, but she'd felt it clear as day with the... the pill bottle...

She shook her head and rubbed her hands together. This was crazy. It was *impossible*. Except she'd felt that tingle before, and every time she'd felt it, it would happen. Her keys, a soda can, or even that stupid cassette tape would be closer than it had been before... all the way back to when it had been one of her toys, and she'd been barely old enough to hold onto the memory. She'd always managed to tell herself it was nothing, shoved it down inside her, even when it started happening more often. But it had always hovered there inside her, that splinter of knowledge, that feeling that she was different. That she was special.

She stepped into the room, and her eyes landed on the superhero doll. That red and gold breastplate, that emblem portraying strength and power and the ability to do things no mere mortal could do. Suddenly it hit her. *That's* why, out of all the dolls in that store, she'd chosen the superhero. Even back then, somehow she'd known.

Sue reached out her hand. Her fingers stretched out, and she felt her mind stretch with them—across the distance, to the superhero doll on the desk. She felt the tingle ignite in her palm. But more than that, she felt the doll. In her mind, she *felt* it. The doll jerked an inch closer to her. She clenched her jaw tight. The tingle in her hand surged. The doll quivered on the desk. Then Sue pulled. She didn't know how even as she was doing it, but she pulled. The doll launched itself up, through the air, straight to her hand.

She stared at the doll, into those fierce, determined eyes painted on the hero's face, and for the first time, Sue looked into that face and saw herself looking back.

She was different now. There was no denying it, and there was no going back.

She wondered, if she *could* go back… if she'd want to.

***

The slamming of the front door woke her. Sue shook herself awake, shocked that she'd slept, and looked to the window for a clue at how long she'd been out. The sun was still bright, but it had traveled a long way in the sky since she'd laid down. She rubbed her eyes. After the adrenaline of everything had worn off, she must have...

She heard the muffle of her dad's voice through the wall, and her mind rushed with the image of his red face struggling to breathe. Suddenly the only thought in her mind was whether he was okay. She sprang off the bed and bolted out the door.

Rachel was there with him in the hallway, her arm around his shoulder, supporting him. He stumbled a step but pushed her arm away. "I'm not a damn invalid," he grunted at her.

"Of course not, Chief," Rachel said, "but you've had a busy day. You need to take it easy."

"If you think I'm going to sit in some rocking chair and knit a sweater, you're—"

He stopped dead when he saw Sue. He stumbled again, and Rachel braced to catch him.

"Dad!" Sue ran to hug him, but Rachel held up a hand.

"Easy now," Rachel cautioned her.

Sue probed his face. "Are you okay, Dad?"

His eyes wouldn't meet hers. He didn't answer.

"Your dad's fine," Rachel said, either not registering the tension or ignoring it. "He gave us all a little scare, but he's too tough to let something like that stop him. Of course, if you hadn't found those pills when you did..."

Chuck's eyes flicked to hers for just a moment, then went back to the floor.

"Well," Rachel said, "let's not stand around here. Come on, Chief, let's get your feet up so you can rest."

"I told you already, I don't need to rest," he protested.

Sue stepped forward. "Yes, you do, Dad. You need to take care of yourself. We'll get you in your favorite chair, then—"

When she put her hand on his shoulder, he flinched. Violently. His whole body jerked back, pulling away from her.

His eyes bulged and his cheeks blanched white. Rachel grabbed him and fought to keep him upright.

"Whoa!" Rachel said, steadying him. "Are you okay?"

Chuck wiped the fear off his face and forced a smile, but his cheeks were tight. "I'm fine. Sorry, I... you startled me, is all. I was... it's been a long day." He reached his hand toward Sue, hovering above her shoulder; then he pulled it back without touching her. His eyes went to the floor again.

"Maybe I do need to sit down," he said.

"Sure, Chief," Rachel said. "You've earned yourself a break."

Sue stepped aside as Rachel guided him past her through the hall. His eyes never left the floor. And for the first time since that Tuesday morning all those years ago, that day he'd found her in front of the fire station, Sue couldn't look at him either.

SIX

SUE'S EYES STARED RIGHT THROUGH THE pages of the book in front of her; through the library study table, through the floor underneath that, and on, and on.

"Sue? Earth to Sue!"

"Hmmm?"

She turned to see Tanya looking at her with a raised eyebrow.

"You okay?" Tanya asked her.

The murmurs of other kids' conversation faded back into Sue's ears, and she glanced around the library to see the bookshelves and tables and the maybe brown, maybe orange carpet.

"I'm, uh…"

"How long have you even been sitting here?" Tanya asked. "I didn't see you in English."

Sue shook her head. "Sorry about that. I just couldn't deal with that right now."

"Are you worried about your dad's blood pressure thing?

I'm sure he's going to be fine."

"That's not it, it's... never mind."

"What is it?"

Sue chewed her lip. "I finally know why I don't belong."

"Are you still on about that? Sue, seriously—"

"I am serious. I'd always felt it, tried to pretend it wasn't there, but now I know *why*. I can't hide from it or pretend anymore."

Tanya cocked her head. "Did something happen, Sue?"

She felt the tingle in her hand. Saw the image of the pill bottle flying toward her, her hand closing around it. "I... I did something."

"Did what?" Tanya said, her voice growing concerned. "Are you in trouble?"

"No. Not exactly. It was... a *good* thing. But my dad saw, and he didn't understand, and he looked at me like..." Sue shuddered. "I don't even know how I did it. I didn't know I *could* do it. I mean, I guess I sort of knew, deep down, but I'd never done it like *that* before. When he saw it, he freaked out, and... God, it freaked *me* out too! I mean, what the hell *was* that? But I... I helped him with it. That's a good thing, right? If I can do something no one else can do, if I can help someone with that... shouldn't I do it?"

Tanya sat down and stared into her face. "I don't know what you're talking about, Sue."

"No, of course you don't. No one would." Sue glanced at the floor. "Maybe I should've just kept this thing buried. Maybe I should bury it again."

Tanya put a hand on her arm. "Hey, don't talk like that. Whatever this is—I mean, you'll need to explain it better, but I'm sure we can figure it out. Just tell me. Or show me, even! I'm here for you, Sue."

"Just show you..."

Sue looked down at her pen on the desk, and the tingle started in her fingers. She could do it right now. She needed a friend, an ally, and Tanya could be that. Sue held her hand out over the pen. *Just show her. She'll be on your side.* The pen started to tremble.

She glanced at Tanya's eyes, thinking of all the times they'd laughed together, cried together, all the secrets they'd shared. This wouldn't be any different. She repeated that to herself, willing it to be true. The tingle surged in her hand. *Just show her.*

She wanted to; she wanted to believe it would be that easy, that Tanya would know and understand, that they'd hug and carry this thing together. But finally she let the tingle fade, and the pen lay still against the tabletop. She pulled her hand back.

The bell rang overhead. Sue stared at the table, unable to look Tanya in the eye. There was a long silence.

"I guess we should head out, then," Tanya said.

"Yeah." Sue pushed herself up from the table, which felt like it took everything out of her. She shuffled behind Tanya toward the door.

Out in the lobby, everyone was talking over each other, laughing at jokes, griping about flunking that test, talking about that boy or girl they had their eye on. Joe the custodian was perched on a two-story ladder right over the Badgers emblem in the middle of the floor, working on one of the overhead lights. The herd flowed around the ladder on either side, intent on getting out of there. Sue followed them all, feeling numb. Twice she opened her mouth to say something to Tanya, to just tell her and get it over with, but nothing would come out.

She heard a few male voices hollering above the rest, and glanced back to see Ryan, Brett, and Carl shoving each other and laughing it up. Tanya looked back, too, and winked—Ryan was one of the boys she'd had her eye on. Ryan winked back, with a look like he was about to do something stupid to impress her. He pulled a football from his backpack. "Hey, Carl, go long!" he shouted.

Carl took off to the other end of the lobby. Tanya kept her eyes on Ryan with a smile.

Ryan let the ball fly—not some light toss that would only get him a talking-to, this was a detention-level launch if Sue had ever seen one. But just as he threw it, Brett shoved him again.

The ball sailed off course. Away from Carl, straight toward Joe on the ladder.

Sue watched it in slow motion. Everyone did, as Ryan and Brett and Tanya all dropped their jaws. The ball hurtled straight for Joe's head like a missile. The impact was inevitable, and it would send him tumbling from the ladder, down to the hard tile floor fifteen feet below.

Sue held up her hand. The tingle ignited out of sheer instinct. The ball curved slightly—not enough. She pulled harder. The tingle raged to a full burn, and the ball jerked violently. Three feet from Joe's head, it spun on a dime and shot off at a ninety-degree angle, straight toward Sue.

She ducked at the last second, and the ball flew over her head and hit the floor with a thud, bouncing away harmlessly. Her eyes darted back to Joe on the ladder, who looked confused but otherwise just fine. She let out a breath, and found herself smiling. She'd done that. With this... Ability, she'd done it. She was the *only* one who could have—

Her smile faltered. Everyone was staring at the ball on the ground like they'd just seen bigfoot.

"What the hell..." said Ryan, Brett, and about half a dozen others.

Sue flushed crimson. She realized there had been warning bells going off in her head, but she'd listened to them too late.

Brett shoved Ryan again. "How the hell did you do that?"

"Me?" Ryan protested. "No way could I make it curve like that!"

The voices in the crowd spread like wildfire. Sue caught snippets of "some kinda magic trick" and "freaky" and "flippin' awesome." Everyone kept staring at where the ball had rolled to a stop, and since it had sailed right over Sue's head, she suddenly realized that most of them were staring at *her*. She shuffled to the side, keeping her head down. As she glanced up, she noticed that several of the stares followed her.

"Are you okay, Sue?"

She turned to see Tanya. There was a searching, questioning look in her eyes, just for a moment. Then Tanya shook her head, and the look was gone. "That ball almost hit you. Crazy, huh?"

"Yeah... crazy."

Sue looked over the crowd of students. Most were already laughing again, herding toward the doors like nothing had happened, but a few of the faces still had that look on them. Like when a math problem doesn't add up right, or... make that a physics problem. She felt herself getting hot.

"I... I have to go..."

"What's the matter, Sue?" Tanya asked.

"N-nothing. I just... have to get out of here..."

"Don't you want a ride?"

Sue didn't respond, and she didn't look back. She pushed her way through the crowd, through the front doors, and then ran with all her might until she couldn't run anymore.

SEVEN

BIRDS CHIRPED IN THE TREES, BUT Sue didn't hear them. The only thing she did hear as her steps plodded along the sidewalk was the voice in her head, and it was *screaming* at her.

What was she thinking? Her dad seeing the pill bottle was bad enough, she hadn't even dealt with that yet, and now she did *this?*

That was the problem, she *hadn't* been thinking. She'd just done it.

But it was good that she'd done it. If she hadn't, Joe would be in the hospital right now, or worse. No one else there could have done anything to stop it, but *she* could, and she did. She had an Ability, and she'd done something *good* with it.

But that look on everyone's faces...

They don't know it was you, she told herself. *They don't know. They don't know.*

She kept repeating that, over and over, but it didn't make the pit in her stomach go away.

The train horn sounded, and Sue found herself smiling just a little. "Where are you going today?" she whispered to herself. She stopped to listen to the rumble of the train cars, clattering on their way, until the sound gradually faded into the distance.

Sue reached her house. A tightness constricted around her chest with each step up the front walk, the back of her mind prodding her with fears; she forced it off and took in a deep breath. *He loves you,* she told herself. *You're just being silly.* She convinced herself that she believed it and then turned the doorknob.

"Dad?" she called. She chided herself on how timid her voice sounded, and forced the jitters out. "Dad?" There, that was better. It sounded like her.

"In here," he called back. It sounded like him, too... almost.

She walked toward his voice, her steps just a little slower than usual. She forced her thoughts down and stepped into the kitchen. He wasn't there; but the counter was full with a bunch of potatoes stacked in a heap, along with some pork chops and a dozen spice bottles.

Chuck shuffled in from around the corner. His eyes flicked up to hers for just a moment, then back down again. His back hunched him forward slightly. They both stood there, a few feet apart, the silence painfully thick.

Chuck cleared his throat and forced the words out. "I was... making dinner." He reached his hand toward the potatoes. As soon as he touched them, the whole pile toppled, sending three of them rolling and tumbling to the floor. He flailed to grab them, only to knock over half the spice bottles too.

Sue laughed. The same sweet, innocent laugh she'd always had. Chuck looked up at her, a snicker finding its way to his lips. Sue found herself smiling, and the tightness in her chest disappeared. Well, almost.

"You always do make a mess when you cook," she said.

"I have to," he said. "The bigger the mess, the bigger the flavor."

Sue bent down and picked up the toppled potatoes. "Here, I'll help you. I'll take care of these. You can do the meat."

He gave her a half smile. Not a full one, but it would do. She laid the potatoes out, being careful so they wouldn't roll away again, and grabbed a pot to fill with water. Chuck picked up a meat tenderizer and started tapping it against the pork chops. Sue flicked a glance toward him as she filled up her pot.

"That isn't all you've got, is it?" she asked, with as much playfulness as she could muster.

He looked up. "What?"

"Come on," she prodded him. "Let 'em have it."

He hesitated a moment, then brought down the hammer hard. It made a dull *thud* against the meat. Chuck's smile spread a little wider, and his back straightened up. He raised the hammer and started pounding away. Sue smiled.

She carried the pot to the stove and busied herself with piling the potatoes into the water while her dad kept pounding the pork chops beside her. She glanced at him, and it felt right. She'd helped him cook since she was little, since she'd had to stand on a step stool. Her mind wandered to images of herself with pigtails, standing on her tiptoes on that stool, with him beside her, joking, laughing—

She reached for the salt, just as Chuck reached for it too. Their hands brushed against each other. Instantly he jerked away and staggered backward, knocking into the counter and sending the spice bottles clattering. Chuck's face bleached white and his eyes began to dart around, looking everywhere but at her.

Sue stood there, her mouth trembling. "It's... it's just me, Dad," she said.

His back hunched forward and he rubbed his hand where he'd touched her. He didn't say anything, but he didn't have to. Sue tried with all her might to summon those images back of her in her pigtails, laughing with him, but the image wouldn't come. She wondered if it would ever come again.

 EIGHT

THE LAUGHS AND NOISY CONVERSATIONS SUDDENLY muted themselves when Sue stepped through the school doors. Everyone carried on, but there was a hesitation, the briefest moment where their eyes flicked toward her, before they continued talking at half their previous volume.

That ladder was still stretched over the Badger emblem on the floor, standing as a haunting reminder of yesterday. Sue froze, staring at it, and thought about turning around and walking right back out the doors. But she knew going home wouldn't be any better.

She pushed herself forward, one step in front of the other. All day it was like that. Like walking through a haze; like a fish swimming against the current. People moved aside as she passed by, and conversations grew quieter. There was something questioning in their glances at her. Did she imagine all that? Was she making this worse than it really was? Every time she'd almost convinced herself of that, she'd walk into another classroom and there it was again.

At last the final bell rang, the sound shrill through the haze in her head. She shuffled toward the doors, when she saw Tanya up ahead. Her heart jumped with hope that she could put all this behind her.

"Hey, Tanya!"

Tanya kept walking. Sue hurried to catch up with her.

"Tanya?"

"Oh… hey…" There was a hesitancy when Tanya turned.

"What's wrong?" Sue asked.

"Why would you say something's wrong?" Tanya replied defensively.

Sue glanced from her to the rest of the students. "Well, isn't there?"

Tanya chewed her lip. "Look, it's that crazy thing with the football yesterday."

"T-that was just a weird fluke," Sue said, her words rushing out.

"Sure." Tanya nodded, as if she were trying to convince herself. "Sure. Probably. But, I mean, it was freaky, right? And you know nothing ever happens around here, so people are talking about it, and you know how rumors get started—"

"Rumors about what?"

Tanya darted her eyes away. "Nothing. It's just that the ball went flying straight toward… you."

Sue fought hard not to break eye contact with her. "That doesn't mean anything."

"Sure," Tanya said. "Most of the kids laughed it off, but a few people…"

Sue grabbed her shoulder. "You can't listen to them, Tanya. You *know* me."

Tanya's eyes searched her face for a long moment. "Sue, is there anything you want to tell me?"

"What?" Sue said, barely a whisper.

"Well, yesterday you started to tell me something, about... doing something people wouldn't understand. And then, that thing with the ball happened, and I just... is there something you want to tell me?"

Sue stared into her friend's face. If she was still her friend. "It's me, Tanya. Just like I've always been."

They stood there for a moment looking at each other. It hadn't been said but they both knew just the same. Tanya turned and started to walk away.

"I did something good with it!" Sue called after her, her voice desperate. "Please, I... maybe there's a reason for this! If I can do something good, shouldn't I do it?"

For a moment, Tanya paused, then she kept walking without looking back.

Sue stood there, watching her go. Her lungs heaved and her eyes stung. She was in a crowd of people, and yet she was completely, utterly alone. She shoved her way through the bodies, and through the doors, bursting out into the sun. With the dark cloud of emotions thick above her, she barely felt the warmth on her skin.

Her footsteps wandered, and the sun wandered in the sky along with her. She walked from one end of town to the other, but her path steered clear of her house and the fire station. She couldn't bear to face Chuck; to see him flinch away from her again. But as the sunlight began fading in the sky, she finally found herself at her front door. She couldn't avoid it forever. She took a deep breath and stepped through.

The kitchen was dark and quiet. Then, she heard a yell.

"Dad?" Her voice caught, and she ran to the living room. "Dad, are you okay?"

She burst into the room, and saw the glow. The TV screen.

Another yell came, but it was a cheer this time. There was a crack of a bat, and a baseball went soaring across the screen.

She stood there waiting for her eyes to adjust. There was no sound except the game on the TV, and for a moment she thought she was alone. Then she saw him on the couch, sitting limp in the flickering glow of the screen.

"Dad?"

He sat unblinking, like a wax figure. After a long moment, he raised his arm and took a slow swig of beer, then he set the bottle back down on the tray set in front of him. His plate was picked over; the chicken cut up, the peas pushed around, but it didn't look like he'd eaten much. She looked back at his face; his eyes never left the TV, dulled by the screen's glow.

His shoulders moved with his breaths, slowly, up and down. His cheeks were pale, and the gray in his hair seemed starker than she'd remembered. Maybe it was the light. He breathed out another long rasp.

"Are you okay, Dad?" Sue asked hesitantly.

"Fine." It was more of a grunt, barely audible. He took another swig of beer.

She looked back at his tray. "Are we... eating in here tonight? We've always eaten at the table, you know, but this could be—"

"I set you a plate," he said, his voice flat. He nudged his head toward the dining room. "In there."

She stood there, hovering. The crowd on the screen cheered again.

Sue turned and stepped into the darkness of the dining room. She could just make out the shadow of the plate sitting on the table. The plate was full, but the smell drifting from the food was cold and thick.

"Dad?" Her steps were quick, back to the living room. "We

can... we can still talk, can't we?"

She reached out toward him; he flinched back. He didn't say anything.

"It's still me, Dad," she said, her voice choking.

"Is it?" he said. He still wouldn't look at her. "You know, I'd always wondered. Ever since I found you at the front door of the fire station. What could've made your parents leave you like that? Such a strong, beautiful little girl. I could never come up with a reason that made sense. But now, after all this, I could almost... understand..." He took a long gulp of beer, draining the bottle.

Her mouth quivered as she looked at him. And then a memory tugged at her, the hazy whisperings of one that her mind had barely been able to hold onto; or maybe her mind had tried its best to flush it away.

The orange carpet in her playroom. She didn't remember anything else about the house where she'd spent her first four years, but that carpet, that vivid color; and the patch of sun through the window shining on it like fire. Her toys all spread across it in a heap. Her parents were there, in the doorway, watching her. Their faces were vague and blurry in the memory, not quite formed in her mind, but she could feel that they were happy as they watched her.

She reached for something... a ball. It was out of reach, in the corner. She stretched her little stubby fingers toward it... and that's when she'd felt the tingle. She'd laughed, she remembered, as the ball quivered, then rolled toward her all on its own. She clapped her hands. A fun new game. Did Mommy and Daddy want to play the new game with her?

Whatever her parents said, the words don't make it through the memory. Just a blurred wash of sound, but the tone of the voices carried through just fine. Fear and shock and horror and…

Sue shuddered and found herself back in the dim living room with the crowd cheering on the TV.

"Dad, please—"

"Chuck," he said.

She blinked at the tears forming in her eyes. "What?"

"My name is Chuck."

Sue stood there, all the feeling in her body pulled away to numbness. The space between them, not more than a few feet, suddenly felt like a canyon. His eyes gazed off a mile away.

Finally she pulled herself away and plodded with painfully slow steps; past the table with the cold smell of her food, through the dark emptiness of the house, to her bedroom that her dad… that Chuck had painted for her. With her last ounce of energy, she dropped onto the bed, and then she couldn't hold back the tears any longer.

NINE

SUE SLIPPED OUT OF THE HOUSE the next morning without even looking for her dad. If he was still in the house, she didn't want to see him.

Tanya wasn't there to pick her up. No surprise there. What really hurt was that Sue realized she didn't want to see her, either.

She walked toward the school. On any other morning, she would've thought how pretty it was, with the warm sun and the birds chirping. But right now, Sue didn't care. She reached the school and looked up at it, feeling her chest tighten... and she kept walking. She kept on, putting the building and everyone in it behind her.

She ended up downtown. People shuffled in and out of the storefronts, intent on wherever they were going. They all had a purpose. What was hers? For a moment there, she'd thought she'd known. The painted face on her superhero doll back home was so confident, so determined. She'd thought that could be her. How stupid was that? Things don't work like that in the real world. People don't cheer like they do in the comic books; they don't thank you or—

"Help!" A shrill voice cut through her thoughts. "Someone, help!"

A middle-aged woman waved frantically up ahead. Sue took off along the sidewalk, sprinting up to her. "What's wrong?" Sue asked her. "Are you all right?"

"No, I'm *not* all right!" the woman shrieked. "It fell off!"

"What fell off?"

"My ring!"

"Your... your *ring?*" Sue huffed out a long angry breath. "That's all? You shouldn't go yelling for help over something like that. Some of us have *real* problems."

"But it's my wedding ring! I can't lose that, not after... oh, it's all the way down there!" She pointed frantically toward the storm grate at the curb.

Sue cast a glance in that direction. She almost said *I don't care* before she stopped herself. It's not like she had anywhere to go anyway. She shuffled over and squinted into the shadow.

"You can see it, can't you?" the woman prodded.

"Yeah," Sue said, catching a glint in the depths of the storm drain. "But it's way down there. You're gonna need a new ring." She stood up to leave when the woman burst into sobs. Heaving, guttural sobs poured out of the woman in a torrent. Sue felt her own heart catch in her throat.

"I'm... I'm sorry," Sue said, hesitantly patting the woman on the shoulder. "Don't cry, okay?"

"Tom would be so proud of me," the woman sniffled through her sobs. "I did it for him, you know? I told him I'd get myself in shape, to live a full life for him. And I did. I lost weight! But it made my ring loose, and it slipped right off!"

"Oh," Sue said, searching for something to say. "You lost weight? I mean, of course you did, you look great—"

"I can't lose that ring!" the woman burst out. "Someone has to be able to get it out from there. I'll... I'll call the fire department!"

"The fire department?" Sue jerked back. "Not him! I mean, them. They, uh, can't help with this."

"But *someone* has to!" the woman choked out. "I can't lose it..."

"Look, it's just a ring. I'm sure your, uh... Tom? He'll get you another one."

The woman stopped between her sobs and looked Sue in the eye. "He would have, I know he would have. But he *can't*, not anymore. Right before he... he passed last year, that's when I promised him. I told him I'd live a life for both of us."

Sue's mouth hung open, suddenly without any words to say.

"I *am* going to call the fire department!" the woman blurted out. "I'll make them get it. I'll make them tear up half the street if I have to! I just need to find a phone..."

As the woman turned toward one of the shops, Sue stood staring into the storm grate. The ring glinted from down below.

Her hand tingled.

No, she told herself. She squeezed her fist tight.

But the ring kept glinting in the darkness. Sue glanced at the woman, hurt etched on her face like a scar. She looked back at the grate.

NO! came the voice in her head again. *Don't even think about it.*

But the pain on the woman's face...

Remember last time. Remember how they looked at you.

She stifled a shudder. She'd already lost Tanya, and her dad... she couldn't bear anyone else looking at her like that.

But her hand kept tingling.

She could get the ring out. No one else could do that, but *she* could. She had an Ability. This was more than a coincidence; it was a purpose. Maybe there was a reason for it after all.

Sue held her hand over the grate and let herself feel the energy in her fingers. The sparkle of the ring trembled, then hovered... then rose. She watched it float upward, slowly, evenly, gliding through the air, until it slipped through the bars of the grate and right into her hand. Sue closed her fingers around it, squeezing tight until the diamond pinched against her palm. She felt her heart skip.

"Ma'am?" Sue jumped up and rushed across the sidewalk.

The woman stood hyperventilating in front of the hair salon, her voice nearing a shriek. "I don't care if your phone is for employees only! This is an emergency!"

"Ma'am, it's okay!" Sue touched her shoulder. She held out her hand and opened her fingers, revealing the ring inside.

The woman froze, her mouth wide open. She stared with a desperate intensity, then reached out and carefully grasped the ring between her fingers. "How... how did you..."

"I couldn't let you lose it," Sue said.

"But *how?*"

Sue felt her cheeks flush, knowing there was no way she could answer that question. "It was nothing," she said.

"Are you kidding? It's a *miracle!*"

"It's... not a miracle," Sue insisted. She took a step back. "I have to go."

The woman grabbed her arm. "You can't go! I have to thank you!"

Sue glanced around at the people on the street, who were beginning to stare at her. "You've already thanked me," Sue said quickly.

"No, I mean like… oh, you should have your picture in the paper!"

"M-my picture?"

"Of course! Young lady, you must have a superpower! Oh my, but here I am babbling… I never even asked your name. Who are you?"

Sue could see it all unfolding in painful clarity—word spreading like wildfire, from one end of Laurel to the other. There would be no containing it. *Everyone* would know; everyone would give her that look. And they wouldn't call it a superpower, they'd call it something else. They'd call *her* something else.

"I really have to go." Sue pulled her arm away from the woman and stepped back.

"Oh…" The woman's face dropped. "Well, if you must… oh, but at least let me give you a reward!" She stuck her hand into her purse and rummaged through it. When her eyes dropped to look, Sue turned and slipped away. She was gone before the woman found her wallet.

Sue heard the woman calling out for her, the voice fading into the distance, but she kept walking.

She wished she could feel proud. She *should* feel proud. She'd done the thing that needed to be done, that helped someone, that no one else could do. That's why she had this Ability—to help people. And she had helped that woman, and Joe, and her… Chuck. But she couldn't feel proud or special, she had to hide it, bury it and pretend to be someone else. And the real problem, the thing chewing at her from the inside, was that in this town, there was nowhere to hide.

As long as she had this Ability, as long as she used it to help people—even if she *didn't* use it—she'd be hunted down with pitchforks and torches. Because she was different from the rest of them.

Because she didn't *belong* here.

The train horn startled her. She stopped and listened to the clacking of the wheels carrying it out of Laurel. Carrying it away from the walls of this town, away from everyone who knew her secret. Carrying it to places where her Ability could bring good, could bring hope; where she could use it as a gift, not a curse.

Suddenly, she turned and started off. Walking quickly, resolutely, toward the tracks. Toward the train.

She wondered where it would take her.

YOU MIGHT ALSO LIKE...
LOST IN FANTASIA

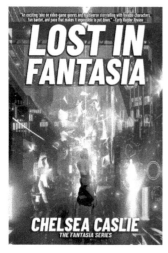

When virtual reality takes over, it's hard to tell the difference between what is real and what is a part of a game. Having all memories of life before The Game erased, Tack's experience is altered when a glitch infiltrates her world. After her partner disappears, infected by the glitch, she is forced to find answers to the mysterious Game malfunction to determine if he is dead or alive.

Her home, partner, and game are seemingly destroyed. Glitched herself, Tack embarks on an adventure to unfamiliar and new worlds, including the largest Fantasy role-playing game, Fantasia. However, this glitch isn't like anything else the Gaming world has experienced. With no one respawning and the Game's Production team in a communication blackout, the lines between what is virtual and what is real are blurred even further. If Tack can't stop the glitch, she risks more than just losing her partner forever—everything she knows and loves might disappear.

"A surprising and engaging Lit-RPG adventure set in a future where gaming was so evolved (or decadent, depending on your point of view) that humans were employed as avatars... kept me involved in both the game world and the mystery."

—*Reader's Favorite*

SCAN ME

YOU MIGHT ALSO LIKE...
HONEY BEAUMONT

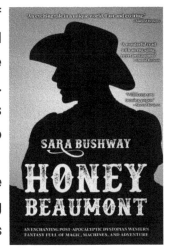

An unlikely hero was born out of servitude: Honey Beaumont. He strived to do right by everyone and see justice prevail no matter the consequence. He dreamt of the intrepid Adventurer's Guild and helping those who can't help themselves.

Every day our hero persevered the wrath of Byron, his owner. Helping those around him doesn't fill Byron's pockets, bringing out anger in his boss.

One day, Byron brutally attacks Honey after a wealthy client offers to help Honey leave the life of servitude and be free. After the attack, Honey was scarred, disfigured, and with a grudge. He begrudgingly left his home and the love of his life behind to move into a new and luxurious home. Honey mingles amongst those in the new house and learns about the world's inequalities, especially between the nobodies and humans. But with his new owner forbidding him from being independent, Honey has no other choice but to leave this new luxurious life behind.

Freedom for Honey meant joining the Adventure's Guild, becoming a hero, and helping his family leave the horrible place he used to call home. Will Honey be strong enough to take on Byron? Only time will tell.

"An exciting tale in a unique world featuring Honey Beaumont's magical journey from who he was when he was born to the hero he was meant to be. A fast and exciting read. I couldn't put it down!" — *Starred Review 5/5*

SCAN ME

YOU MIGHT ALSO LIKE...
THE ART OF BECOMING A TRAITOR

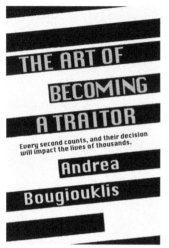

THE ART OF BECOMING A TRAITOR

Every second counts, and their decision will impact the lives of thousands.

Andrea Bougiouklis

A young woman with a larger than life legacy and an incredible sense of self truly believed that what she was doing was right. With all of her being, she thought that she was helping to serve a long-overdue justice.

When Eleri learns that she had been used as a pawn in a larger, evil plot, she has to find it in herself to right her wrongs - even if it means going against everything and everyone she ever loved. The war had been raging since she was a young child, and she had never thought to question it.

When Eleri and her best friend Fyodor discover that their leaders have been doctoring and altering history and are planning to disintegrate an entire population, they realize that they may be the only two who can prevent this atrocity.
In a race against time, power, and their own morals, they can only hope that their willpower and strength are enough to overturn a war that has already begun.

"Young adults who enjoy girls who kick ass and take no names will like this dystopian fantasy as it resembles many of the same themes as action movies... I saw many parallels to this story to events happening to today. What do you do when you discover you are fighting for the wrong side?"
—*Veronica Krug, author and educator*

SCAN ME

Ingram Content Group UK Ltd.
Milton Keynes UK
UKHW012130280623
424228UK00002B/25